THE OPIUM EQUATION

LISA WYSOCKY

T I T L E S

Published by
Cool Titles
439 N. Canon Dr., Suite 200
Beverly Hills, CA 90210
www.cooltitles.com

The Library of Congress Cataloging-in-Publication Data Applied For

Lisa Wysocky—
The Opium Equation

p.   cm
ISBN 978-1-935270-06-5
1. Mystery 2. Horses   3. Southern Fiction   I. Title
2011

Printed in the United States of America

1 3 5 7 9 10 8 6 4 2

Book editing and design by White Horse Enterprises, Inc.

For interviews or information regarding special discounts for bulk purchases,
please contact cindy@cooltitles.com

Distribution to the Trade: Pathway Book Service,
www.pathwaybook.com, pbs@pathwaybook.com, 1-800-345-6665

Other Books by Lisa Wysocky

The Power of Horses
Success Within
Front of the Class (with Brad Cohen)
My Horse, My Partner
Horse Country
Success Talks

DEDICATION

To all of my friends: human, equine, canine, and feline.
Thank you for all you do for me.

CAST OF MAIN CHARACTERS

Cat Enright: A horse trainer near Nashville, Tennessee. She is twenty-nine, single, impulsive, vulnerable, a tiny bit rude, and the owner of a small stable.

Bubba Henley: Budding juvenile delinquent and ten-year-old son of a neighboring trainer. Cat worries when no one can find him.

Hill Henley: Bubba's no-account father and fourth generation Tennessee Walking Horse trainer.

Glenda Dupree: Retired movie star and neighbor of both Cat, and Hill and Bubba Henley. She's the kind of person everyone loves to hate.

Adam Dupree: Glenda's nephew. He is a failed actor, a songwriter wanna-be, and likes Cat very much.

Opal Dupree: Glenda's aged mother. Opal knows a terrible and ancient secret that may help Cat, but her mind wanders.

Fairbanks: The ancestral antebellum home of the Henley family, now owned by Glenda Dupree.

Col. Sam Henley: Long dead Civil War-era builder of Fairbanks, and Hill's great, great grandfather.

Agnes Temple: Eccentric woman of a certain age with electric blue hair. She owns two horses in Cat's barn.

Hank: Cat's incorrigible Beagle-mix puppy.

Martin Giles:	Local cop. Young, but smart.
Jon Gardner:	Cat's stable manager and right hand. No one, Cat included, knows exactly where he's from, which is the way he likes it.
Darcy Whitcomb:	Seventeen-year-old daughter of a prominent dot com entrepreneur. She's a little spoiled, but Cat loves her like family.
Carole Carson:	Riding student neighbor of Cat's, and wife of country music super star, Keith Carson.
Keith Carson:	A neighbor and country music superstar. Keith is out touring and has only a very small part in this story, which is too bad as he's really quite a hunk.
Robert Griggs:	Quiet hospital nurse and a riding student.
Frog:	A trouble-making punk friend of Bubba's.
Brent Giles:	Martin's older brother. A small animal veterinarian from Clarksville.
Buffy Thorndyke:	Young reporter with blue blood in her veins and air in her head.
Sheriff "Big Jim" Burns:	An election is looming and the sheriff wants an arrest. Any arrest.
AT's Sally Blue:	Young, (possibly) psychic, red roan Appaloosa mare bred and owned by Agnes Temple, hence the initials "AT" at the beginning of Sally's name. Sally is loyal to Cat.
Peter's Pride:	Tall, older black gelding owned by Darcy Whitmore. Petey is a calming influence on Darcy, but he also likes to play.

Hillbilly Bob: Bay, aged gelding owned by a local orthopedic surgeon. Cat swaps training fees for treatment of broken bones and has won several championships on Bob.

Glamour Girl: Fun-loving yearling filly. Gorgeous, but immature and unfocused.

MAP OF CAT'S NEIGHBORHOOD

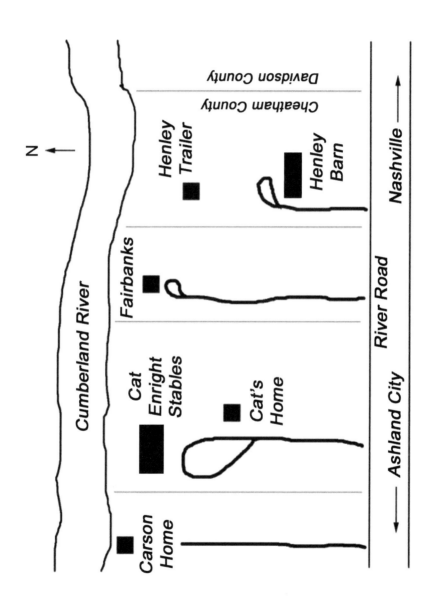

1

THE ROCK WAS THE SIZE OF a baseball. It missed my driver's side window by inches, skimmed over the roof of my truck and landed in the ditch. I skidded to a halt and threw open the door. The little menace had it coming.

The little menace was Bubba Henley, a ten-year-old who lived two farms up from mine. I caught him by the back of his shirt fifty feet up his father's driveway.

His father, Hilton Jefferson Henley III was a tall, skinny, balding piece of trash. The first three characteristics were obvious. That last part was my own conclusion. Hill Henley professed to be a trainer of Tennessee Walking Horses, but he really was a bully who cowed his client's horses into obedience. Did I mention I didn't like him much?

Hill's farm was typical for Walking Horse trainers in Middle Tennessee: small house shadowed by a long barn with a wide aisle that served as an indoor training area. The Henley farm also had a profusion of rebel flags, a tribute to Hill's "distin-guished" Confederate ancestors, a fact he never failed to bring up in any conversation.

"Bubba," I said, as I grabbed him by the back of his shirt, "if you throw one more rock at my truck I'll have you locked up in juvie jail until you're thirty!"

"Go ahead, Cat," he said, calling me by the nickname I'd had since infancy. "Go ahead. I don't care."

And the truth was, he didn't. Even though a mixture of rain and sleet fell on this cold February morning, Bubba wore only an old Walking Horse Celebration T-shirt, jeans that had long ago seen better days, a filthy Atlanta Braves baseball cap, and tennis shoes with holes along the front and sides.

Bubba still held the long, narrow wooden twitch (a tool nor-mally used to restrain horses during veterinary procedures) that he used to bat rocks at passing cars. I was so mad at Bubba and his dangerous prank that I could have thrown both Bubba and the twitch across the road. The sad fact is, I doubted his dad would care. Nor would his mother, who had become fed up years ago and left Bubba and Hill for a better life in parts un-known. But, one had to try.

"I'm going to talk to your dad about this," I said, as I snatched the twitch out of the hands of the heir to the Henley clan and stalked past the troubled youth toward his house.

"He ain't here."

"What?" I asked, still walking, not fully hearing.

"My dad ain't here," Bubba shouted. "He took a mare to Shelbyville last night to get bred and he ain't back yet. He's been slower than cold molasses in getting back, he has."

Shelbyville is a small town an hour's drive southeast of Nashville and a good hour and a half from our neighborhood northwest of Nashville. It is the center of the Tennessee Walking Horse industry. Bubba's voice held a touch of concern, and I guessed, in spite of everything, that he loved his dad.

This wasn't the first time Hill had stayed out all night, cruising bars and going home with who knows what. He'd even gotten himself shot once; overslept and the lady's husband found them. Fortunately for Hill, the husband had poor aim and didn't hit any vital parts.

Many Southerners talk about the Civil War, or "The War of Northern Aggression," as if it were a recent event. Hill was no exception. According to Hill, his ancestors saved our neighborhood from battle during "The War." But the truth was that the Henley family used every opportunity the war presented to gain from their neighbors' misfortunes.

Our area had not seen gunfire because a nearby powder mill supplied gunpowder to both the Union and Confederate armies. As neither army wanted to cut off its supply of ammunition, both stayed clear of battle here. The great statesmanship of the Henley clan had nothing to do with it.

Not much had changed for the Henley family in the last one hundred fifty years. Hill was out for everything he could get, and it looked as if the latest generation would be no different.

I sighed and handed the makeshift bat back to Bubba. The kid needed love and counseling—neither of which I could give. Unlike his emaciated father, Bubba carried a few extra pounds, undoubtedly the result of ingesting one too many frozen pizzas. I realized the way to get through to this kid, and prevent my truck from future assault, was through his sizable stomach, so I did the unthinkable and asked if he wanted to join me in town for breakfast.

Bubba gave my offer serious thought, but declined.

"I need to stay home and wait on my dad," he said. "But hey now, if my dad ain't home by noon, I might wander on over for lunch."

"Okay," I replied, "but you have to promise to leave me, and my horses, off your prank list. Agreed?"

He nodded his assent, reluctantly, but then perked up.

"Maybe I will see you later. A body's gotta eat sometime, don't they?"

Those words would soon come back to haunt me.

Cat's Horse Tip #1

"The best teachers of horsemanship are horses."

2

AFTER LEAVING BUBBA, I HEADED EAST on River Road and zoomed into town at the blazing speed of thirty miles per hour. Well, it *was* icy. I'd woken this morning to the familiar rattle of my bedroom window just before sleet came and, sure enough, a few hard pings soon fell on the glass. Ice and sleet were not unusual in February in Nashville. Then again, sunny and seventy wasn't unusual either.

I wanted to load up on supplies in case the sleet turned into a major ice storm. Worst-case scenario was that my farm was right on the Cumberland River and we could haul water up for the horses, but the nearest store was miles away and we could be iced in. My supply of hot chocolate was running low and I sometimes got cranky if I missed my daily dose. Trust me, no one wanted that to happen.

If a big storm didn't develop, I didn't mind a little bad weather driving. Traveling the Appaloosa horse show circuit I had hauled my six-horse rig through all kinds of weather. Most Nashvillians, I'd found, didn't like to drive when the weather was cooler than thirty-three degrees, but somehow they could strip grocery shelves bare at the slightest hint of snow. I hoped this early in the morning I'd catch all the hypocrites who claimed never to have left their homes, yet were sure to leave the stores with empty shelves by noon.

Normally the drive into town was pretty, especially in the spring when, just past the Henley house and continuing a half mile or so, there were scattered fields of wildflowers. But today, ice, sleet, and fog kept any of the fields from being visible.

I ate a hearty breakfast at Verna Mae's, a local "Mom and Pop" that featured the mouthwatering Southern specialty of "meat and three," one choice of meat served with three vegetables and a slice of corn bread. Most meat-and-three's were only open for the noon meal, which Southerners call dinner, but the food at Verna Mae's was so good they couldn't accommodate just the noon crowd. They were open for breakfast, dinner and "supper." After listening to other diners speculate about the weather, I joined a herd of frantic shoppers at Walmart, and gathered enough food to keep me going for a few days.

By the time I arrived home at Cat Enright Stables, the sleet had turned into a cold mist and the sun was trying to break through the murky sky. I am, by the way, Cat Enright, owner for the past seven years of said stables. I'm twenty-nine, single, come from mostly Irish stock, and am just beginning to have some national success on the show circuit.

As I inched up the icy walk to my farmhouse, arms laden with heavy shopping bags, a wriggly half grown puppy burst out of the front doggy door to greet me. I'd found a cold, sodden, shivering Hank sleeping on my porch last November when we returned from the world championships. He is a sweet and happy soul, and it wasn't long before he moved from the porch into the house. Hank is definitely part Beagle. The other parts are anyone's guess.

"Arrrrr. Rrraaaarrrrr," wiggled Hank, meaning, "I'm so happy you're finally home. I've tried to be good while I've been waiting."

I opened the farmhouse door and Hank and I tumbled into the living room. Or what was left of it. While I had shopped, Hank had happily destroyed what used to be my sofa. After my brain registered what my eyes saw, I realized he had taken the foam stuffing out of the cushions and scattered little pieces all over the room.

"Bad dog! Bad! Dog!" I yelled, shaking my finger at Hank and dropping a bag of groceries in the process. It would have to be the bag with the eggs and pickles in it.

I was so mad I felt like shaking *Hank* instead of my finger. But when I approached to toss him out of the house, Hank rolled on his back and wagged his tail. I never could figure out how he could wag his tail so joyfully while he lay upside down.

"Okay," I relented. "But you have to help clean up."

Hank knows I'm a sucker for a tail-wagging dog. He jumped up and contributed to the project by running circles around me, making the tiny pieces of the sofa's innards airborne in the process. I was too busy grabbing soft white flying objects out of the air to see that Hank's circles had gradually changed from fun loving puppy romps to something on the more frantic side. Too late, I realized what it meant. I made a mad dash to grab him, but only got half way there before Hank showered his intentions into the furnace's floor grate.

That's when I knew I was having a bad morning.

This was not the first time Hank had "watered" the furnace, but he had never before been quite so generous. The fragrance of warm dog urine quickly permeated the house. Hmmm. Dog pee in a potentially explosive gas device. I should call the gas company. The lady who answered the phone had a Southern drawl deep enough that I could barely understand her, but she said she could send someone right on out. That was a surprise. With luck, I thought, I would be able to sleep in my own freshly scented bedroom that night.

I opened the door into the mist and dumped Hank outside, knowing he'd happily make a beeline for the dryness of the barn. Peering into the wet murk, I knew I'd be happy if we had an increase in temperature. With Nashville's unpredictable weather, that wasn't impossible. Then again, a hurricane wouldn't surprise me either. In the meantime, I didn't want to spend another minute in my now pungent home, so I cleaned up the broken eggs, the pickles, and the broken pickle jar. Then I put the rest of the groceries away, threw on my barn jacket, and followed Hank to the stable.

At the door to the barn Jon Gardner presided over a snow shovel, aided by an apologetic, tail-wagging Hank. As I approached, Jon put the shovel aside and helped me over a treacherous ridge of ice that had collected in front of the door. He wore a heavy olive-green parka, tan Carhart pants, knee-high muck boots with several colorful layers of socks peeking over the top, and a huge fur-lined cap that looked as if it might have been daily wear somewhere in Siberia. His liquid brown eyes twinkled in spite of the weather.

"Well," I said in lieu of greeting, "you're the only one I've seen this morning who looks as if he's enjoying all this."

I wondered as I spoke if Jon had grown up in a colder climate, as he seemed not to mind ice or snow—though he didn't seem to mind heat and sun either. Although I'd known him for almost three years, my assistant was still an enigma. He had called one day to say he wanted to take a look at the barn and horses. It was a slow day, so I told him to come on over. Two hours later he was moving his things into the small apartment I'd recently had built in the loft of the barn. Although we now worked together every day, I didn't know much more about him than I did three years ago, except that I couldn't get along without him.

"Some things," he said with a grin that split the strong features of his face, "ought to be appreciated. The ice, for instance. Turn around."

His gloved hands spun me around and I found I was facing a fairyland. The sun had finally broken through just over the roofline of the house, and illuminated both it and the ice covered pasture. It was too beautiful for words.

When I bought my farm about seven years ago it featured a seventy-year-old run-down farmhouse on twenty acres complete with a tobacco barn that needed a new roof. In the last few years I had done well enough to add to the barn, re-fence some of the property, paint, build a much-needed covered riding arena, and make minor repairs to the house, but much more needed to be done. In the ice-filtered sunlight, though, the old place looked enchanting.

I watched until I saw a car making its way slowly up the drive. I'd completely forgotten about my ten o'clock riding class. With a sigh, I turned from the sparkling scene and went into the converted stall we used as an office. I needed some thinking time to prepare for my students.

As I walked in, the office phone rang. I debated answering and regretted my decision the moment I lifted the receiver.

"Shopping malls!" cried a familiar voice. "It's perfect—"

"No. No shopping malls," I said, rolling my eyes and unzipping my jacket at the same time. "No cheap promotional stunts, Agnes. Do you understand?"

"Yes, of course I understand, dear. But certainly you can see the advantages."

"No."

"Oh, pooh," she replied. "You don't actually mean that, do you?"

"Agnes, I've had a rough morning. I can't deal with this right now. But I can tell you that no horse in my care will ever be displayed at a shopping mall where the general public can come to gawk."

Agnes was silent for a moment. Unfortunately, the moment didn't last.

"Cat, dear. Please listen. You know you have to promote to keep your name—"

Agnes is a wonderful person and I never forget she owns two horses in my barn and therefore has a vested interest in how I promote those horses. If that weren't the case I wouldn't put up with her, as she is the most exasperating woman I have ever met.

"—in front of the public. Then there are the horses. Such wonderful creatures. Why, if a little girl were to lay eyes on my sweet, psychic Sally Blue—"

"Agnes! Sally is a horse. She is not psychic."

"Of course she is, dear. You must remember last fall? The

world championships? Every day Sally bumped something blue with her nose. Blue is the color of champions. Sally knew she was going to win that class."

Agnes, who saw her seventieth birthday last year, had dyed her short, spiky hair electric blue in honor of both the championship and her horse's name, Sally Blue. If she hadn't gotten blue-tinted lenses in her bifocals, the look never would have worked. I reminded myself that Agnes always paid her bills on time and never complained about the fees. I didn't even mind that she carried the ashes of her three dead husbands around with her in her purse and talked to them all the time, although it sometimes made having a conversation with her difficult, as you never knew who it was that she was talking to.

"Cat, are you listening? Ask Sally. The shopping malls are a great idea."

"You want me to ask one of the horses I train if it is a good idea to display her at a shopping mall?" Agnes was out there but this was a bit much, even for her. "You know that grubby kids will poke at her and try to climb into her stall and tired mothers will ignore their little monsters who are pulling Sally's tail and sooner or later one of the kids will get trampled and we'll get sued?"

Tact is not one of my better qualities. I was afraid my outburst would cause me to lose a good client and—if I were honest—a good friend. So I tried again.

"Agnes, it's not the direction we need to go. Today is Monday. Barely. Drive down Saturday for lunch and we'll figure out a great promotion."

Agnes was silent again. This made twice in a single conversation. Probably a new record.

"I'm only looking out for you," she said in a small voice.

"I know, and you are so wonderful for all you do for me. Now go think up some fun ideas."

I hung up the phone wondering if it was possible for Agnes to come up with anything remotely reasonable.

Cat's Horse Tip #2

"People expect respect. With horses, you have to earn it."

3

THIS WOULD BE A GOOD TIME to mention that most of my business involves the training of Appaloosa show horses. Walk, trot, and canter along the rail, nice and pretty, both Western and English pleasure. I have always loved the distinctive spotted breed, and was thrilled when I was able to assist a now rival trainer when I was in college. Seven years later I am even more enthusiastic about the versatile, intelligent, gentle horses—so much so that I can't imagine doing anything else.

In addition to the training, I give a few lessons to promising students, especially during the off season. And February is about as off as you can get.

This morning's class consisted of four students who were thinking about competing in the show ring. That was three more than I usually handle a lesson. But they all had the same goal so I took them on, as I hoped they would learn as much from one another as they did from me. For the most part, I was right.

Carole Carson was the first to come through the door. My neighbor to the immediate west, Carole was the wife of the very hot, very hunky, country music star, Keith Carson. They had a slew of young kids, a few of whom I gave lessons to on the odd days when I was home in the summer. Did I mention that her husband was gorgeous?

Carole was a good rider, but I guessed that her enthusiasm came more from wanting to establish an identity of her own, away from her famous husband and ever growing brood, than from a true love of horses or competition. Tall and fashionably thin with loose dark auburn curls cascading down her elegant back, Carole fit in with the other students more easily than I'd ever dreamed. There was no star trip from her, but that may have been because one of the other students was a very retired, very theatrical, film star.

Glenda Dupree had to be well into her middle sixties, although she insisted she wasn't a day over fifty-eight. But I'd peeked at some of her early film credits so I knew better. She had come into her own at the tail end of the glamour girl era and she'd played "diva" to the hilt on the silver screen for many years. Off screen . . . well, you'll see..

Tall and curvy, Glenda's aging hourglass figure was holding up remarkably well, assisted, I'm sure, by at least one Hollywood plastic surgeon and a stem cell face-lift or two. She had been born in Nashville, gone to Hollywood while still a teen, made her mark and her millions, and retired here several years back. She wasn't a recluse, but she was adamant that the film star era of her life was finished. Like Cary Grant, she had opted out while she still photographed well.

Glenda owned the farm just east of mine, so she had the pleasure of being sandwiched between Hill Henley and me.

Lucky her. Actually, her home, Fairbanks, had been the original residence of the Henley plantation. Hill had let the towering two story antebellum mansion, complete with lofty white columns, slide into a horrible state of disrepair. Glenda purchased the house just months before I moved in, but it was several years before the extensive renovations on Fairbanks were completed and I had a genuine former movie star living next to me.

Today, an enormous cobalt blue scarf hid Glenda's shoulder length, fashionably streaked blonde hair. The scarf also hid most of her face. I knew her, though, from her runway model strut, her designer jeans, and her theatrical gestures as she entered the barn office. Saying that Glenda Dupree was a pain in the ass to work with is like saying Hannibal Lecter was a little bit danger-ous. But if Glenda ever learned to ride, she'd be great in the show ring.

My third student, Robert Griggs, was a hard one to figure. By profession he was a nurse. By personality he was an absolute stick in the mud. After a few lessons I got the feeling there was a sensitive side to him, but I couldn't quite find it. Everything, from the way he moved to the words he spoke, was controlled and devoid of emotion. He even combed the long bangs of his salt and pepper hair forward, almost to his eyebrows, as if form-ing a barrier to keep intruders out of his mind.

At our first meeting Robert told me that a former girlfriend had gotten him involved with Morgan horses, but as he was no longer seeing the girl, he no longer wanted to ride Morgans. I wondered if the ex was the source of his suffering. But in spite of the lack of personality that surrounded Robert, I liked him. His rare smiles were charming and you could tell he had a real rapport with the horses. He not only liked them, he loved them. I hoped he had the same relationship with his patients.

My last student, Darcy Whitcomb, was, as usual, late. And, as usual, I decided not to wait for her.

We had been working the past few weeks on how attitude affects performance in the show ring, and at the last lesson had videotaped a mock competition. I had spent much of the previous evening reviewing the tape and had typed what I hoped were constructive critiques for each student. With a bright look, I passed out my summaries. Hank assisted by wagging his tail.

The relaxed mood of my three pupils tightened perceptibly as they read my remarks. They finished reading within seconds of each other and turned to me as one, their faces registering emotions that varied from indifference to anger to absolute surprise.

"Now, I understand that some of you may not agree with my comments," I said.

Glenda muttered something unprintable.

"But you all signed up for this class for a reason," I continued. "You want to excel in the show ring, and I intend for you to do just that."

This time Glenda sent a frightful look in my direction. Apparently what she was looking for was affirmation of her already perfect talents.

"If I only mentioned areas where you already excelled," I went on, "if I didn't offer comments on specific areas where you needed to improve, I wouldn't be doing my job. You are all here to gain insight into the show ring, not to receive senseless adulation."

This last part I directed in Glenda's direction. Glenda frowned, her collagen-injected lower lip swelling into a familiar pout. Actually, her showmanship in the ring was superb, instinctive, the obvious result of her many years in front of a camera.

But the mechanics of her horsemanship left a lot to be desired and I'd told her so in my critique.

By far, Carole had turned in the best performance. Entering the ring quietly with her chin up, heels down and shoulders back, she'd turned her head slightly and given the camera an "I am going to knock your socks off" stare and had me won over before the competition even began. I turned on the small TV/DVD combo we kept in the barn and asked the class to watch the tape with the emphasis on Carole's ride. My students watched with the same expressions of indifference, anger, and surprise.

By the time the tape ended, Glenda's anger had turned to a smirk.

"You know, Mary Catherine," she said using my full name, even though, or maybe because, she knew I hated it, "I do treasure your wee efforts to educate us."

Glenda lounged in the one good chair in the room, her jacket unzipped, her scarf and kid leather gloves on my desk. Now that her warm outer clothes had been removed, I saw that her face was as immaculately Botoxed and made-up as ever. Never one to be underdressed, she wore an exquisite cable knit sweater that looked as if it had recently hung in one of the upscale shops in Belle Meade. Her jeans hugged her curvy hips to perfection.

"My wee efforts?" I repeated.

"Yes, wee. It's a good word for you, don't you think?" she asked. "Considering your Irish heritage and all. Too bad, I can't take them seriously. Your efforts, I mean."

Somewhere along the line I'd forgotten that Glenda was a first class bitch. Why in the world had I let her in this class? I'd known her for years. I knew she always had to be the center of attention. When Glenda was around no one else could be recognized for any accomplishment, no matter how insignificant. I knew better, but I let it happen because she'd pestered me so. Glenda, it seemed, always got what Glenda wanted.

"I've been talking with another trainer," she continued, nodding at the others, "and this, well . . . other trainer . . . thinks I'm ready to compete in shows right now."

She stopped, drinking in the astonished looks of her classmates. They were as aware of her lack of riding ability as I.

"In fact," she added, "I've already made plans to compete in several small shows next month."

Embarrassed celebratory mumbling hailed her announcement. But Glenda was oblivious to the uncomfortable feelings of those around her. She shot a dramatic and superior look around the little room, then continued.

"You all know how excited I've been about the possibility of competing in real horse shows. I decided I just couldn't stand another day of those tedious drills and silly exercises we all do," she said with a wave of her hand. "So I talked to this other trainer and, well, he had some fabulous ideas. And here I am, ready to go."

So Glenda had trekked through the cold and ice just to make her big announcement. Her very own mini press conference—without the press. She couldn't have called me on the phone, or even dropped by privately to discuss this. Not once had she indicated that she was unhappy with her progress, or that she wanted to hurry into the show ring. Not that she was anywhere near ready, no matter what the "other trainer" had told her.

We all jumped as the office door banged and a colorful whirlwind of wet mittens and boots burst into the room. My tardy fourth student was once again making an entrance.

Darcy Whitcomb was seventeen going on forty. The only child of Mason Whitcomb, a prominent dot-com entrepreneur, Darcy was, to put it mildly, a spoiled brat. I know, because she'd been training with me since she was thirteen. Since our first meeting four years ago, Daddy Mason had divorced exotic Asian wife number two and was now engaged to number three, a twenty-two-year-old party girl he'd met on a boat off Myrtle Beach. Darcy's mother, wife number one, had long been jet setting in Europe. No one knew when or where she'd turn up, or which duke, prince, or count she'd have in tow. In spite of all the parental marrying and divorcing and spoiling, Darcy was a good kid and I had a feeling she'd turn out okay.

Of the four, Darcy was the only one with show ring experience. Until eighteen months ago she'd been one of the top youth competitors in the nation. But she lacked the ambition—the drive—to be successful on a regular basis. She stayed out of competition all last season and spent the summer being a regular teenager. Regular teenaged life, apparently, wasn't all it was cracked up to be and Darcy decided to take this class to see if she was ready to come back to give it a better shot. Secretly, I thought she came back because there was no other place for her to go where people understood her. Either way, she was a good addition because she willingly lent her wealth of experience to the others in the class.

Darcy shook her thick, waist length blonde hair out of a Santa stocking cap, turned her huge blue eyes toward me and said, "What's up?"

The room couldn't have been any quieter if the Pope had walked through the door.

"I was just telling the others," Glenda finally drawled, "that I have decided to switch to a new trainer. Hill Henley."

My first reaction to the name of the trainer was to collapse into the scarred wooden desk I was leaning against. The shock was as real as if someone had punched me in the stomach. But as the full impact of the name Hill Henley whirled through my brain, a comforting thought popped in: the two deserved each other.

"Hill is just full of wonderful advice. Which, naturally, I am all ears for. It's been a while since I had any good advice," she said.

Glenda was in the middle of quite a performance and by now she knew she owned the small audience.

"Of course Hill is a fourth-generation Walking Horse trainer. This business of training horses is in his blood. He grew up around it. His ancestors even saved the area during The War of Northern Aggression. Did any of you know that?" Glenda's look was condescending. "No, of course you didn't. How silly of me."

It was all I could do not to throttle her right then and there. Have I mentioned that I have a very small anger management problem? Nothing serious, really, but it does pop up from time to time. Recognizing that I was on the verge of losing my temper, I instead bit my tongue. It would prove to be a life-saving gesture. Well, my life, anyway.

I, as did the others in the room with the possible exception of Robert Griggs, knew all about the Henleys. Furthermore, we all knew much more than she about the highway robbery and horse thievery that permeated the Henley ancestral tree. Not that I planned on filling Glenda in on the gory details. I'd let her find that out for herself.

"Hill says I am going to become the next Champion Rider of the Year," Glenda announced with a grand sweep of her arm.

Carole looked up from the melting globs of ice she'd been intently inspecting on the floor. Her face only partially contained a smile. Robert looked blankly around the room. Like the rest of us, I imagined he wished he were somewhere else. Darcy, ever loyal, looked ready to pounce.

"I'm also going to tell everyone just who helped me get to the winner's circle, and," Glenda added, "who didn't."

I knew very well that it was ridiculous. Hill Henley could never make Glenda Dupree champion of anything. Not in his wildest dreams. If you throw money around right and left it will only get you so far in the show ring; eventually you have to actually stay on the horse. But like it or not, Glenda was a famous film star. Excuse me. Former film star. Either way, people would believe what she had to say. At least at first.

I didn't believe she could do me much damage as far as prospective clients go. Due to the very different build and use of each breed, Appaloosa people and Walking Horse people did not mix all that often. It was like the difference between a dentist and a podiatrist. Both were doctors, but at different ends of the spectrum. We did use many of the same veterinarians, feed suppliers and other vendors, however, and I realized it was a situation that would have to be handled carefully.

For the first time since she exploded through the door Darcy moved. Crossing the tiny office to stand directly over Glenda, she looked down at her.

"Like that idiot next door could teach you anything. Get real," said Darcy with all the sarcasm her seventeen years could muster.

Glenda gave Darcy a bemused look. It was clear that Glenda thought Darcy's intelligence was somewhere in the neighborhood of owl poop.

"Honey," she said, sarcasm dripping all over the word, "Why don't you go play with your little girlfriends or whatever it is that you do? You'll be so much happier if you stick to your own kind and stay out of important business that can't possibly concern you." Then she laughed and flung her hand in a cruel and dismissive gesture.

Robert tensed and I thought for a moment that this was the time he was going to let out all those pent up emotions. His face was snow white; his already thin lips were bloodless. He opened his mouth several times, but when he realized nothing was going to come out, he grabbed his coat and hurried from the room.

"You bitch," spat Darcy. "I used to think you were cool. I admired you. But you're totally fake. I hope you die a thousand deaths!"

Darcy had a good thing going, but then emotion welled up in her eyes and she, too, stormed out. Never one to enjoy an argument, Hank quickly followed. Through the open door I saw Jon frowning in at us, but I shook my head and he shrugged back, letting me handle it.

As all but one other member of the class had already run out the door, Glenda could see that if she didn't leave soon, there would be no one left to witness her grand exit, so she dramatically gathered her things and swept herself from the room.

Maybe if I'd known it was the last time I'd see her alive, I would have gone after her. Then again, maybe not.

4

OKEY-DOKEY THEN. I FORCED MYSELF to turn my attention to Carole, who made up the entire remainder of my class. Our time was almost up, and trying to continue at this point was useless. I apologized for the loss of class time, and reminded her that we would be back in the saddle again next week. Of them all, I thought Carole had been least disturbed by the incident. In fact, she seemed to be amused by the unusual turn of events. Her amber eyes had danced throughout the messy scene. Being married to a country music superstar must be an unconventional life, so maybe she came up against emotional incidents all the time. If so, she had my sympathy, for this was the kind of stuff I had no wish to handle.

Alone at last. I closed the office door, sank into the good chair Glenda had so recently occupied, closed my eyes, and allowed myself a huge sigh. We Irish people are big on sighing. It helps diffuse all the emotionally draining confrontations we seem to have.

I told myself that I'd trade a thousand clients like Glenda for one ditsy client like Agnes in a heartbeat. Agnes's motives were pure; she just wanted to help. Come to think of it, Glenda's motives were pure as well, because when you broke it down, Glenda was a very simple person. Glenda was all Glenda ever cared about. I had forgotten that and had considered myself her friend.

Glenda, I knew now, had no friends, only adversaries that she sometimes used to her advantage. And if the adversary happened along the way to think that friendship was included in the deal, well, then someone was going to be disappointed. I'd dealt with disappointment before and surely would again. Losing a friend you never had was not the end of the world. The problem now, I thought, was to keep Glenda from becoming my enemy and I wasn't quite sure how to do that.

I opened the old wooden door that led from the office to the barn and found Darcy stomping up and down the aisle. Her short body had not yet lost all its baby fat and the layers of winter clothes made her look as round as a cartoon kid. I took one look at her and pointed her in the direction of stall number four.

A tall, black ten-year-old gelding with irregular white spots across his body inhabited that stall. Petey always had the ability to calm Darcy down, and vice versa. I'd found Petey for Darcy four years ago, when she first started training with me. Their temperaments were perfect for each other, and the years of hard work and play had forged a very strong bond.

Petey was also a real ham. He liked to hold the end of a cotton lead rope in his mouth and "lead" himself down the aisle. In the crossties Petey flapped his lips together in pleasure when Darcy groomed him, but wouldn't "flap" for anyone else. He whinnied when he heard her car and, if he was in the pasture, ran to the gate to see her. It was a big deal for a horse to choose to leave the security of his pasture mates—and his food—to spend time with a human. Horses always feel safer in numbers. Petey, however, left his equine friends for Darcy all the time.

I could see Darcy's facial muscles relax as she opened Petey's stall door, and I knew that in a few minutes she'd be fine. That made me glad; I loved that kid like a sister.

I turned to find Robert directly in front of me. Jon once commented that Robert was so thin he'd have to stand up twice to cast a shadow. Looking at Robert now, I knew Jon's assessment was accurate. Additionally, Robert wasn't much taller than my five-foot-six. Seen straight on, Robert's long, narrow nose had an odd bump halfway down, as if it might have been broken at one time and hadn't healed properly. A small gold hoop adorned his left ear.

I'd noticed before that Robert walked silently. He could appear out of nowhere and vanish just as abruptly. Maybe it was a technique he'd learned in nursing school. Floor Walking 101. It might work in a hospital, I thought, but in the barn it was a bit disturbing.

"I, well . . . I wanted to say something," he said.

"All right." We walked toward the now brightened outdoors, passing the stall of Agnes's (possibly psychic) prize mare, AT's Sally Blue. Sally stuck her mottled red head into the aisle and I gave her a friendly pat. Psychic or not, it was easy for me to love a horse who so readily loved me back.

Once outside Robert gave the briefest of smiles. "I just wanted you to know that I never liked Glenda and I know that the horses didn't either."

"The horses? What do you mean, Robert?" I asked, turning toward the house. The magical sunlit fairyland I had so enjoyed a short hour ago was now gone, melted by the sun that earlier had given it its glory. What a day this was turning out to be. All I wanted now was a cup of hot chocolate and some peace and quiet.

Robert stopped my musing by staring earnestly into my eyes. "The horses are always tense when Glenda is around. Haven't you noticed, especially with Sally Blue? When Glenda is in the barn the horses rustle around in their stalls more. And in lessons they are always watching her. It's like the horses are uneasy because they don't know what to expect from her. And they're right. You taught us that animals, and horses in particular, pick up on things that have been educated and civilized out of humans, and you're right. So it's good for all of us that she's gone and I just wanted to say I hope you don't try to bring her back into the class. She's an evil person. The further away she is from everyone the better."

I sighed and said, "Robert, I think some things were meant to be, and for now, I think Glenda and Hill Henley are meant to work together. If that's the case, we won't be seeing much of her."

He gave what passed for another smile and nodded. Then he walked soundlessly toward his car without a word of farewell. He was strange, that one.

Ahead of me, the van from the gas company headed down the driveway. They must have arrived after my students had. Jon had probably let the technician into the house. Hopefully this meant my damaged furnace been revived from Hank's morning shower.

To my left, Glenda's Fairbanks loomed, looking cold and pale and unfeeling, its shadows creating grotesque patterns on the melting ice. I shuddered and half walked, half ran, to my kitchen to indulge myself in a thick, rich comforting mug of hot chocolate.

Cat's Horse Tip #3

"Horses hear and smell things that humans physically can't."

5

AFTER A QUICK LUNCH I TOOK a long time to think about my disastrous morning. To be honest, I have never dealt well with disasters. Add confrontations and arguments to that list. My grandma always claimed the Irish way was to avoid problems, so I come by my aversion honestly.

At least the furnace still worked and the house didn't smell too bad. Well, okay, I'm lying to myself. The house still smelled like pig doo-doo after it had baked a while in the sun. Maybe by nightfall the odor would be gone. Thinking tends to tire me out, so I grabbed a catnap and woke suddenly after about an hour with the perfect plan to deal with Glenda.

Pulling from my purse a crumpled business card with a hand-drawn map on the back, I ran a wide tooth comb through my tangled mop of mouse-brown curls, started up the truck and headed for Music Row. It was an easy twenty-five minute drive with little traffic along the way. I took the Demonbreun exit off

I-40, drove past the row of renovated buildings that now housed several of Nashville's most popular places to "eat, drink, and be merry," navigated the new circular roundabout with the controversial nude sculpture, and finally hooked a left on 18th Avenue South.

Reading the map on the back of the card, I found the house a few blocks down, but had to drive past and double back in the alley behind it to find parking. That was okay, because Adam's office was located in the back of the house, second floor, accessed by a set of rickety black metal stairs. Under the stairs three yellow daffodils were bravely blooming through the bleak winter sun. Some years there were scores of early spring flowers tucked away in corners throughout Middle Tennessee. These were the first I'd seen this year.

I sat in my truck for a few minutes before I got up the nerve to knock on Adam's office door. It was silly, really, because I hardly knew the man. On the other hand, I thought my feelings were justified, because what I knew I didn't like. Adam had moved here from California last summer and I'd run into him at a few neighborhood parties. There was something about him. Too much ego. Too much cool. But he did say if I ever needed anything he'd be glad to help. So here I was.

I climbed the stairs to a small porch and knocked on an imposing metal door. I heard a few scuffled movements inside and then the door cracked opened.

"Why, Cat," he said. "How wonderful to see you! Please, please come in."

Adam's office was quite upscale for someone who had just embarked upon a songwriting career. Although it consisted of a single room about the size of an average living room, Adam's aunt had had the room "done" as a welcome-to-Nashville gift for her only nephew. Thick black carpeting sank under the weight of my feet. What looked an awful lot like polished oak paneling—and probably was—lined the walls, while a heavy beveled-glass coffee table sat in the far corner. It was surrounded by a plush black leather couch and matching chairs.

Next to the door was a brass coat rack, a combination refrigerator and microwave, and a black four-drawer filing cabinet. Straight ahead was a modern black desk with a laptop, and one of those nifty machines that phones, faxes, prints and would probably do your laundry if you knew how to program it. To my right was an impressive looking stereo/TV/DVD unit with speakers spread throughout the room. Most songwriters would give anything to have a writing room like this.

"Excuse my attire," Adam said, indicating his disordered clothes. His starched jeans were rumpled and spattered with mud, his long sleeved T-shirt partially untucked, his spit-and-polish loafers scuffed and streaked with dirt. "I pulled over on I-40, just by the 440 split to check a tire I thought was low and a semi came by and splattered me with road sludge."

The mussed clothing did nothing to diminish Adam's rugged good looks. His dark blonde locks were attractively disheveled, his six-foot-one body, if a bit on the thin side, was well proportioned, and his face reminded me of a young Robert Redford. He invited me to sit on the leather couch, and I did.

"I hope I'm not interrupting anything," I said. "I can come back another time if this isn't convenient. On second thought, maybe I'd better do that. It was rude of me to stop by without calling first."

Being around Adam always made me babble. I couldn't figure out if it was his money, his good looks, or his infamous family tree, but I just couldn't relax around him.

"No, no. Oh, please stay, Cat. I'm so glad you've finally come to visit," said Adam. Then his nose twitched. "Do you smell something?"

I flushed beet red. Hank's mutant urine vapors must have attached themselves to my clothes and hair. Can I just die of embarrassment right here and now?

"Uh. No. I don't smell a thing." I began twitching my own nose in an exaggerated manner, followed by equally exaggerated shrugging, as if to prove any odd smell must be his imagination. Probably I should have showered before I headed over here, but I was so determined to find a solution to the Glenda situation that when one presented itself after my nap, I dived right in without thinking. Fact is, not thinking tends to be a habit of mine.

Adam gave one final, uncertain sniff, then said, "You know, I said to my aunt just the other day, 'I need to call Cat, it's been weeks since I've seen her.' And here you are."

"Well, Adam, that's why I'm here."

He laughed, but the light had gone out of his eyes, "I . . . I see. You're here because my aunt sent you."

"Oh, no," I protested. "I'm here, well, let me just dive in on this. There was a nasty scene at the barn this morning. I'm not sure what to do about it so I came to you because the source of the trouble was your Aunt Glenda."

Adam Dupree rubbed a weary hand over his face and paced the small room as I nervously explained what had happened. "I don't care if she goes to Hill. I couldn't work with her anyway, under the circumstances," I concluded. "But I also don't want her to spread false rumors about me, my horses, my clients, or my stable. I just want her to go her way and leave me alone. No hard feelings."

"I'm sorry she embarrassed you," he said, sitting on the arm of one of the matching chairs. "But if you want her to keep the rumor mill from rumbling, you have to make Aunt Glenda think it's in her best interests to keep quiet."

"I'd love to, but how do I do that?"

"For it to work, you need to march right over there and confront her, just as she did you. Firmness is one of the few things she respects, but you'll have to grovel a little, too. Tell her you admire the courage it took to make such a decision and that you realize you are not worthy of her time. Wish her well. But you've got to play it just right. End it by making her think it was her idea to leave you alone."

I took in his words of encouragement, but Adam's expression left me dubious about any success for my mission.

"You mean just go over to Fairbanks and ring the doorbell and barge in?" Glenda was notorious both for her privacy and her formality. One didn't just barge in on the diva.

Adam stared at me without saying anything. Then he raised one eyebrow. At least his nose was no longer twitching.

"I guess you're right," I sighed. "But I'm just not good at that sort of thing, confrontations and all."

"All you have to do," he told me, "is look her straight in the eye. Don't waiver. Don't back off. She abhors people who are weak. Stand up to her. She won't give you an inch, but she'll listen."

It was a task much easier said than done.

6

NOW THAT I HAD MADE UP my mind to deal with Glenda, I wanted to get it over with as soon as possible. I decided to drive straight from Music Row to Fairbanks. I was just ahead of the rush hour traffic, but it was windy and almost dark by the time I turned off River Road onto the paved drive of the stately antebellum home. When I got out of the truck I noticed the air was still damp from the morning's sleet. If the wind kept up, it was going to be a cold and miserable night.

As I started toward the steps I tripped on something soggy and fell, scraping the heel of my right hand as I landed in a damp puddle. Great. I'm going to intimidate the hell out of Glenda looking like this. Wind tangled hair. Pants soaking wet. Bloody hand. Oh right, and no lip gloss. I hadn't put any makeup on today. Imagine that.

I rolled out of the puddle and sat there in Glenda's wet driveway, as the emotions of the day washed over me. I don't know why I allowed Glenda get to me. Maybe it was the celebrity. Don't we all treat celebrities a little differently? With Nashville being the country music capital of the world, we bumped into our share of the rich and famous at the Waffle House, grocery store, or even Walmart. And you find that, just like regular folk, some are nice and some you wouldn't walk across the street for. So what was it about Glenda that turned me into a quivering pile of jelly? Why could I not "cowgirl up" and stand my ground with her?

I pondered the question as I stared at the object that tripped me. I thought I'd tripped over a rag that had been carelessly left near the steps, but when I reached out to move the object away from my rubber muck boot, I saw it was a baseball cap. Or had been. Now it was splattered with a dark, sticky substance and the bill was partially torn off. There was an Atlanta Braves logo above the torn bill, and Bubba Henley had worn a cap like that just this morning.

I scrambled up the steps, ran across the deep porch, and pounded frantically with my uninjured fist on the massive seventeenth-century slab of wood that served as Glenda's front door. She'd had the door imported from a castle in England and had to enlarge the door frame to accommodate it. At the time, Hill had been horrified at the break from traditional Southern architecture. Guess he'd gotten over it.

"Glenda," I shouted above the wind. "Glenda, are you home?" I switched from pounding on the door, which was beginning to hurt my fist, to sinking my finger into the doorbell. The door was so thick, I couldn't hear if the doorbell was working or not.

"Glenda, please come to the door. It's Cat. It's important."

The house remained as dark and silent as when I'd arrived.

I took the cap and hurried around the right side of Fairbanks. Then I crawled through Glenda's pristine, white post-and-rail fence to the Henley farm. This reeked of one of Bubba's pranks, but I had to make sure it wasn't something far more serious.

"Bubba," I shouted as I banged on the metal trailer door. "Bubba! Hill! Open up." Around me the wind swirled a fine mist from the river. I banged some more, then I jiggled the doorknob and the flimsy door swung open.

Inside, the place had that deserted feel, that emptiness when you get home and know deep down that no one is there, not even the cat. I flipped the light switch next to the door. Nothing. Hill must have forgotten to pay his electric bill. I hadn't thought to bring a flashlight, but there was still enough light outside for me to peer into the dim interior.

I stepped into the house and just as quickly stepped out. It felt spooky and I realized that someone could be in there after all. On the other hand, I reasoned, if someone was in the house, it would most likely be Bubba or Hill, and I had a perfectly good excuse for breaking and entering. Well, Hill might not think so, but probably I could convince Bubba.

I hate dark places. I stood in the mist, my heart thumping, trying to gather up the courage to go back in the house. Only the thought of a child who might be hurt made me step back across the threshold. I wasn't going to leave, I told myself, until I'd either found Bubba or found the house as devoid of life as it appeared to be. Missing child or not, the thought of searching the dim rooms made me as tense as a mule in a submarine. I am such a chicken.

The flimsy trailer wobbled slightly as I walked into the living room.

"Bubba," I forced myself to call out in a pleasant voice. "Bubba, are you here?"

There was enough illumination to see general shapes and not much more. Was that a rebel flag tacked to the ceiling? I believe it was. I put my hand on the wall to guide me but jerked it back to my side when I encountered something slimy. On second thought, there was enough light that I didn't have to touch anything.

I could tell that the far wall held the outline of a couch. A table in front of it was littered with what looked like trash. On closer inspection it could have been fast food containers. Maybe.

"Bubba?"

I took a left into the kitchen. It was small and messy, but a quick glance told me Bubba was not there. I took a couple of deep breaths to try to calm my shakiness. Snooping through someone else's house was not my idea of fun. I wanted nothing more than to get out of there. Now. But if Bubba was inside the house and not answering, he was probably unconscious and in need of help. I took a left out of the kitchen and doubled back into the narrow hall behind it. It was darker back here and I felt, more than looked, my way through two bedrooms and a bath.

The fact that I felt with my boots more than my bare hands is not important. I searched well enough to know with certainty that Bubba was not there. I finished with a fast but thorough search of the yard around the trailer, then ran back to Glenda's driveway and to the safety and comfort of my truck.

I sat there for a few minutes, Bubba's bloody cap in my hand. My heart thumped and my legs shook as I wondered what the hell to do next. Bubba was not my kid. But Hill wasn't home and Bubba was a human being who could be bleeding profusely.

Either that or he had just pulled off the prank of the century. If so, I was going to be thoroughly pissed.

Maybe I should head over to Hill's barn to see if his horses had been fed their evening meal. That would be an indication that Hill or Bubba had been present somewhat recently, unless the hired help had done the feeding. Or maybe the horses were fed later in the evening. I didn't keep up with Hill's schedule.

I sighed, got out of the truck, and made a brief foray to Hill's barn. I was able to snag a quick peek through the window in the office door before Hill's two snarling Dobermans raced to the glass from inside the barn and made a beeline for my throat. Sadly for them both the door and the window in it held firm. It was the lack of human noise more than anything that convinced me that, other than me, dogs and horses were the only beings present. If a person were in there, he or she would have to be as deaf as a Moon Pie not to investigate the racket the dogs were making.

I thought angrily about the filth that Bubba was living in; surely Hill's precious clients never saw that. The one time I had been inside his barn, it had been immaculate. Poor kid. No mother, and a father who was just plain sorry. Bubba certainly hadn't had it easy. I wondered briefly if my concern for Bubba meant my biological clock was starting to tick a little louder. Nah. I shook my head. Not yet.

So, damp, scraped, and bedraggled, I drove the short distance home. When I picked up the phone to call the Cheatham County Sheriff's department, I remembered that Bubba had not shown up at my place for lunch. If Bubba had missed an opportunity to eat, something was seriously wrong.

7

CHEATHAM COUNTY IS A MUSHROOM SHAPED piece of land just west of the combined city and county of Nashville/Davidson County. It is bisected north and south by the Cumberland River, the south shore being where my farm lies. The particular stretch of River Road that my neighbors and I shared was kind of a stepchild of both Cheatham and Davidson Counties. We all had Nashville addresses, phone numbers, and electrical service; but our water, gas, and law enforcement came from Cheatham County, where the properties were actually located. We weren't offered sewer service from either county. So close were we to the county line that a small section of the Henley property was actually in Davidson County.

Hill claimed his ancestors planned it that way so they could have their say in both Davidson and Cheatham Counties. I always thought the original Henleys messed up and put the county line in the wrong spot. But we'll never know, will we? Regardless of the intent, the actual site of the Henley home was in Cheatham County. That's why I gave the sheriff's department across the river in Ashland City a call.

The deputy who arrived a few minutes later was a member of the Giles family. I knew that even before I looked at his name tag simply because he had the prominent chin, pale hair, and jug ears that all members of the Giles family are afflicted with. There were lots of people with the surname Giles in Cheatham County, which was odd, as Giles County is in south central Tennessee and nowhere near here. There must have been a very prolific Giles who moved here years ago to account for as many of them as there were. A look at the deputy's nametag confirmed that he was indeed Giles, Martin.

Giles, Martin was somewhere in his mid-twenties. He wore the standard brown and tan county deputy uniform along with a thick down jacket. He was of stocky build, around six feet tall, and still had a bit of peach fuzz on his doughy face. I had heard that Cheatham County deputies came and went pretty quickly due to the county's low pay scale, but I thought this one might stick around for a while; he had a lot of family in the neighborhood. Besides, Hank's frantically wagging tail confirmed that the deputy was indeed one of the good guys, and I guarantee that there is no better measure of the human spirit than Hank's tail.

As I sized him up, I could tell the deputy was doing the same for me—masses of curly, mouse-brown hair, thin but muscular body, long nose a little too large with a rash of freckles spread across the bridge. My pointed chin was a little too small, my teeth a little too large. On the plus side was the fact I'd once been told that my bright green eyes saved my face from utter plainness. A former boyfriend made the comment about my eyes while he thought he was breaking up with me. In reality, it was I who was breaking up with him, and it wasn't because of what he thought of my eyes, or my face. Looking into Deputy Giles eyes, I knew I passed inspection.

I could see by the polite twitch of the deputy's nose that my house was still faintly scented with dog urine. But the deputy looked to be a well-bred Southern boy, which meant he was too mannerly to say anything and I, not quite as well-bred but possessing just enough breeding to be thoroughly embarrassed, did not mention it either.

After we dispensed with the niceties, I found that Bubba Henley was no stranger to Deputy Giles. He was, in fact, kin, as Deputy Giles's maternal grandmother had been a Henley. The genealogy out of the way, I showed him what was left of the cap and explained where and how I found it.

When I finished, he stared at the dark red stains on the cap. "Guess I'd better call it in. The lab will know whether or not these are human blood stains," he said slowly.

I got the feeling that Deputy Giles did everything slowly.

"The kid's another matter," he continued. "We don't know for sure if he's hiding, or missing, or off somewheres with his dad. But knowing the background of the family and looking at the weather out there, we'll round up some guys and start a search. Check the barn out first. I can tell you though, folks won't be real happy about it. On top of the weather being bad, Bubba's not the best liked kid around. We've dealt with him before and it's usually some childish game he's playing. Either that or he's done run away again."

He took his time as he carefully placed the cap in an evidence bag. "On the other hand, looking at that bloody cap, assuming that it *is* his blood, is enough to make you want to search all night."

While Deputy Giles called in his report, I began to worry that Bubba would show up of his own accord. It would be just like Bubba to wait until we got half the county out here and then wander in on his own. If that were the case, I made up my mind to thrash his pudgy bottom myself. Of course, Hill would probably sue me for child abuse, but what the hell.

It wasn't too many minutes after the deputy called in his report that I began to see the lights of several vehicles over at the Henley place. The big sliding door to the barn was opened and I thought of the brave person who dared face Hill's dogs. I hoped he (or she) remembered to bring along a tranquilizer gun. Beams of light from portable lanterns started to bob in erratic patterns in the pastures of all our farms.

I remembered my mission to confront Glenda, but one look at the clock and another at my grimy face, and I decided it could wait another day. As much as I wanted to stay up for Bubba reports, by midnight I was exhausted. I took a quick shower, bandaged my still oozing hand, and dabbed my face with an organic cream that Agnes swore also brought about positive karma. Then I said a quick prayer for Bubba as I slid between the clean warmth of my sheets.

8

I ROSE EARLY THE NEXT MORNING in preparation to feed. Unless it was my or Jon's day off, I fed in the morning, and Jon in the evening. Hank and I headed for the barn at six o'clock sharp under the cover of a dawn that promised nothing but thick gray clouds and more damp air.

I loved mornings. I loved the cool stillness of the air and the sound of stomps and whinnies as the horses greeted me. There is something very relaxing about watching a horse eat and I treasured my morning minutes with my equine friends.

Hank did, too. He supervised as I pulled hay from the feed stall and distributed it to each horse. Hank's morning ritual was to stick his nose into every flake, as if he was a quality control expert. Then he sat by the grain bin as I measured the correct amount of feed for each horse and mixed supplements that were formatted for that horse's individual needs. Hank then personally inspected each horse's stall as I looked over every horse for the odd bump or scrape he or she might have acquired overnight, and as I cleaned and checked the automatic waterers. By the time I was done, we were both ready for our own breakfast.

On a sobering note, this morning, on my walk back toward the house, I noticed there was still a county vehicle over at the Henley place and I assumed that the fact it was there meant the searchers had found nothing.

I was back in my kitchen by six-thirty and had just poured a cup of coffee when the doorbell rang. It was Deputy Giles come to tell me they had called off the search of the immediate area. For now.

"We did an inspection of the area and we know the kid is not in the neighborhood. But," he said, silencing my protests before I could voice them, "we've stationed a guy at the Henley house. That's standard procedure. Chances are that Bubba's run away, but we take runaways serious like and won't give up 'til we find him."

Wishing that I'd never heard of Hill or Bubba Henley didn't do me any good, for it wasn't much more than an hour after Deputy Giles left that Hill himself banged on my door.

"I been talkin' to cops for half an hour and I want to know what makes you and them think that by Bubba bein' out all night Bubba ain't doing just what he wants?" he demanded as he barged in to my living room. Have I mentioned that Hill Henley is dumb enough to throw himself on the ground and miss?

Hill wore a long-sleeved denim shirt that had seen better days, and filthy jeans that could have been kin to those worn by his son. What hair remained on his head was black and stringy and his face had not seen a razor in at least two, three days. The whole package made me want to dunk him in the horse trough. It would have been a big improvement.

"If I thought Bubba was somewhere safe, I wouldn't have called the sheriff," I said calmly. The fact that I could handle Hill's wrath without batting an eye, but being around Glenda made me want to cower like a kicked dog, flickered through my mind.

I led Hill through the living room and back into the kitchen where he helped himself to the last of my coffee and sat down at the kitchen table. At that point I was so mad at Hill that I almost forgot to worry about Bubba. A ten-year-old does not stay out all night in the cold and rain voluntarily. The house, with no electricity, would be cold, but at least Bubba would have been out of the wind and dampness.

"Oh yeah," he sneered, "go right ahead, call the law on my boy. That's how you people handle ever'thing. Get them hard-asses to snoopin' through all my stuff, and without a warrant, I might add. You ain't any different from the rest of 'em. You don't give a shit about ol' Hill."

He jumped up and ran cigarette stained fingers through his straggly hair. "An' just what were you doin' with my boy anyhow? That's what I wanta find out. Just how the hell did you know he warn't home and who invited you to call the po-lice? Whyn't you mind your own god-damned business? I try my damnedest to raise him in a God-fearing manner and here's what goes an' happens."

I wondered if ignoring his son for years on end was Hill's definition of God-fearing child raising.

"Yesterday morning he was cold and hungry," I said, "and quite worried about you. He was at the end of your driveway batting rocks at passing cars with a twitch, so like any friendly neighbor, I invited him to lunch. But he didn't show, so I assumed you were home to—"

"Whaddya mean, 'He was hungry?' I went all the way up to Ashland City and bought him a couple o' them happy meals afore I left. Bubba's too fat anyway, it's embarrassin' the way he eats all the time. If'n he were an inch taller, he'd almost be round. He jus' don't need to be eatin' ever'thing in sight."

"So is that why you didn't take him with you, because he's too fat? Because he embarrasses you? Because—"

"I didn't leave him by hisself. My man come in twice a day to feed. Bubba coulda told him if he needed anythin'. My Bubba ain't all that smart, but he knows how to use a telly-phone."

"Let me see if I have this right. You haul a mare to Shelbyville, leave after supper Sunday night and don't come home until Tuesday morning. In the process, you leave a ten-year-old boy home alone with no food and no supervision, no electricity, no place where he could reach you, no one to call if—"

"Now you hold on just a god-damn minute, Missy. I—"

"Have you ever heard the phrase 'child neglect,' Hill? Do you understand the concept? Do you realize that if anything has happened to Bubba, it's your neck they'll hang? Not mine, not the 'law's,' no one else's. Just yours."

"What the hell—you tryin' to scare me? He's my kid and I'll raise him as I see fit. Plus, I don't want to see him 'round this here place no more. He comes back from here and tells me how to run my barn. I try to lead a horse the civilized way with a chain over its nose and he says, 'No. Cat does it this way,' and wants me to take the chain off. He says if I need a chain the horse don't respect me none. Well I been doin' this a long time and I don't need no learnin' from no kid or no silly-ass girl."

"You assume Bubba will be back."

"Now what's that supposed to mean? A course he'll be back. But things'll be different 'round here when that happens I can tell you. The law crawlin' all over my place ain't doin' my business no good. It'll mess me up good for years to come, I can tell you. And it's all your doing. You'll hear from my lawyer. That I can guarantee."

He stood, belligerently, in front of me. A stupid, selfish man overwhelmed with his own importance. Overwhelmed, and losing sight of the fact his son was missing and probably in need of medical attention. But then, as if he could sense what I was thinking, that realization started to sink in.

"What am I goin' to do now?" he said softly, his head sinking into his hands.

Gee, maybe there was a real person in there somewhere, for Hill looked like he was afraid. Of losing Bubba, of losing face, of what the "law" might find in its search, I didn't know. But there was a glimpse of real emotion in his eyes.

"You're going to do everything you can to find him," I said as I led him back to the kitchen table. "Who are his friends from school? What does he like to do? What kinds of games does he like to play? You're his dad. You know the answers to those questions better than anyone else, and those answers will help lead the searchers to Bubba."

Hill just shook his head. "I don't know. I jus' don't know."

I sighed and wondered about Bubba's mother, if he could have run to her, or to another relative, but before I could ask, Hill stopped that idea cold.

"It's just me an' him. With all the relatives I got 'round here, there's never been no family that'd help us. Not even his ma. Oh, man alive, I don't know what I'd do without that boy."

Hill now looked trapped, like a fox who realized he'd no place left to run. I wondered just where it was that Hill had been these past few days.

He sighed, muttered what sounded an awful lot like an apology, and let himself out the front door. I got an empty feeling when I realized there was nothing I could do to help.

Cat's Horse Tip #4

"Home is where the horse is."

9

WHEN I GOT TO THE COVERED arena later that morning, Jon was already there, longeing a yearling filly we hoped to take with us on the show circuit that summer. I think whoever invented longeing should be elected president, as it's about the most efficient way to exercise a horse there is. If a horse is too young to be ridden, or suffers from stiffness and needs to loosen up, longeing is the way to go.

All one had to do is attach a long rope—or longe line—to the horse's halter, then just stand there as the horse moves around him or her in a large circle. The human controls the horse's speed by positioning his or her body either toward the horse's neck or the tail, and this positioning also helps the horse understand that the person, and the not horse, is in charge.

Using body language to teach a horse trust and respect for the human partner is a basic concept, but not one that is easily mastered. It is best done is a circular enclosure called a round pen, where the horse can be "free longed," or longed without the halter or longe line. But, I didn't have a round pen. Most of the show grounds we went to didn't have one either, or if they did, there was often a long line waiting to use it, so we longed a lot. Besides, longeing was a great training tool to help a horse become supple; and for teaching voice commands such as walk, trot, canter, and the all-important whoa.

The name of the filly Jon was working with was Glamour Girl G, and it was an appropriate name, I thought, as I watched her taut muscles ripple through her glistening chestnut coat. As far as I'm concerned there isn't a bad color as long as there's a horse attached, but Gigi was exceptional. Her breeding was impeccable. Her legs moved fluently, gracefully; her head tapered to a small muzzle and large nostrils, and her neck arched with the knowledge that she was perfection itself.

I might also add that the gorgeous Gigi was nuts. She was, simply put, scatter-brained, which was unusual in the Appaloosa breed. I thought of the coming horse shows with a mixture of pride and trepidation. On one hand, I knew there wasn't a filly in the country that could compare to her breeding, conformation, and beauty. On the other hand, the thought of hauling that silly youngster miles on end, show after show, week after week, was enough to make me think seriously about leaving her home. But Darcy's dad, Mason Whitcomb, owned the filly. He'd been a good client throughout the years and I knew he had a real shot at a national or world championship with her.

No question, I sighed to myself, the filly was going on the road. We'd been using a lot of natural horsemanship techniques on Gigi—plus relaxation exercises, music, massage, acupuncture, and chiropractic—but so far it had only calmed her down a little. I'd also consulted with an equine nutritionist, and had recently changed her rations. It was too soon to see if that would help or not.

After calling a greeting to Jon, I checked the cinch on the well-used western saddle I preferred to use at home because it fit almost every horse I rode, and climbed aboard an old friend called Hillbilly Bob. My very first client, an orthopedic surgeon, owned Bob and the good doctor had set more than a few of my broken bones over the years. I never said training horses was free of risk.

Never one to be flashy, Bob was a steady western pleasure horse who excelled in consistency. A large, dark bay with a small "blanket" of white lace over his hips, Bob won as often as he did mostly by default. He wasn't the kind of horse that judges and spectators oohed and aahed over, but sooner or later the other top contenders in the class would bobble here or there and Bob, by virtue of his easy, plodding regularity, would come out the winner.

As my mind was still overloaded from yesterday's events, Bob was a good choice for me. Teaching horses new skills demanded a lot of concentration, and concentration was something I had little of at the moment. I didn't have to think much when I rode Bob. He rarely needed schooling and he didn't have any bad habits, so this was more of an exercise period for both of us than a skills-sharpening lesson.

Hank was not allowed in the arena, as it was dangerous for a little dog to be around all those big, moving hooves. But early on Hank had claimed a spot right at the gate that was not really *in* the arena, but not completely *out* of it either. He knew better than to think about chasing, or playing, with a horse, so now he lay in his usual spot chewing on one of the big sticks he always seemed to find.

Bob and I had settled into a nice, slow jog along the rail when Jon spoke up. "I ran into Jim Ed at the Ashland City Co-op this morning," he said after a warning glance at Hank, who had crept a fraction of an inch farther into the arena. Jim Ed was a talkative, older member of the Giles clan who'd had a five-way heart bypass a few months ago. The fact that he was out and about at the co-op was a good sign. "Jim Ed asked about Bubba and somehow we got talking about Colonel Samuel Henley, the man who originally built Fairbanks in the 1850s."

I didn't ask how Jon knew about Bubba. The police had probably questioned him last night. I should have talked about it with him, but with all that had gone on, I'd forgotten.

"Apparently Jim Ed's grandpa, or maybe his great-grandpa, was a cousin of Col. Sam's. Jim Ed said his grandpa told him that Col. Sam made his fortune buying things that soldiers needed, smuggling them in and then selling the items to whichever army could afford what he had."

I smiled as I made an automatic adjustment to the set of Bob's head by raising my hands and squeezing my pinky fingers a fraction of an inch. I also sat a little deeper in the saddle and squeezed my lower legs. Once in a while Bob over-flexed at the poll, which made him pull from his front end, rather than push from his hindquarters. "That sounds just like the kind of ancestor I'd have expected of Hill—a true blue, loyal Southern patriot. So Jon . . . just what kinds of things did Col. Sam smuggle in?"

"Don't know. Jim Ed didn't say and I didn't think to ask," he said, slowly reeling the filly in and setting her off very carefully in the opposite direction. To help her stay calm, Jon always kept his body posture and facial expressions relaxed but businesslike when working with Gigi. It sometimes affected the tone of our conversation, but never the words. "He did say that whatever was smuggled in was rumored to have been kept in a secret hiding place somewhere in the house. What do you think, Cat? Does that house next door have any secrets?"

"Oh boy, if that house could only talk," I laughed, circling Bob at a slightly faster trot, using my seat, legs and hands to make sure he didn't get lazy and drop his inside shoulder. "But I'm sure a lot of the older houses around here have stories to tell. What's that house south of here in Franklin with the bullet holes still in it—the one with the cemetery next to it?"

"Carnton," supplied Jon.

"That's it. The Carnton Plantation. Now that house played a big role in the Civil War."

"Well, maybe our Fairbanks did, too, only it was all secret and no one knows about it."

"Could be," I agreed, "but unless Col. Sam's ghost comes back to tell us about it, we'll never know."

Bob and I loped the arena in a slow, rhythmic three-beat gait a few times in each direction. He seemed as bored with it all as I did, so we called it quits. Besides, my scraped hand was throbbing to beat the band. I had just finished brushing Bob and had snapped the last buckle on his blanket when Sally Blue began banging her hoof against the stall door. Sally did that when she thought she wasn't getting enough attention, or maybe when she was channeling Seabiscuit.

I slid open Sally's stall door and went inside to spend a few minutes with Agnes's intuitive marvel. Sally lifted her head and put her chin on my shoulder, a sign she wanted her cheeks rubbed. This actually was an excellent poll release, the poll being the tiny bump horses have at the top of their head just behind the ears. Think of human fingers massaging the hollowed out point at the base of your neck and you get the idea. I obliged and Sally sank into the moment, closing her eyes and groaning. I wish people could be so easily pleased.

After a few minutes, Sally declared she'd had her fill of poll stretching and cheek-rubbing and set her nose to inspecting my clothing. As inquisitive as Sally was, she should have been a dog, I thought, not for the first time. Sally bumped my left hip, a signal that she thought I had a carrot in my pocket. I knew I didn't, but Sally bumped my hip again.

"Look," I said reaching in to turn my pocket inside out. "No carrots."

But my pocket wasn't completely empty. I pulled out a small leather notebook. I knew I had never seen it before. Turning it over I gasped to see gold letters embossed on the other side. GLENDA DUPREE.

How in the world, I thought, did that notebook get into my pocket? Better yet, could Sally have known it was there? Nah, I thought. Now I'm starting to sound like Agnes. I flashed back to the scene in the barn. Glenda must have put it on my desk along with her gloves and scarf, and forgotten it when she had stormed out of the room. Somehow, without thinking, I had picked it up and put it into my pocket. I hate it when I zone out and do stuff I don't remember doing, but how else could it have gotten there?

Jon finished with Gigi and brought her, prancing, to the barn to put her blankets back on. Gigi pranced even when she was in her stall. Thank goodness she also liked to eat or it would be difficult to keep weight on her.

Before I could ask Jon about the notebook, the phone rang. Jon was still with Gigi at the other end of the aisle so I closed Sally's stall door and jogged down the aisle to answer it.

"Cat Enright Stables," I said, stretching the long cord over to Bob's stall door to double-check the latch.

"Yes, hello. Is Cat there?"

"Speaking."

"Oh hi, Cat. This is Buffy Thorndyke at the *Ashland City Times*. I wondered if I could ask you a few questions?"

Buffy was a snooty young reporter from the local weekly paper who had interviewed me after I'd returned from the world championships last fall. Her parents lived in the Belle Meade area of Nashville, one of the ten richest neighborhoods in the nation. We're talking old, old money, so I had no doubt that Buffy would soon move on to bigger and better things, thank God. Even though the *Times* was owned by a major newspaper conglomerate, they were similar to Ashland City's police department in that they didn't keep their staff very long.

"Questions? Sure. Fire away."

"Okay. I got a phone call yesterday morning from Glenda Dupree, the film star?" Buffy was one of these people who talked in question marks. She probably thought it was cute. I just found it irritating. "She said she was severing her ties with your stable and had chosen Hill Henley as her new trainer? I wondered if you had any comment?"

A phone call to the press! This was carrying things too far. Just announce to the world that Glenda Dupree thinks Cat Enright is incompetent. If Hill thinks Bubba's disappearance is going to hurt business, wait until his star client announces he's a has-been. That'll shake him up some. The more I thought about it, the madder I got. I fought to keep my Irish temper battened down, but it took longer than I would have liked.

Buffy mistook my silence to mean I didn't want to comment. "Well, it's just that Glenda Dupree is an international film star?

Anything she has to say is news around here. Anything. If you don't—"

"Of course I have a comment, Buffy," I said, recovering my composure. "I was just checking on Sally Blue." Agnes's young mare was a favorite of Buffy's. I thought if I reminded her of a positive thing, she wouldn't totally trash me in her story. Well, one can always hope.

"Let's see . . . okay. 'Glenda and I both decided that her talents lay more in the direction, style, and glamour of the Walking Horse industry rather than in the direction of stock breeds such as the Appaloosa. I applaud her decision and wish both her and Hill the best of luck.'"

When I have to I can b.s. with the best.

"Oh that's great, Cat. Sorry to have bothered you."

Anytime, Buffy. Just any old time at all.

The call from the *Times* made me angry enough to confront Glenda and finally have it out with her. I was so frustrated and mad at the woman I decided I would put her in her place once and for all. Before I had time to think about it, I stuffed Glenda's little notebook back into the pocket of my jacket, strode across my pasture, and swung under the post and rail fence that divided our properties. We'll just see who has the upper hand here.

10

THE MORNING'S CLOUDY SKIES FULFILLED THEIR promise. It began to rain as I raced up Glenda's front steps and across the porch. Exactly how I was going to confront Glenda and what I was going to say, I wasn't sure. I had no time for thought, though. I knew Glenda took suggestions about as well as a mud fence. However, I was determined to give it my best try. With a deep breath, I tucked my resolve close to my heart and knocked on her impressive front door. Several times. With no luck.

The rain was coming down harder every second. Maybe, I thought, if she was in the back of the house she couldn't hear, so I trotted around to the back, to the door that led into the kitchen. Here there was only a small overhang above the door and I quickly became soaked. Maybe she wasn't home. But I thought it was more likely that she was avoiding me.

Glenda wasn't going to like my coming over unannounced. Unannounced guests denied Glenda the satisfaction of letting people know that she created time for them only under extreme hardship on her part. And when she came to the door—if she came to the door—Glenda was sure to tell me she was too busy to see me now, that I'd have to schedule an appointment with her at a later date.

Considering Glenda's "manners," I wouldn't put it past her to comment unfavorably on my now soaking wet attire and muddy boots. Anything to make me feel inferior.

But I wasn't going to feel inferior, no matter how she treated me. This time I was going to give as good as I got. In the meantime, I was getting wetter and she still wasn't answering. I banged harder on the back door—a little too hard maybe because it slipped open. Apparently no one but me locked their doors around here. Oh well, guess who's here.

"Glenda," I called. "It's me, Cat. Sorry to barge in, but I've got to talk to you." There was no response.

The door opened onto a large, square kitchen that featured a real brick floor and textured lemon-yellow paneling. The appliances were dated, but fit perfectly with the room. I wondered if Glenda brought them in, or if Hill had left them when he sold the house. Mindful of my muddy boots, I moved drippingly ahead toward the front of the house, to the fully restored dining room, calling Glenda's name.

By antebellum standards, Fairbanks was not a large home. It was originally built in an L-shape in 1857, with each room approximately fifteen feet square. The kitchen that I'd just come through was not part of the initial structure, having been added in the early 1900s when some Henley ancestor discovered the luxury of indoor plumbing. The attached laundry, bath, and storage room had been the pantry and was almost the size of the kitchen. The remains of the original kitchen, which had been detached from the house, now served as the floor of the patio, just outside the back door.

The dining room ahead of me featured a perfect reproduction of the original red wallpaper, flocked with a profusion of leafy gold flowers. The large dining room table was made of a polished gold wood, possibly a match to the yellow poplar that had lain on the floor for the last one hundred fifty years. Glenda was very proud of her one hundred-fifty-year-old floor, so proud, in fact, that she had chosen to cover most of it with a thick red-and-gold Oriental rug. For protection, she'd once told me. Polished wooden chairs with red brocade seats matched the curtains in the floor-to-ceiling windows and surrounded the table. *Architectural Digest* had praised the room as a masterpiece, but altogether it was a bit too intense for me.

Still calling her name, I figured Glenda either was not home or she was hiding. The way I screech no one could miss the fact that I was here.

To the right of the dining room was the entrance hall. Here, the polished floor was bare for all to admire. A narrow but beautifully curved staircase rose from the right of the entry hall to a balcony on the second floor. From the one time I'd been up there, during the party Glenda threw when she opened the house, I knew there were three bedrooms, two of which shared a full bath, along with one plush master suite with oodles of closet space and a Jacuzzi tub in the adjoining bath.

I thought that if Glenda was home, she was probably upstairs, but I felt uneasy about invading her privacy that deeply. What the hell. I was this far. I may as well see this through. Better finish the downstairs first, though.

The living room was across the hall to my left and was dominated by photos of Glenda. Small, candid shots in silver frames sat on dark and ornate antique tables, while larger, poster sized publicity shots graced the white lacquered walls. The sitting down kind of furniture was bright and soft and modern, the antique floor once again uncovered. It was an unusual contrast, but it worked well with the high, molded ceilings and the large marble fireplace.

There was something strange about the fireplace but I couldn't figure it out at first. It was a two sided affair, located to the right of the room, next to the wide, open passageway that led to a den. I knew if I went into the den that the fireplace would look exactly the same in there as it did from here. Well, not exactly. I looked at the hearth carefully from across the room, looked away, then back again. Then the bottom dropped out of my stomach and my mind twisted with horror as I realized a hand was reaching out from the front of a sofa near the fireplace. A very still hand. What the hand meant didn't register right away.

My heart thumped for all it was worth but I stepped closer, struggling to force order into my brain. I tried to understand exactly what it was that I was seeing. Long moments passed before I realized that the intricate marbling of the fireplace was, in fact, dried blood. Long moments passed while I stared at the mutilated body that lay on the stone hearth. Glenda's body. Longer moments passed before I realized that Glenda Dupree had been brutally murdered.

I staggered back into the entrance hall and collapsed on the magnificent curving staircase. The room spun uncontrollably as I puked violently all over Glenda's one-hundred-fifty-year-old floor.

11

TEN MINUTES LATER I WAS SITTING on the front steps of Fairbanks, my head pressed against my knees, waiting for the police. The rain had slowed to a fine mist, but at the time, I couldn't have told you that.

I lifted my head at the sound of an engine. I looked up, expecting the police, but was dismayed instead to see Adam's bottle-green Jaguar turn into the drive. He pulled up in front of the steps and got out.

"Don't tell me," he said with a warm smile. "Aunt Glenda got the best of you."

She sure did, I thought. Glenda brought me down to size real good this time.

Adam walked lazily toward me, carrying his black leather briefcase. I noticed dully that he still wore the same unkempt clothes as he had on yesterday. He must have pulled an all night writing session at the office. Hope it was worth it and that he wrote a big hit. If he took any notice of my disheveled state, he made no mention of it.

"I take it you had your talk?" he asked.

I shook my head.

"Then let me get Aunt Glenda for you," he said as he slid past me and started up the steps.

"Adam," I croaked. "Adam, don't . . . don't go in there."

He looked at me with a mixture of surprise and amusement.

"But this is my home, Cat. I live here."

"I know. But don't go in."

I could tell he was becoming irritated with me.

"And just why not?"

I took a deep breath. "Because Glenda's dead. I'm sorry, Adam. She's in the living room and she's dead. I've called the police. They'll be here soon. I think we should wait out here."

Air left his body with a big whooshing sound, as if he had been punched in the stomach. Color drained from his face and he plopped down on the step beside me.

"Are you sure?" he asked quietly.

"Very."

"I can't believe you . . . ah, I mean . . . I know you were upset, but—"

"I didn't kill her, Adam," I cried, outraged at the idea. I was surprised that I could speak so vehemently, that I could feel any emotion. Maybe the numbness that had enveloped my entire being the moment I saw the body wasn't going to stay with me forever. I hoped not. Then again, considering the horror of it all, permanent emotional numbness might not be all that bad.

"No. Of course not, Cat. I'm sorry. I'm a bit stunned. Then it was you who found her?"

"Yes."

"Oh, my God. Just now?"

"Yes."

Neither of us noticed the police had arrived until the patrol car came to a halt behind Adam's car. A weary-looking Deputy Giles eased out of the car, pulled on a rain slicker, and shut the door with a thud.

"Hello again, Miz Enright. Sir." He nodded slowly at Adam. "The lady's inside?"

"Yes." The reality of it all began coming back in vivid waves, like the nausea. My heart began thudding and my body began to shake. Yes, the blissful unfeeling state was definitely leaving. I tried to grasp on to it, to hold it close to me like a protective shield, but it slipped away and I began to cry, my tears mingling with the rain.

The deputy nodded at me as if in approval, but here, on the steps of Glenda Dupree's mansion, his eyes looked far older than his years.

"I'd better take a look," he said finally.

I stood on legs that didn't seem to want to support me, feeling more queasy than I ever had. Deputy Giles noticed and shook his head.

"Let me go in alone, Miz Enright. You sit yourself right back down here and let your friend help you."

I thought introductions should be made and did so in a small voice that I didn't recognize as mine.

"You're her nephew, Mr. Dupree?" asked the deputy.

"Yes, sir. I've been living here with my aunt since last summer."

The deputy sighed and glanced up River Road. "A swarm of folks are fixing to be here in a few minutes. I need to get this over with."

He went in and came out, grim-faced, in less than a minute. "There don't seem to be signs of a struggle," he commented.

"No," I agreed.

"'Cept of course for that mess on the floor. By the steps." He looked inquiringly at me and then it was my turn to nod. He patted my shoulder awkwardly. "Don't worry. I've done it myself. More than once. But, Miz Enright," he continued more harshly, "did it occur to you while you were so gleefully breaking and entering, that whoever did this to the lady might still be in the house?"

"Cat."

"Cat? You trying to get me to believe a cat did this?"

"No. My name. It's Cat. And no, I didn't think of it."

"Didn't think so," he said quite sternly for someone so young. "But next time you go poking around in someone else's house and find things out of order, you get right on out of there. Better yet, don't go in in the first place. Just call me." He consulted a little notebook. "If I'm right, this is the second time in less than twenty-four hours that you've nosed around in one of your neighbor's houses. Plan to make a habit of it?"

"No. No, I—"

"'Cause if you do, you need to let me know, preferably ahead of time." He paused. "Miz Enright, you ever hear the story 'bout the three farmers?"

I shook my head.

"Well, my Uncle Estes once told me there are three kinds of farmers. There's those that learn by reading 'bout farming. Then there's those who learn by watching others farm. Then there's the rest of 'em that have to pee on the electric fence for themselves. My point is, ma'am, if you keep this up, sooner or later you'll end up in the same shape the lady is in and I'd rather not be around for that if you don't mind."

I was learning rather quickly that even though Deputy Giles moved slowly, his mind worked at warp speed.

Someone hung a blanket over my shoulders, and I pulled it close to my body. I hadn't noticed that the deputy's "swarm of folks" had started to arrive. The sheriff showed up in due course and said rather imperiously that I'd have to make an official statement. I said, yes, that I would. He added that I'd have to be truthful in said statement. I said yes, I would be. He then said that over the course of the next few days I'd have to answer a lot of questions and I said yes, that I would.

After a few minutes of this I could see why Sheriff "Big Jim" Burns was not well liked in Cheatham County. A former state prosecutor, he had defeated former Sheriff Rollo Crowell in the last election. Old Sheriff Rollo had been sheriff here for eighteen years. But apparently, over those eighteen years, Sheriff Rollo got in the habit of bending the rules a bit, for certain folk. Okay, to be honest, he was as crooked as a barrel of snakes. Newcomers to the area, hearing how the land lay, didn't like Sheriff Rollo's system at all, and recruited Burns for the job. Burns won by a very small margin, putting Sheriff Rollo back on his tractor seat.

When Big Jim Burns took office he cleaned house, hired new deputies, new secretaries, and a new jail warden. He cracked down on crime, did no favors for anyone, and followed the letter of the law. With Sheriff Burns there was no bedside manner, so to speak. The *Times* was even bold enough to call him "slicker than a greased hog and tougher than a one-eared alley cat."

That was all fine and dandy, except that wasn't what the people who helped put Sheriff Big Jim in office expected. Turns out they didn't want a straight arrow sheriff. Turns out all they wanted was a sheriff who would cater to their own causes. A new blood sheriff who wouldn't obliterate the good old boy system practiced for so many years, but who would create a new system, with them smack in the middle of it. So now Sheriff Burns had the old guard against him, the new blood mad at him and an election coming up in August.

Eventually, the coroner came and asked a lot of questions, as did Deputy Giles, the sheriff again, and the inevitable reporters. Buffy Thorndyke showed up, Harry Giles represented the South Cheatham paper. Reporters from the *Nashville Ledger* and *The Tennessean* were close on their heels. I was sure WSM radio would show up, but they were on the other side of town, out by the Opryland Hotel, and it would take them a little longer to make the drive. Thank God there weren't any television cameras out yet. Maybe they were busy with Al Gore, who had a home in Nashville. Local reporters followed him around a lot.

To get it over with more quickly, I said I'd answer all the reporters' questions at once. If someone showed up late, too bad. I was only going to do this one time. I huddled inside my blanket and tediously told them yes, I had found her. No, I didn't know who killed her. And no, I didn't kill her. No, I continued, I could not comment on the condition of the body. And no, I didn't know how long she'd been dead but she'd been very much alive in my riding class at ten-thirty yesterday morning.

I knew right that away letting go of this last bit of information was a mistake and I mentally gave myself a swift kick in the shins. The small group of reporters jumped on my blunder and bullied me for information on the riding class. Rightly so, they sensed a scoop with local color that would add to this story. It wasn't often that our area had something of national interest.

Without giving the names of the other students (although I was sure the press would come up with them somehow), I said the class was a routine prep for students who were considering show ring competition this summer. Chuck Dauphin, a print and radio journalist from Dickson, Tennessee, had interviewed me before. Now he asked if any member of the class might harbor a grudge against Glenda, and also if any class member was unusual in any way.

I laughed, which seemed to me like a deranged thing to do, but this whole scene was deranged and I forgave myself. This wasn't exactly what I had planned to do when I got up this morning.

I forced my mind back to Chuck's question. How should I answer it? Each of the class members, in their own way, was unusual and each held a grudge against Glenda. But that didn't necessarily mean any of them had killed her. Glenda, by far, had been the most unusual of the bunch. As for the grudges, I debated telling them about the blowup Glenda instigated and decided to let the press do its own dirty work.

As far as I knew, Buffy, the *Times* reporter, was the only one who had talked with Glenda recently and if she was smart, she'd hold that bit of information and break it herself. Although, come to think of it, Buffy might not be that savvy. Some of those wealthy Belle Meade people she was related to didn't have both oars in the water and I had no reason to believe Buffy was an exception. Probably all that blue blood floating around in her veins. Couldn't be healthy.

I didn't think there was any member of the riding class who liked Glenda, but again, that was not an indication one of them had committed murder. Thinking back, Glenda threatened me when she promised to tell others in the horse community that she had left my stable because I was incompetent. Darcy had threatened to kill Glenda for the nasty, public way Glenda informed me of her decision, but that was the way Darcy always talked. Robert made it a point to tell me he didn't want Glenda back under any circumstances. But other than his love of horses, what did I really know about him?

And then there was Jon. Jon was a loose cannon. Would he take revenge against someone who threatened me—or my livelihood—and by virtue of that indirectly threatened him and his livelihood? I didn't know. Of them all, I thought Carole was the only benign one in the group. But, appearances can be deceiving.

I decided not to pass any of this along to the reporters. Instead, I called a close to the impromptu press conference. When the reporters realized I was serious, they quit clamoring and rushed off in search of other leads.

No longer the center of attention, I turned from my damp place on the steps to find Deputy Giles and Sheriff Burns comparing notes in the much drier entrance hall. The sheriff was clearly instructing the deputy in a task he wanted no part of. The laid-back deputy stood rigidly, with his chin up and his arms held stiffly at his sides. His pudgy face had turned to stone and you could almost see the sparks fly from his eyes. But he didn't say a word. After a moment he nodded at his superior and disappeared into the back of the house. What, I wondered, had all that been about?

Sheriff Burns saw me peering in and came over.

"I believe you're now free to go about your day, Miss Enright."

I looked at him in amazement, for it never occurred to me that I had not been "free to go about my day."

"We'll be in touch, of course," he said, "but I'd appreciate it if you kept us informed of your whereabouts."

My whereabouts! I didn't know whether to be furious or frightened. Gee, let's see . . . I'll pick furious. It's more productive.

I let him have it. "Sheriff, I'm getting the damnedest impression that you are treating me as a suspect. If that's the case, you let me know right now because I didn't kill Glenda Dupree and I have no idea who did. So listen up and remember this: I just happened to stumble across her body. Period."

Sheriff Big Jim glowered. "Enough information has not been amassed to comment on who may and who may not be a suspect in this case, Miss Enright. But still, we'd like to know where you are."

Before I could reply, a reporter caught his eye and he marched over to give a statement.

"What was he talking about, Cat?" asked Adam as he came out of the house.

From the movement of the people who came regularly to these things, I got the impression that they were ready to move the body. Ambulance doors were opened and uniformed people scurried about in all directions. We walked down the steps, away from the activity, and propped ourselves against his cold, wet car.

"Just off the top of my head," I said in a carefully controlled voice, "I'd say he's talking about the coming election." I took a deep breath and slowly released it. "I think he wants to make a quick wrap to this case and use it in his campaign. I only hope he finds the right person to arrest."

"Don't worry," Adam said, "you didn't do it, and hey, whoever did is probably miles from here by now."

"Why do you think that?"

"It's just an idea. I'm not sure." He massaged his temples as we leaned against the side of his car. "Remember that murder in Dickson just after Christmas? Then there was one in Springfield a few weeks ago, and now this."

I'd heard of the Society Lady murders, of course. It had been hard not to as every news station in town had carried some angle of the murders as a lead story for days. In each case a wealthy, middle-aged or elderly woman had been found clubbed to death in her home. Bashed several times in the head, just as it looked like Glenda had been. Nothing had been taken; homes had not been trashed. No notes had been left and no cult or group had claimed responsibility for the crimes. The police had not released much on the alleged murderer and I could only suspect they had little to go on.

"My best guess," Adam continued, "is that this is some weirdo striking at random."

"With nothing stolen, nothing disturbed? Glenda was wearing diamond earrings and a Rolex—"

"The other women were also well-to-do and were wearing expensive jewelry. Okay, maybe not in the same category as Aunt Glenda, but worth something all the same."

"Adam, I agree that whoever the Society Lady murderer is, he or she is after the thrill of the kill, or maybe it's some wacko who is afraid of these women for some reason. But I'm not so sure that this murder ties in with the others."

"Well, that's for our esteemed sheriff to find out isn't it? And speaking of the gentleman, if I may call him that, it looks like he is headed our way. Since he has already spoken to you, I can only assume that I am his intended target." And with that Adam went to join Sheriff Burns.

I felt lost. Obviously, I was supposed to go on with my day. Just pick up where I'd left off and go about my business. But I couldn't do that. My mind was spinning and I knew if I set foot in the barn I'd transmit my extreme unease to every horse in the stable. Horses are sensitive to the moods of the people around them. A single session with a trusted person who was upset could undo weeks of careful work, and could also possibly cause digestive problems in the more delicately stomached equines. Gigi and Sally both came to mind.

Suddenly I wanted to get as far from Fairbanks as possible. I pulled the blanket tighter around me and ran back across the field and down toward the river. Let them add blanket theft to the murder charge I already knew Sheriff Big Jim wanted to hang on me. I didn't care.

Water had always soothed me. My property sat high above the Cumberland, but there was a steep, narrow path that led down about ten feet to a huge maple tree that hung diagonally over the river. I could sit on the base of the trunk, totally hidden from view, and watch the river traffic and think. It was a place I'd come to many times before.

Today the rhythmic quality of the river was broken here and there only by the occasional barge or adventurous fishing boat from the marina up the road. The cold and dampness that surrounded me were the least of my worries as I tried to order the chaotic mess of my mind.

First Bubba and now Glenda. Not friends—certainly not friends—but daily acquaintances. Neighbors. I didn't know how to deal with it, how to absorb it all and move on. Or even if I could.

I wasn't used to people being murdered practically in my back yard. I came from a small town where everyone knew each other. And while we didn't always like our neighbors, no one ever got killed. Bucksnort, Tennessee (population eighteen), got its name back in the 1880s from a man named Buck Pamplin. Before the Civil War, Buck owned and lived on the site that later became the town. The story is that Buck loved whiskey. He would frequently get soused, and when he did, he'd snort louder than a sow in heat. His neighbors would shake their heads and say, "Listen to Buck snort." After a while people began running the two words together, and the place where Buck lived became Bucksnort.

When I left home after graduating from high school it was to pursue my dream of studying horses at Middle Tennessee State University in Murfreesboro, not to become part of a murder investigation. I'd graduated from MTSU seven years ago, about the same time my grandma died. It surprised everyone—including me—when her estate brought enough for me to buy the farm and start a training stable. Grandma always was a frugal one, but who knew she had saved more than eighty grand and stashed it under her mattress?

When I hung out my shingle, there were those who said I needed to work for an established trainer for a few years before breaking out on my own, but I never did go much for what other people said. In the early years there had been a lot of hard times. The past three or four years I'd done pretty well, having brought home several national and world champions, two of them just this past fall. I'd weathered many storms and enjoyed every minute of it. Until now.

Now I was inches away from being accused of murder. If Hill thought a police investigation that looked into the disappearance of his son was going to damage his career, what would a murder investigation do to mine?

Eventually, shivering with cold, I went back up to the house, choked down some hot soup and got ready for bed abominably early. When I woke the next morning before dawn I felt somewhat better. But not a lot. Bubba was still missing. Glenda was still dead. And both my doorbell and telephone were ringing.

Cat's Horse Tip #5

"The safest way to lead a horse through a gate is to push the gate the same direction you are going."

12

I PEEKED THROUGH MY BEDROOM WINDOW to find Carole Carson standing in the pre-dawn on my front porch. She looked wide awake, and impatient, as if she thought I should have been up long ago.

Deputy Giles, on the phone, shared her opinion. I rubbed the sleep from my eyes, told him to wait, let Carole in, and told her to wait. Then I let a squirming Hank out the kitchen door, and told him not to wait.

Carole looked apprehensive as she stood in the kitchen doorway. Was that a sniff? Were the last of Hank's mutant urine vapors still hanging around? Surely not. I took a tiny sniff of my own and couldn't detect anything. Carol must have super sensitive nostrils. However, I decided if my house did still smell like warmed over road kill, it was the least of my worries.

I waved Carole toward my grandmother's wooden breakfast table and pointed to the coffee maker. She shook her head. It was just as well, as I was out of coffee. Hill had downed my last cup yesterday.

I picked up the conversation with the deputy on the cordless extension by the hall table.

"I don't guess Bubba showed up to your place last night?" he asked.

I almost reminded him that, according to my watch and the current position of the sun (still somewhere over the Atlantic), five twenty-six in the morning was still night time, but there was a sharpness in his voice and I held my tongue. By my calculations he had been up for the better part of two days and he didn't need any lip from me.

"No, Deputy, he hasn't. Why? Have you found anything?"

"Maybe," he said in his slow drawl. "I talked to the sheriff a bit ago. We might have a lead."

I immediately forgot my promise to thrash Bubba within an inch of his life. I just wanted him to be safe and unharmed.

"We might've found the murder weapon," the deputy continued. "The boys searching the river bank found it yesterday evening—in front of your place."

My heart sank and I sat down abruptly, feeling sick. Next to me, Carole chewed on a fingernail that was painted a delicate pink. Her entire body was tense.

"My place. But surely, Deputy, you don't think—"

"I don't think anything at this time, but no, my gut says you're clear. Sheriff Burns, now. He's another matter. I've got to tell you . . . according to him you are a number one prime suspect."

"But—"

"But nothing, Miz Enright. You were there. You found the lady. You were seen heading toward the riverbank after finding the body. We got to follow up on every lead. If you're innocent, time will prove it."

I hoped. I was quiet for a few seconds, and then I asked, "What is it?"

"What is what? Oh, the murder weapon?"

I nodded my head and he went on as if he'd heard me.

"It's the wooden part of what I think you horse people call a twitch. We're pretty sure it's the murder weapon. It's got the initials H.H. burned into the wood near the bottom and I remember you saying you saw Bubba playing with something like that the day he disappeared."

A twitch is normally used for restraining horses for veterinary purposes. Wooden ones have a wood base about eighteen inches long and are as thick as small person's wrist. Attached to the end is a loop of chain about a foot long. To use it, you grab the horse's top lip, insert it into the chain and twist the chain with the wooden end until the lip is solidly caught in the chain.

It sounds horrible, but if a horse needs medical attention and becomes dangerous to himself or to the handler, it is safer for everyone involved to use the twitch. Pretend you had to get a shot that would save your life, but you hated needles so much that you wouldn't allow the person holding the syringe close to you. If someone else came up and twisted your ear so badly that your ear hurt more then the shot, you'd let them give you the shot. Same principle and, like the ear twist, the twitch does no lasting damage.

I was a bit concerned about the twitch being found on my property. "Deputy, in this neighborhood twitches are a dime a dozen. There are probably any number of them lying around." Okay, so I lied. Pastures where horses grazed were kept notoriously clear of debris to prevent injuries.

"Not twitches with Hill Henley's initials on them," he reminded me, "and not with the chain broken off."

I'd forgotten about the chain. The twitch Bubba had used as a bat had been missing the chain.

There was a moment of silence before the deputy cleared his throat. "Well, listen. If Bubba shows up, call us without him knowing about it if you can."

"Call you without him knowing . . . you can't mean that you think Bubba killed Glenda."

"Miz Cat, right now I believe everything and I believe nothing. All I know is I've got a dead lady. I've got a murder weapon that was seen by you in the kid's possession, and I've got a missing kid I want to question."

I admitted that I could see his point all too well and told him I would call if Bubba turned up.

"Just one more thing," he said. "Someone got into Fairbanks last night. Ignored all the purty crime scene tape we wound around, opened a window, and went right on in."

Sheriff Big Jim wasn't going to be happy about that, I thought. I wondered if the sheriff already knew of the break-in, or if Deputy Giles still had that unpleasant task ahead of him. I was sure that the sheriff would place 100 percent of the blame on the deputy's shoulders. For his sake, I hoped the deputy had finished gathering evidence from the house.

Detective Giles seemed to read my mind. "It's not like this was downtown Nashville," he said in defense. "It didn't occur to me that we'd have to sit on the front steps all night. We sealed the house up proper like and someone came right on in anyway. Whoever it was left a couple of lights on. Old Jimmy Johnson saw the lights and called us 'bout four-thirty on his way out to do the milking at the dairy."

"So you think because I slipped into her house unannounced before that I went back in again last night?" I asked. He probably thought I went in to check out Glenda's precious Limoges china. It was well known how much Glenda prized her china, and she did have a beautiful pattern.

"No. I mention it because you are . . . were . . . her neighbor. You knew her. You might have heard or seen something. Or someone. You might even," he added, "know why someone would break in. As far as we can tell, nothing was taken— including the china."

Well that was a relief. I didn't think my clients would approve of my overseeing their horses' progress from a jail cell. Although according to Sheriff Burns, jail was still a strong possibility for me.

"Kids, maybe," I said. "Or Adam. After all, he lives there."

"Nope. Far as we can tell, the nephew is still tucked away safe and sound in his Music Row office. But come to think of it, it coulda been kids. We'll check it out."

He reminded me to call him if I saw Bubba and said he'd be in touch later.

I looked at the clock. Almost six. If the rest of the day was going to be as unpleasant as the last half hour, I didn't want any part of it. I wondered, not for the first time, if I wouldn't be better off waiting tables at Verna Mae's. It certainly would be less stressful.

I turned to Carole and held up a hand to stop the words that were beginning to burst from her lips.

"I'm out of coffee so I'm going to make some hot chocolate," I said. "You can watch me drink it, or you can help me drink it. I don't care. But I'm not going to listen to a single word you have to say until I have had a cup. Any questions?"

Carole shook her head, and her eyes glinted with a touch of the amusement I'd noticed the other day at the barn. I didn't know her well, but so far I liked her. She seemed to have her own way of looking at the world, one that mixed tragedy, joy, and strength. When I first met her, I'd thought her silly and spoiled. But instead of silliness, I now saw someone who was fun loving, someone who was vibrant, who enjoyed the little nuances of life and chose to embrace them with every ounce of her being. Instead of spoiled, I saw someone committed to excellence in everything she did, from parenting to organizing a charity event. So much for first impressions.

It was clear Carole wanted to talk, but now that she knew she'd have my full attention soon, she waited. I studied her as I set out a pair of mismatched mugs. She was tall, about five-ten, and fine boned, but there was a strength in the way she carried herself that belied any notion of fragility. Her hair, like mine, was long and wavy. But on her it worked. She had chiseled cheekbones and a set of arched eyebrows. Her mouth was full, her chin strong. I'd heard that she had been in a number of music videos before she married Keith and I could easily believe she'd been a popular celluloid love interest. This morning, though, she looked drawn and pale, and faint shadows of dark purple sat under her eyes.

Carole waited until I'd drunk the last of my hot chocolate and set my empty mug on the table. Then she said, "I don't always look this bad in the morning. Our youngest has a bad cold and I've been up all night. For safety with the kids, Keith insists we keep all the heavy duty medicines, the ones with codeine and stuff, locked in the safe in the basement. We don't use the medicines a lot, but when we do, it means I've got to trudge up and down all those steps. It's tiring."

Like a number of entertainers, Keith Carson had a history with drugs, and the first thought that came to my mind was that Keith kept the stronger medicines locked up not for the kid's safety, but so that he wouldn't be tempted. He'd given up all the drugs, the partying, and his wild ways when he met Carole, and was now committed to keeping the past just that—the past. But we all had our temptations.

Carole held her mug of cocoa close to her and blew on it gently. "I assume that was Deputy Giles on the phone. He called me earlier and came right out and said that while Sheriff Burns thinks you killed Glenda with that twitch, he thinks Bubba did it. I know you didn't do it. I need to know if you think it's possible that Bubba did?"

"No," I shook my head. "Bubba plays a lot of nasty pranks, but he's never done anything to hurt anyone. Not on purpose, anyway. I'll admit some of his actions, like batting rocks at my truck, could have caused quite an accident, but Bubba doesn't think things through; he doesn't bother to consider the results of his actions."

"I agree," Carole said. "We've had him over to play with our kids several times and I've seen him do things that do not turn out the way he intended. Bubba is an immature boy in need of attention, and he's not overly bright. But once you get to know him there is a sweetness in him, so I can't imagine he'd hurt Glenda. Besides, he's always been in awe of her."

"So what do you think? Did he run away, or has something happened to him?"

"I think," she said slowly, "that he saw something—or heard something—that scared him. I think he's hiding and if the police find him, whatever scared him has frightened him very badly and he'll just run away again."

She finally took a sip of her chocolate, and raised an eyebrow in appreciation. Next to pizza, root beer, and chocolate chunk cookies, hot chocolate is the best comfort food in the world. I can't cook, so homemade pizza and chocolate chunk cookies aren't frequent visitors to my house, but I do make a mean cup of hot chocolate. "Unless, of course," she added, looking me right in the eye, "you find him first."

"Me? Oh, yeah, get real," I laughed.

"Cat, I'm serious. You can do this, and it might be a matter of life and death that you find him. Your life and Bubba's."

"You believe that, don't you?" I asked, staring at the earnest expression on her face.

"Yes, I do."

"I don't get it. What possible good could I be to the police investigation?"

"Screw their investigation," she said. "We all know you are the only one in this whole neighborhood that Bubba trusts. That includes his so-called father. That man is about as useful as a trap door on a canoe. I'm convinced Bubba saw something. He has information about this, information that could keep both of you from being arrested. If you found Bubba, you could talk to him. If you could convince him to tell you about whatever he saw or heard, you could go to the police. Don't you think that would be a lot better than Bubba being so scared that he kicks Sheriff Burns in the balls and runs away?"

While the thought of Sheriff Big Jim getting the stuffing kicked out of him was enticing, I agreed that it would be better all around if Bubba came forth on his own. But I was still skeptical of Carole's idea.

"What's your interest in all this, Carole? Bubba didn't stop by last night to have a little chat with you, did he?"

"No." She put her mug down and took a deep breath. "My interest comes as a friend and as a mother. First of all, I don't want to see you wrongly accused. And secondly, and more importantly, I can't imagine any of my kids outside in that awful weather, scared and lonely. I have four kids and a husband to take care of. Not to mention work on several charitable committees. My time is limited and with four young kids in tow I can't go traipsing around town asking questions. But you can.

"And," she continued, "here's another perspective you've probably not had time to consider. As far as the sheriff is concerned, *you* were upset with Glenda, *you* found the body, *you* reported Bubba missing, and the possible murder weapon was found on *your* property after *you* were seen going down to the river. Now put yourself in the sheriff's shoes. The entire county is mad at him and there is an election coming up. If you were the sheriff, what would you do?"

This train of thought was starting to sound like a broken record.

Carole gave me a searching look as I pondered what she'd said. "Maybe I've misjudged you, Cat. You have to realize that much of the evidence points toward you. I thought you cared enough to want to help save that boy, and to save yourself. Maybe I was wrong."

"Now wait a minute! I didn't say I wasn't concerned. Actually, I'm more worried about all this than I'll even admit to myself. And I didn't say I wouldn't help. I just want to be sure I'm going about this the right way."

I stopped for a moment. Did I just agree to try to find Bubba? I think I did. Besides, Carole was right. Bubba needed help and I wasn't all that sure there was anyone else who was up for the job. Then there was the Big Jim angle to consider. He viewed me as a suspect and I didn't trust him not to arrest just anybody so he could wrap up the case. I didn't know who killed Glenda, but I did know I didn't want to be the one the police pointed their fingers at. Bubba was the key to clearing up this mess.

"Okay," I said. "I'll try. But I don't have any idea if I can help or not. The police will be covering this pretty thoroughly. You're right in that I know Bubba better than they do. Maybe I'll come up with a plan."

The tired look on Carole's face was replaced by one of animation. "Oh, thank you," she said. "Now I can rest a little easier. I know whatever you do may not help, but I'm so worried about Bubba. At least I'll know someone is out there who has his interests in mind."

I walked her to the door, thinking that Bubba deserved a lot more than a couple of worried neighbors. The sixty-four-thousand-dollar question was . . . what? I didn't like the fact that the twitch had shown up and Bubba hadn't. Deputy Giles thought that Bubba killed Glenda with it, then tossed it and went into hiding. But I didn't. Knowing Bubba, I thought it was a great deal more probable that someone had taken the twitch from him. Maybe, I thought, whoever took the twitch from Bubba had taken Bubba, too. Maybe, just maybe, Bubba wasn't in hiding. Maybe he'd been kidnapped—or worse.

This thought was just unpleasant enough to get me moving. By the time I got out to the barn, I was more than an hour late and several of the horses showed their displeasure by stomping their feet as I gave them their morning feed.

Petey and Bob both gave me looks that said "finally." Gigi was racing around her stall, so I turned on the CD of waves crashing onto a beach that sometimes took the edge off her nerves. Two other horses, Chico and Dolly, a big dun-colored Quarter Horse gelding and a mare who was a gaited draft cross, belonged to a guy in Kentucky who wanted some miles put on them for the upcoming trail riding season. Neither seemed particularly put out by the lateness of their breakfast.

Nor did Dondi's Dancer, an older bay leopard gelding of Agnes's. We campaigned Dondi in driving, native dress, sidesaddle, and a few other of the less mainstream classes.

Agnes's Sally Blue was another story, however, She was especially displeased, so I took an extra few minutes to rub her neck and talk softly to her as she started in on her breakfast. Sally never quite settled in to eat, though. Instead, she took an occasional quick mouthful, then walked to the stall door, and stuck her head out to look east, toward both Fairbanks and the rising sun. Her skin was tense and she was as alert as I had ever seen her. Did Sally actually sense what had happened next door, or was she just greeting the day uneasily?

After Sally had eaten about half her grain I left a long note for Jon. Then I made a quick run through the shower, swabbed on far more mascara than usual, and headed into Ashland City.

13

AS I PULLED INTO THE PARKING lot of the Ashland City Co-op, I saw Jim Ed holding court from a rocking chair on the porch. He didn't look much the worse for wear due to his recent surgical ordeal. His thin body was clad, as usual, in an endless series of white undershirts, dark blue work pants, black suspenders, white tube socks, and black lace-up shoes with thick soles. As a concession to the cold weather, he had added a bright red coat that looked as if it might have once resided in his wife's closet. The thinning hair on his scalp had been dyed bright yellow, and his full set of ill-fitting uppers and lowers had been scrubbed to an unnatural whiteness. Before he'd had all his teeth pulled, Jim Ed had looked something like Bugs Bunny, so this was a marked improvement

As I got out of the truck, Jim Ed greeted me as a long lost old friend. Not that I was either long lost or an old friend; Jim Ed greeted everyone that way.

"Miss Enright, how very nice to see you on this cold morning," he said, dismissing the two older men he had been speaking with. "I ain't seen you, seems like, in a month of Sundays. Can I help you find something inside? There's a new line of hay nets just come out, guaranteed for a year."

Listening to him, one might swear that Jim Ed was employed by the Co-op. But he wasn't. Since his retirement ten years or so back, Jim Ed had hung out at the Co-op just about every day. Rain or shine. Good weather or bad. He once told me, in the strictest confidence of course, that as much as he loved his wife, they drove each other crazy. So he wandered down to the Co-op every morning to keep his marriage intact. The fact was, Jim Ed was Cheatham County's biggest gossip. He thrived on it. I think the Co-op figured out early on that having Jim Ed ensconced in a chair out front was the equivalent of several thousand dollars of advertising each week. With Jim Ed around, everyone came to the Co-op to find out what was happening. I was no different.

"No, no, Jim Ed. No hay nets today. I came by to see you. Jon told me you were doing pretty well since you had your heart surgery and I just stopped by to say hi."

From prior experience I knew I wouldn't be able to rush Jim Ed. Jim Ed freely peppered his gossip in Southern analogies so we'd have to sit around and b.s. for a while before I could get to the real reason for my visit. I hoped my extra coat of mascara would hurry him along.

"Well, that's mighty kind of you, Miss. Mighty kind," he said, settling me on a bench next to the rocker. "Since my op-e-ration I'm finer than frog hair. In fact, if life gets any better, I'll have to hire someone to help me enjoy it. Say, you don't know how that old mare of Hello Holderman's is doing, do you?"

Hello was an elderly farmer who lived on Pond Creek Road. He was nicknamed for obvious reasons; he, like Jim Ed, had never met a stranger. Hello had never gotten around to modernizing enough to use a tractor and still plowed using a team of Belgian mares as ancient as he. Hello was older than dirt, but he still did all right. If he'd ever married, it was so long ago no one had ever heard about it. The same goes for any kids he might have had.

"No, I haven't heard a word. The mare had a bout of colic, didn't she?"

"Boy howdy, did she ever. Doc Giles said her gut was twisted tighter than a fiddle string. Didn't know if he'd ever get the kinks out. Guess he did, though. Guess I'd have heard if she didn't make it. Boy now, that'd be hard on old Hello, losing one of his team. That old boy is as tough as leather, but it'd plumb kill him to lose one of them."

I agreed, then said, "I think it would be even harder to lose a child. I wonder how Hill Henley is doing? You've heard Bubba is missing?"

"Oh yeah. Yep, gotta be tough, but that young 'un is sorry as a two-dollar watch."

"You haven't heard anything about where Bubba might be, have you, Jim Ed?"

He looked surprised. "Ain't you heard? That boy's done gone off the deep end. He's out hiding, made hisself as scarce as hen's teeth. He's going to be charged with murder. Turrible thing it turned out to be. Now I know you know the boy. Personal like. I warn't even gonna bring all that up, with you finding the body and knowing Miss Dupree. But if you're thinking of sticking up for that boy, I'd say don't. Leave it to the sheriff. That boy is plumb dangerous."

Jim Ed apparently had Bubba tried, convicted, and sentenced.

"What makes you think Bubba is guilty?"

"Well, the murder weapon belonged to the boy, didn't it? Well didn't it?"

I nodded my head.

"It was found there on your land, but the weapon belonged to that boy. I mean it don't take no genius to spot a goat in a flock of sheep. It's very simple. Miss Dupree's done been murdered horrible-like and Bubba's implicated you and gone missing. That's why I know Big Jim Burns is on the right track."

It sounded to me more like Sheriff Burns and Jim Ed had breakfast together. Sheriff Big Jim knew Jim Ed's visible location on the porch of the co-op, combined with his propensity for gossip, could do a lot to sway voters his way so he made it a point to cultivate the older man. But my big question was: why did our lofty sheriff implicate Bubba—and not me—to Jim Ed when he'd told his deputy the opposite?

"So tell me now, Miss Enright," Jim Ed said, leaning in close, "you having found the body and all. Were she in purty bad shape? I mean, I've heard different things from different people." Jim Ed's old eyes glittered and he licked his lips in anticipation of my answer. When I didn't say anything, he continued, "You having found her, well, I'd like to know, so's I can put to rest all them nasty rumors that're floating about, if you understand my drift."

Oh, I understood completely. I knew Jim Ed spread rumors quicker than horses stomped flies, to use one of Jim Ed's own analogies. He lived for gossip, the more outrageous the better, and I took a bit of perverse pleasure in telling him briefly and factually about the body.

"There wasn't much to see," I said. "There was some blood and it was obvious that she was dead."

"I see." Jim Ed tried his best to look satisfied with my answer, but he didn't quite pull it off. Eventually curiosity got the better of him. "So now, what did you do when you found her?"

"What did I do? Well, Jim Ed, I puked. Right there on Glenda's precious antebellum floor."

Jim Ed had the presence of mind to choke on that last bit. When he stopped gasping for air and the tears cleared from his eyes, he asked eagerly if there was anything else I could remember.

"No, that's about it, Jim Ed," I said as his face fell. He looked like a kid whose last piece of candy had rolled into the gutter. "If people start any rumors about this, you tell them you talked to me and that's the way it was," I said as I rose to leave. "Oh, and I am so glad you're feeling better."

"Me, too," he said sadly. "Me, too."

Cat's Horse Tip #6

"When a horse backs up, she moves her legs in a reverse trot with the diagonal pairs of legs moving together."

14

I WENT THOUGHTFULLY FROM THE CO-OP to the Cheatham
County Rest Home, driving over the "new bridge" across the
Cumberland River. The new bridge had been in place for a while
and was a nice, safe, generic structure, but I'd liked the old one
better. If you discounted the fact that pieces of its roadway regularly fell into the Cumberland and that it was so narrow that
two trucks couldn't pass, causing a lot of traffic to stop and back
up, the old bridge had character.

I am of the opinion that planning commissions ought to in-
clude a hefty dose of character along with their so-called
progress. Guess it comes from my small town upbringing, but
I'm not convinced that progress is always what we need.

And speaking of truth, it still bothered me that Sheriff Big
Jim told Deputy Giles that I was a suspect, and then turned
around and told Jim Ed that he was going to arrest Bubba.
Maybe we were both suspects, or maybe he was just testing the

water. Dipping his toe, so to speak. As I parked in the shady lot, I dismissed such thoughts from my mind. I didn't have enough information to figure out the sheriff's motives, and besides, I had a different problem facing me.

I could hear Opal before I even got to her room.

"I took one of those an hour ago," she said loudly, and she clamped her lips together as I entered.

Physically, her private room at the home was only a few miles from Fairbanks, but culturally it might have been worlds away.

"That was yesterday. Remember, Gran? These pills are the ones the nurse gave you to take today. See?" Adam's voice was a smooth mix of persuasion and determination as he set three pills on a tray in front of Opal Dupree.

He spoke to me in a stage whisper that Opal could hear only too clearly. "It's good that you came now. She's not what she was before she heard about Aunt Glenda's . . . ah . . . passing. I thought I'd start coming by twice a day. Don't take too much notice of her ramblings, will you?"

Adam poured liquid the color of aged port into a small shot glass. "Here's your morning tonic, Gran. The pills on the tray are your blood pressure pill, muscle relaxer, glucosamine, and your vitamins." He lined up the capsules in a row while Opal sat in her custom wheelchair in a lavender designer robe.

I could see why Opal Dupree looked as delicate as the china in her late daughter's dining room. If she took all the pills on the tray she'd be too full to eat lunch.

Opal grumbled a few unintelligible words as she eyed the medicine suspiciously from under wrinkled lids. Then, with a resigned glance at her handsome grandson, she began to dutifully swallow the pills, her gnarled hands creeping slowly from the tray to the creases that made up her mouth and back again.

The hospital bed to her right was industrial, as was the metal stand beside it. But the room itself had been painted a warm beige and had generous accents of deep green at the window and door. The floor was a uniform tile that spread throughout the home, but it was well polished and shone where the sun peeped in through the window. The room itself was quiet, yet there was a comforting buzz of activity out in the hall. I got the sense that the activity could have included this room, had the occupant wished.

"That's great, Gran," said Adam, as Opal slowly swallowed the last pill. "And now you have a nice visitor. Cat Enright is here. You remember our neighbor, Cat."

The heavy lids glanced in my direction. She gave another unintelligible muttering and waved her shot glass to emphasize her point.

I molded myself to a tan plastic chair that looked as if it belonged in the dining hall, or maybe the rec room. I wondered if the choice of chair was Opal's and, if not, why Glenda hadn't brought her something more comfortable. Surely cost was not an object here.

While Opal studied me wordlessly, I studied the multitude of paintings that hung on the walls. They were quite good and ranged in subject matter from delicate portraiture to exquisite still lifes.

Adam, meanwhile, shifted uncomfortably from foot to foot. "That's Colonel Samuel Henley. He's the one who built Aunt Glenda's house, Fairbanks," he said as he saw me studying the portrait of an elder statesman in a long frock coat and stiff white collar. White muttonchops matched his shirt, and his flowing head of hair meant either that the artist took exceptional license with his subject, or that Hill's balding head did not come from

Col. Sam. This was the man that Jim Ed claimed made his fortune smuggling during the Civil War. Just what, I wondered, was it that he smuggled?

"Well," said Adam nervously, his eyes on his watch. "I'm not due on Music Row until this afternoon. You two don't mind if I sit here with you for a few minutes, do you?"

His eyes, sea blue today, gave his grandmother an inquiring glance. Sensing no opposition, he perched on a corner of her bed. In the hall, I heard the tinkling of laughter followed by the almost silent hum of a wheelchair as it passed by.

"You're not her," Opal conceded brusquely.

I looked at Adam, not sure what Opal meant.

"No, Gran. This is Cat Enright. With the horses. Remember?" He turned to me. "She thought you might be the physical therapist who comes several times a week. Gran, well, let's just say Gran doesn't think much of her."

There was another unintelligible grumble from Opal. "All you young girls look the same. And I'm just as glad that you aren't her. Aren't you?"

I said that, yes, I certainly was glad I wasn't her, although I was still not certain who "her" was.

"I get confused sometimes," said Opal, her creased mouth quivering, her eyes misting.

I said that it was all right. That I sometimes got confused, too. I looked again at Adam, who was now swinging his left leg back and forth in a charmingly distracting way. He gave me an encouraging smile and I turned back to Opal.

Opal took a big gulp of her "tonic," the glass gripped vice-like in her clawed hands. "Damned pills make my mouth dry."

I nodded again, not knowing what to say. I'd come to see Opal to pay my condolences on the death of her daughter, but the change in her since I'd last visited a few weeks ago was disturbing. At her eighty-fifth birthday party in early January she'd been a lively, striking woman, handicapped only by the arthritis that crippled her limbs.

Now Opal's eyes were dull and vague, her disposition peevish. I forced myself to remember that she'd lost her younger daughter, Adam's mother, in a tragic car accident many years ago and now she'd lost her one remaining child in a brutal murder. Hardships aside, the change in Opal was extreme all the same.

"I need some money," she said, leaning imperceptibly toward me in a confidential manner. "That's why there's no furniture in here. I had to sell it to pay off the nurse. She wants to kill me but as long as I keep giving her money, she'll leave me alone."

It was utter nonsense of course. Wasn't it? Adam agreed calmly that it was.

"Now, Gran," he said. "Don't you remember you wanted all the furniture moved out? You said it was hard for you to move your wheelchair around with it in here and you never used the furniture anyway. Remember?"

Opal ignored her grandson. "My dear," she continued, "you must try the pâté. It's wonderful." She held her empty shot glass toward me and with a nod from Adam I accepted it and pretended to sample its contents.

I was at a loss. The Opal Dupree I knew had been a shrewd, dynamic businesswoman. She had encouraged her two daughters in their quest for Hollywood stardom, even to the point of negotiating Glenda's first movie deal herself. Many said Opal Dupree made Glenda the big star she was, continually planting stories in the trades and arranging numerous publicity stunts. Not bad for a widow from Nashville.

As I watched, Opal dug among the many folds of her robe and produced a stylish gold lighter and a very crumpled pack of cigarettes. She withdrew one, examined it thoroughly for some time and finally, with shaking hands, lit it.

"I'm not supposed to have these," she said, her chin raised. "So. Why are you here, Cat?"

Once the cigarette was lit, Opal's mind seemed to come back to her. She was once more the domineering mother, the revered matriarch of the Dupree family.

"I just stopped by to say how sorry I am for your loss."

"What loss? You mean Glenda? You didn't murder her, did you?"

I shook my head.

"Then what do you have to be sorry about? She's gone. It's my loss, not yours."

Even though her words were harsh, this was the woman I had expected to see. I was infinitely more comfortable with the abruptness, the coldness, than I was with her vague wanderings, because this was the Opal Dupree that I knew.

"Is there anything I can do to help you? Funeral arrangements, anything like that?"

"No. Adam is supposed to be taking care of all the details. You are taking care of that, aren't you?" she asked him. He nodded.

"Well you'd never know it by me. He hasn't told me a damned thing." Her head nodded on her thin, wrinkled neck, and for a minute I thought she was going to drift off to sleep. Instead, she heaved a big sigh and frowned at the portrait.

"Col. Sam Henley," Opal said. The words came out slurred. "All he tried to do was better his place in life and help those soldiers. After the war no one gave him the time of day."

"I see." I tried to look intelligent, look as if I knew what she was talking about, but to my dismay, I saw Opal had slipped back into vagueness. I realized that I couldn't tell how coherent she was from sentence to sentence. It was proving to be a difficult visit.

"He gave those soldiers exactly what they needed," Opal said fiercely. "And they should have thanked him. But no. Them Northerners all run off home when the war was over and not a how-de-do from them. Not even a remembrance on the day he died."

She glared at me, and this time even Adam looked uncomfortable.

"Was the war his fault?" demanded Opal, her pasty cheeks finally acquiring some color. "Can you blame a man who was too old to fight for wanting to do his part? Oh, my. Did you think he was a real colonel? No ma'am, he was not. He never fought a day in his life. He just give himself the title because he figured he helped the war effort to that level."

She ended her short tirade abruptly, pointing her knobby finger at me to make sure I understood.

"You must have a great interest in the Civil War," I said.

"My mother died when I was ten."

Not sure where this train of thought was leading, I said, "That must have been hard for you."

"It built character. That's what it did." Her eyes were once more sharp and focused. Her voice strong. "We lived in town. In Nashville. Of course Nashville was much smaller then. Still a city, but it had a small town feel. My father passed shortly before I was born. Run over in Atlanta by a bunch of drunken hooligans during a business trip. I was sent to live with friends of my mother's when she passed. Good people they were. Kind.

My mother was from here, from Cheatham County, and I remember the stories she told me about old Col. Sam. Even then he was a legend out here."

"I'll bet those were great stories."

"He was mad, you know. At the end he went mad. Crazy mad. There was great tragedy in his life. Especially in his later years. He disowned his family. He became a hermit, holed up there in that old house. He became no more than an animal." She turned to look at the portrait, her eyes gleaming, the creases of her mouth moving wildly.

"He was an intelligent man, but there were some things he wasn't very smart about. Oh, no. Not smart at all."

Adam got up from the bed and paced in the small open space of floor that was behind his grandmother. He made a frantic wind-it-up motion with his hand. I supposed it wouldn't do to get Opal too worked up.

She started in again, though, before I could make any noises about leaving. "I was just twenty when I married Alexander Dupree. I loved him. Oh, yes, I loved him. But he, too, had his secrets. In a lot of ways he was no better than Col. Sam. Then he died. Took sick one winter. Today they call it pneumonia. He was burning up. It was a terrible time. Left me with two little girls. No more than babies, they were."

"How did you manage?" I asked.

She looked at me, her expression sly.

"Oh, this and that. You know how it is."

She's hiding something, I thought. She was daring me to challenge her, but I decided against it. What did it matter if the old woman rambled? She was entitled to her secrets. Goodness knows if anyone can get within spitting distance of ninety without a few secrets.

"He never, ever stopped pining for the war," she said, almost shouting. I wasn't sure if she was talking about Col. Sam, her husband, or someone we hadn't even discussed yet. "He needed humoring. Humoring in his old age, but he ended up turning everyone away. Everyone."

Throughout most of the conversation Opal had held her tonic glass to her chest. Now she put it back on the tray. Her eyes slowly moved across the room, settling on everything and on nothing.

"Life is so sad, isn't it, Cat?" she said. "There's no one left who remembers the old days. Glenda gave me the painting of Col. Sam. It was in the house when she bought it. I like it not because of him, but because of what's behind him."

I looked closely at the portrait and sure enough, behind old Sam was an open door and through the door was a glimpse of a beautiful garden. The garden looked old-fashioned and peaceful, a place where there would be no worries, no unhappy endings. I wondered what the real story of Col. Sam might be, and if there was anyone left who knew the truth.

Opal then looked at me with a trace of her old defiance, her eyes once more as clear and as blue as her grandson's.

"There are those who know, those who want us to forget what happened back then. Because the past repeats itself. If we're not careful," she repeated, "the past will happen all over again."

There was a surprising amount of strength in her voice, but the morning had more than begun to place its mark on Opal Dupree. With each passing word, she spoke more slowly, the slurring more pronounced. Adam quit his pacing and came to rest behind his grandmother's chair, and patted her shoulder. She shrugged him away.

"Both of you listen up. I don't care what happened to old Sam, and you shouldn't either. . . ."

Opal seemed to lose her train of thought because she stared blankly at the window for a time before continuing. "But mark my words, children, the past is coming back to haunt us and it's closer than we think."

Her crippled hands fumbled fruitlessly for her cigarettes. Giving up, she turned again to the window, beyond which the sun was continuing to make a miraculous appearance. Then she slowly relaxed, weariness overcoming her body. Her final words were so slurred as to be almost unintelligible.

"Don't mistake me. I grieve for my daughter. Oh, how I grieve. But I can't help the dead. It's the living I want to save."

Her head jerked sharply, but she was fading fast. Adam stepped forward and bent to check on her. It was painful to watch.

Opal started to chuckle. "It's all down in the gopher hole. Adam knows all about it, don't you, dear?" She didn't wait for him to reply. "I know that you know. Oh, yes I do. But don't worry. I won't tell. Never, never, never. Mother said I must never, never, ever tell. And I won't. Oh, no. Bad things will happen. Mother said. . . ."

Beside the chair, Adam raised his eyebrows and sadly shook his head.

"Go away, both of you," she said. "What do you want with an old woman anyway? Leave me to my privacy."

Opal had, thankfully, put an end to the uncomfortable visit. I rose to go, but Opal suddenly reached out and clutched at my jacket.

"Water and darkness," she yelled, jerking my garment with surprising strength. "That's what you need to look for, water and darkness." Her head lolled sideways and she released her iron grip.

"I think we should go," said Adam, stepping in to escort me around his grandmother. "You can see how she is. She's been failing the past few weeks, but since Aunt Glenda . . . well, it's been difficult."

He held out his hands in a gesture of helplessness and before I knew it I had taken them in mine.

"If we are lucky enough to live that long, it could happen to any of us," I said.

In her chair, Opal snored, then jerked awake and began to shout obscenities at us. Adam ushered me toward the door as a nurse came rushing in. As we left, the nurse was trying unsuccessfully to quiet Opal's cackling.

"I'm sorry if my grandmother upset you," Adam said. "Unfortunately, she lives in a dream world most of the time now. You saw how she is. I thought, hoped, she might be better this morning. Mornings are usually good for her, but since she heard of Aunt Glenda's death, she's been pretty unstable. As you might guess, grief affects everyone differently."

We walked hand in hand to our cars. When we reached ny truck he turned toward me and I was surprised to find tears in his eyes.

"Thank you for coming," he said. "You're the only one who has. Out of all the people she knows in this county, no one else has come by to see her. Even though she was difficult in there, I know it meant a lot to her for you to have come. It means a lot to me, too."

When we hugged I was amazed to feel the sharp thinness of his body and thought that Glenda's death must have affected him a lot more than he let on.

"Listen," said Adam. "I know it's almost time for lunch and you probably have things to do, but I haven't had breakfast yet. Would you care to join me?"

Cat's Horse Tip #7

"The wall of the horse's hoof is thickest at the toe."

15

WE HOPPED IN ADAM'S JAG AND SPED up River Road, crossed the river and dropped into Ashland City. There weren't all that many places to eat in our illustrious county seat, but we drove past them all just for the heck of it. Finally, Adam settled on a riverfront restaurant back on the south side of the Cumberland. The new bridge was getting a lot of use today. The restaurant had just opened for lunch, but Adam charmed them into whipping up several stacks of pancakes for us.

Even though I was still somewhat uncomfortable around Adam, it wasn't every day a girl got to eat brunch with a real live soap opera star. I wished I had taken time this morning to tamp down my unruly hair and add a bit of lip gloss, but Adam didn't seem to notice that I was not made up like a Hollywood starlet. If he did, he was a better actor than I had given him credit for.

After settling in at a quiet table next on the river side of the restaurant we started talking about Glenda, but as often happens with people who do not know each other well, we ended up discussing ourselves.

"Of all the professions in the world, how did you get to be a horse trainer?" he asked.

Well this was disappointing. People usually ask that, sooner or later, but I had expected something more original from Adam. Its not as if training horses was the most unusual profession in the world. Not as unusual as, say, writing songs. But people think of training horses as exotic and glamorous, when in reality it is simple dedication and hard work. Plus, I liked what horses taught me about myself. Horses mirror your every thought and emotion back to you.

"I was your typical horse crazy kid who kept on pursuing her dreams when she grew up," I said. It was my standard answer. I didn't go into the "I'll die if I don't get to ride every day" mindset that had dominated my teens, and still did. Instead, I added, "It was interesting to me when Opal said her mother died when she was ten. My mother had breast cancer and died when I was eight, so unfortunately I know what it's like to grow up without a mom."

"We sure are a bunch of motherless people. My mom died when I was nine," said Adam. "Car wreck. I survived, she didn't. I turned to music, but Aunt Glenda convinced me that acting held better prospects. I tried it for almost fifteen years, but as you probably know," he said with a wry smile, "I wasn't very good at it."

Now that he mentioned it, I remember Glenda saying how disappointed she was that Adam had not inherited the family knack for acting. Or maybe, I mused, he had.

"After my mother died, Aunt Glenda raised me," Adam continued. "So when I finally got smart enough to leave acting to the actors I came here, to Aunt Glenda. As you know, I've been staying with her while I've been getting back into my music, but the songwriting is coming along real slow. Nashville is a tough town for those of us who are trying to break into the music business."

Now the details were clicking into place. The *Times* had featured Adam when he moved here last summer. I remember the article had included a section on Glenda's younger sister, Adam's mother, Amie. I had forgotten that Adam had been in the car with her when it crashed. How horrible that must have been. I know how awful it had been for me to lose my mom at such a young age, but to be with Amie when she died in such an abrupt and tragic way would have been terrible for young Adam.

The article also included some juicy gossip about how Amie had never married, and it was rumored that Adam's father was Jacob Katz, who was at the time the very married head of the top motion picture studio in Hollywood. According to the article, Amie Dupree had followed Glenda to Hollywood and had been enjoying some success on her own, in addition to being well-known as a party girl. I did some quick mental arithmetic and figured Adam must be thirty-five or thirty-six.

"Enough with *my* life, or lack of it," he said as he signaled the waitress to bring more coffee. "Now it's your turn."

I told him how my mom and dad met near the 101st Air Force Base in Clarksville. "They were introduced by mutual friends at a dance," I said. "After my dad left the service, they moved to his home in Chicago, and I was born just after they moved. Even as a kid I could tell my mom and dad loved each other above everything else, and I always thought that was so cool. It really gave me a solid foundation. When Mom died, Dad was devastated. Let's just say that he had a hard time coping. He spent more and more time at the corner bar and less and less time with me. When human services found me, I'd been completely on my own for more than a month."

I didn't look at Adam as I was telling him all this; it wasn't a story I told many people as I was never comfortable with the telling.

"Somehow, my maternal grandmother learned I was going to be put in foster care, and she came to get me. She lived in a tiny town between here and Memphis, and I couldn't have had a better place to grow up. Everyone knew everyone and no one locked their doors. My grandma was this great Southern lady. She was everything to me, but just after I graduated from college, she had a massive heart attack and died.

"Grandma left me everything she had. I sold her house, bought the farm and, well, here I am."

"What about your dad?" Adam asked. "Do you ever see him, or did he drop off the face of the earth?"

I smiled and shook my head, just as I always did when I thought of my father. "He pops in every now and then," I said. I had learned over the years to be cautious about my dad, even when speaking of him. In a way, he's like the proverbial bad penny that shows up unexpectedly every now and then; but there is also a vulnerability that endears him to me. He's one of those people that you can't not like. "There's not been much structure in my dad's life since Mom died," I added. "He floats from place to place doing odd jobs, or he has lengthy visits with old friends."

"Well, you certainly are a credit to your family, such as it is. You are doing very well, I hear," Adam said, leaning intently across the wide table. "Tell me about it. Tell me what true success feels like so I have something to look forward to." The gleam I noticed when he welcomed me into his office the other day was back in his eyes, intensifying the sky-blue of his irises to aqua.

"It isn't winning the national and world championships as much as the work leading up to it," I replied after thinking about it. "I remember the little things, like how our halter mare, Sally Blue, is allergic to any kind of fly treatment, even the new organic kinds. We had to douse her the entire season in vinegar and water to keep the bugs away. When she won her halter class at the world show we all doused ourselves with Sally's vinegar. We all smelled so bad! That's the kind of thing I remember more than the nervousness of waiting for the results to be announced, or the cheers of the crowd, or all the hard work.

"And then there's the people. I love my clients. Well, most of them." I added. "Doc Williams fixed a broken arm for me in college and ended up being my first client when I set up shop. He is such a dear. And then there is Agnes Temple. She is the most annoying woman in the universe but she has such good in her heart that you can't help but love her. She is like a little kid in many ways and gets so excited about the shows and the classes. She's past seventy, but she makes it so much fun for all of us. I can't imagine doing this without her. Or Darcy, my youth competitor. In a lot of ways she's like a little sister.

"And I can't forget the horses. It is such an honor for me to work with such wise animals. Every time I walk into the barn I learn something new about them, and about myself."

"So," I said, steering the conversation back to him. "When you finally get a song cut, you won't remember the overall success of the song as much as how the song came to you, where you were, what color the sky was, and how much you love the people you were with that day. To me, those are the true measures of success."

Adam stared at me with a bemused expression. Hot damn, he was a handsome one. We locked eyes and it was several seconds before I could turn away.

"Oh, gee," I mumbled, "look at the time." It was an easy out from a moment that could have led to so much more. A shrink once told me that my mother's death caused some "abandonment issues" and that's why I couldn't stay in a relationship for more than three seconds. But I truly was shocked at how much time had passed. We'd been sitting there for much more than an hour.

Murdered neighbor and missing kid aside, I had work to do. Horses to ride. We hopped back in the Jag and Adam whizzed me the few miles back to my truck. As he drove away I was surprised to find a smile on my face and thought I might have to revise my opinion of Adam Dupree as a shallow party boy. I'd just had a perfectly nice time with a perfectly charming man.

I returned home to find Jon erecting a jump across the front of the driveway, not too far from the road. He had pulled two standards and three ten-foot ground poles from the outdoor arena and was creating a barrier to the television trucks who were parked along the side of River Road near Fairbanks.

"Damned guy from the FOX network showed up in the barn aisle with a camera," he offered in explanation. "He turned the thing on, lights and all, and Gigi about jumped through the roof. I told him if he didn't leave the property immediately that Mason Whitcomb would sue his ass to kingdom come."

Good to know that Darcy's dad's name carried that much weight, I thought. Now if he would actually spend a little time with his daughter. I offered to help, but Jon tilted his head toward the house and I saw two police cars parked near my door.

Jon let me through the barrier and I found Deputy Giles on my porch with a search warrant. He had the grace not to meet my eyes when he handed it to me. I stood in the doorway, stunned, while he and a slimmer counterpart rummaged through my home. When they left with several items in opaque evidence bags, I didn't even have the energy to ask what they had found.

Cat's Horse Tip #8

"Remember to reward your horse's thought or intention."

16

IN THE QUIET OF MY KITCHEN, I made a comforting concoction of hot chocolate using soy milk, dark chocolate, vanilla, whipped cream, and lots of chocolate sprinkles. I thought about adding some coffee-flavored brandy but decided it was too early in the day. Besides, I had horses waiting.

I poured the mixture into a double-sized mug, and Hank wagged his tail hopefully as I took the steaming cup into my living room. His wags lessened considerably, however, as I explained to him that chocolate is not good for dogs. Besides, I realized Hank was still not 100 percent back in my good graces. I don't care what they say. Chewed sofa padding does not come out of Berber carpeting. Clearing the foam-flecked swivel rocker of yesterday's mail, I settled in to think.

I began the day believing Carole was right, that Bubba had seen or heard something that frightened him and he was hiding. But now I felt differently. I was starting to believe that whoever killed Glenda had also done something with Bubba. Whether the killer had hurt Bubba or just taken him somewhere was anybody's guess.

I felt differently about Glenda's death, too. From the first, I had discounted the random killer theory, even though there had been similar murders in surrounding communities. I felt even stronger about it now. And if I was right, that meant someone offed Glenda for a reason. Someone she knew. I shuddered. I didn't like that thought at all. Especially because it meant the killer might be someone that I knew, too. I just couldn't imagine knowing a murderer. I mean, what do you say to them? You can't ask a killer what they did today. They just might tell you.

This morning, Deputy Giles said that someone had broken into Fairbanks during the night. My initial thought that kids were the culprits had also changed. Kids around here don't do things like that at three in the morning. Adults, maybe. But not kids. Not around here—we're too remote. Unless you have a car you can't get here easily. I couldn't see school-age kids walking miles on end down River Road in the dark and cold on a school night to visit a house where a murder had recently taken place. Not even on a dare.

The deputy also mentioned that, as far as he could tell, nothing was missing from the house. Now why, I wondered, would someone bother to break into a house and not take anything? But then again, did the actions of burglars, or even killers for that matter, make sense on any level? No one ever said they had to have a reason for their actions. Even in the best of circumstances, I've always been of the opinion that murder is an unreasonable act.

Unless, I thought suddenly, what they were looking for wasn't there. Unless what they wanted was so small—so obscure an item—that the police didn't know it existed. Unless whoever broke into Fairbanks couldn't find what they were looking for because someone else had it. Someone like me.

My brain finally clicked onto something of importance. Sally Blue. Glenda's notebook. Jacket pocket. Rushing to the old wooden coat rack in the hall, I fished around deep into the left front pocket and pulled out pay dirt. Well, not exactly, but I did find the notebook.

I took it into the kitchen and sat down at the old wooden table. My heart was thumping and my hands were shaking as I examined the leather cover. The book was small, about three inches by five. It was made of a rich, dark brown, beautifully grained leather, and featured a short strap from the back of the book that led to a gold clasp on the front. It was thinner and much more elegant, but the book reminded me of a diary my grandma had given me for a birthday long ago.

Then, I realized, I should not have touched the book. Oops. I wasn't sure if fingerprints could be lifted from leather, or even from paper for that matter. But it was too late to worry about that now. I debated whether I should call the police right away, or if I should open it first. The clasp looked as if it opened with a key, but when I brushed my fingertips along the sides, it released smoothly. So much for any further debate.

Whatever written nuggets of information I half-expected to find inside, they weren't there. Glenda hadn't written on the first page, for example, "if you find me dead, so and so did it." It wasn't a date book that showed the dates and times of her many important appointments, thus indicating an appointment with her killer. Nor was it an address book or a diary. Instead, it looked like a combination recipe book and a place for spur-of-the-moment notes to herself. Only the first few pages were used, but the gum line that stuck all the unlined ivory pages together at the top was a bit thicker, leading me to believe that Glenda tore out the pages when she was through with them. So either she had accomplished the task she reminded herself to do, or she had transferred the information to a more permanent place. The first page read in slanted block letters:

CALL CHARLES T. AT C.S. ASAP

Underneath that, printed in a similar style was:

HAVE H.H. BRING TRANSFER PAPERS TO HOUSE

The first line made no sense to me. The second was somewhat clearer. Transfer papers indicated that Glenda had already purchased a horse. Possibly from Hill Henley (H.H.) or one of his clients. If the note was as recent as I thought it was, Hill had never gotten the papers to Glenda to sign because he had left the house Sunday night to go to Shelbyville.

I wondered if Glenda had already paid for the horse. If she hadn't, that might eliminate Hill from the list of suspects—if he was ever a suspect to begin with. He certainly wouldn't kill a client if she still had to transfer numerous thousands of dollars into his pocket. Or maybe she'd changed her mind about the horse and that's exactly why he did kill her. Just where had Hill been on Monday anyway?

The second page read:

TELL C. LU TO ADD MORE LIME TO SALSA

And below that was:

= PARTS CHEX, NUTS, P. BUTTER CHIPS, CHOCOLATE CHIPS, PRETZ, RAISENS

Two lines here that also made sense. "C. Lu" must be Cinda Lu, Glenda's housekeeper and sometime cook. Cinda Lu Giles, one of the many daughters of our local equine veterinarian Doc Giles, and probably a niece or aunt or cousin to Jim Ed Giles and Deputy Giles, cleaned several of the larger homes in the area in addition to working for Glenda several days a week. The second line looked like a recipe for some kind of trail mix. Hmmm . . . salsa and trail mix. Maybe Glenda had been planning a party.

It was the third, and last written page, that interested me the most. There were only a few words on the page:

$L = OPIUM + SAFFRON + WINE$

What in the world? Opium, I knew, was a narcotic, a highly illegal drug. I knew from watching CNN that opiate addiction accounted for a large portion of deaths due to drugs. Saffron, I thought, was a kind of a flower, or was it a spice? And wine was a given. But what was L? The opium part concerned me. Surely Glenda had not been into drugs? Had her murder been some kind of drug deal gone wrong? If so, then that would remove Bubba as the possible killer. At least I hoped so. I knew kids were getting into hard drugs younger and younger, but at age ten? Here in rural Cheatham County? I didn't think it likely. But it might indicate that Bubba saw Glenda's supplier, and that Bubba didn't leave of his own accord.

On the other hand, Glenda had been a health nut. She had been a strong advocate of organic food, bran muffins, bean sprouts, herbs, and exercise. Although it was possible to combine a healthy lifestyle with drug addiction, I didn't think it very probable. No, the more I thought about the idea, the more I knew it didn't fit.

I got up and paced the room, Hank following doggedly at my heels. My brain was whizzing, and ideas were forming, then spinning out of reach before I had a chance to grasp onto them.

After making a few quick but cautious decisions, I picked up the phone and called Carole Carson.

"Have you found Bubba?" she asked before I could identify myself. What would any of us do without caller I.D.?

"No. But I've got a few ideas. I think you can help me with one."

I asked if she was planning to go to the library in Ashland City any time soon.

"Tomorrow. I usually go Thursday mornings because they have a story hour for the younger kids," she said.

"Could you possibly go today?"

She admitted that, possibly, she could. "Detective Giles is supposed to drop by this evening so I can look over my statement for the police report, but I can be back by then."

"I'm not sure what you should look for other than any information the library might have on Fairbanks or Col. Samuel Henley. I don't get to the library too often now, but when I was growing up our county library had a section on local history. I was thinking that the library in Ashland City might have local information on people or places near here that might not be online."

Before she could question my motives I continued. "I'm not sure it's important, but I've got a nagging suspicion that Bubba's disappearance and Glenda's death are related and that it's all tied in with Fairbanks and possibly even Col. Sam and the Civil War. Who knows? Maybe I'm way off base."

"I can't possibly see any connection," Carole said, "but if you think it will help I'll load up the kids as soon as the older ones get home from school and go this afternoon."

I had to give the Carsons credit. They did have a daily housekeeper/nanny. But Carole was truly a hands-on mother. Their kids went to public schools and she and Keith, when he was not out touring, attended every baseball game and dance recital their offspring participated in. It was a lot more than I could say for the way some other people parented their children.

"One more thing," I asked. "Can you call Hill and find out if Glenda was buying a horse from him, or if she'd already bought one? Oh, and see if you can find out who Charles T. at C.S. might be. I found a reference to that in a note of Glenda's."

My next call was to Darcy, because I needed some of her Internet expertise. I'm probably the only person on the planet who doesn't like the Internet. It just doesn't grab me. I like face-to-face interaction, or barring that, at least voice-to-voice, although I know the Internet can do both of those these days. But not liking to spend time on the Internet did put me at a disadvantage.

Most other trainers around the country had fancy web sites, and many had attracted new clients or sold horses through their lavish, whiz-bang online pages. Some of the star horses even had their own Facebook page and had hundreds of "friends." But I was happy with a simple web site that listed my training philosophy and credits, along with a few photos that Jon somehow put up. Darcy kept nagging me to spend more time online and, with a sigh, I realized she was right. I needed to better utilize the Internet for the great tool it was. But not today.

After the usual hellos and listening to Darcy's amazing, and mostly unprintable, theory about Glenda's death, I asked if she was currently online. It was a dumb question because if Darcy was home, I knew she was surfing the web.

"Oh man, Cat, am I ever. I'm online right now chatting with this way cool dude from Greece. He wants me to come over and check out his ship. Ship. Get it? Like in big, big boat." She giggled. "Think Daddy'd get mad if I charged an airline ticket to Greece?"

"Ah, probably, Darce. But hey, kiddo, forget the ship. I've got a project for you."

I gave her the same spiel I gave Carole, adding that I also needed anything on opium, saffron and wine, specifically regarding their relationship to each other.

"Think you're up to it?"

"For sure, girlfriend. Piece of cake. Hey, let me tell my Greek buddy ta-ta and I'm gone after it. Talk to ya later."

I wondered if Mason knew Darcy spent most of her online "educational" hours chatting with a Greek "friend" about his ship. I thought not. I thought it even less likely that Darcy's chat buddy was really from Greece or that he actually owned a ship. Darcy, for all her teenage bravado, was a somewhat gullible and I resolved to keep an ear tuned to the situation to be sure she never tried to meet the guy. Like Bubba, Darcy wasn't always the best at thinking things through.

Before I could make the last call on my list, the phone rang.

"You planning on coming to the barn today?"

Jon was in even less of a good mood than when I'd met him earlier at the end of the driveway. I knew he had his hands full with his regular chores and the added pressure of the fallout from Glenda's death. I also knew I had been neglecting my own duties. No matter what anyone tells you, it's hard balancing a murder investigation, a disappearance, and a career training horses all at the same time.

"I've got a few more phone calls to make, then I'll be over. What's up?"

"Oh, nothing much," he said. "Just nothing much at all. Before the jerk with the camera showed up Gigi started pawing the stall door because you weren't there to longe her on time and scraped a patch of hair off her shin. Sally didn't finish her breakfast, which as you know, has got to mean something is seriously wrong. There's a spot on the roof over Petey's stall that started leaking and it's past noon and I haven't even begun to get anybody exercised out here or the stalls cleaned because I've either been chasing members of the press off the property or been up on the roof trying to find the problem.

"Plus, Doc Tucker was here to check teeth on Dondi and Bob. It's not right that you skipped out on an appointment with an equine dentist—especially an appointment as important as this that has been on the books for months."

I sighed and felt the tiniest twinge of guilt. "Okay, Jon. It's my fault that Sally didn't finish. I was late feeding this morning and she got upset. I was on the phone with the police," I continued before he could complain about my irresponsibility. "You know how Sally gets when her schedule is out of whack. I'll be out in a few to handle everything else. In the mean time you can move Petey to—"

"The empty stall on the other end," he snapped. "I've already done that."

"Good. Then just to be sure, take Sally's temperature and see—"

"It's one hundred point three. Normal for her."

"Okay, then you can rinse—"

"The spot on Gigi's leg with a Betadine wash and wrap it to prevent swelling."

"Well what in the world do you need me for?" I joked. The silence on the other end was ominous. "Okay, Jon, I know you're upset with me. Please tack Petey up with his hunt-seat gear and I'll be out soon. I'll also call Geoff Tucker to apologize. I really am sorry I've left everything for you to do. It hasn't been fair, but I'm kind of tied up in this Bubba and Glenda tragedy."

"I know, Cat. I'm sorry I got on you. The police have been out here talking to me, too, and that's another reason I'm running behind. And even with the barrier at the end of the driveway, these damn reporters and photographers keep wandering in wanting dirt on Glenda. But if all that wasn't going on, you know this barn is too much for one person. That's why you hired me. We're too close to the start of the show season for both of us to not be here. I'm doing what I can, but you know, you're still the boss."

Of all the people in the world, I certainly did not need Jon to be mad at me. I carried a lot of weight on my shoulders, what with the stable and all the horses, and Jon was the only one who shared a little of that load. I would be lost without him and could not afford to have him jump ship. I'd have to develop a special plan to make it up to him, but just what that special plan was would be difficult to determine.

Jon was very private. He was pleasant, knowledgeable, friendly, bright, and reliable, but after three years of working together I still didn't know what kind of music he liked, where he was from, or if he had family. I didn't know what his favorite color was, or his favorite food. I wasn't even sure when his birthday was. He clammed up so tight when I used to ask him about himself that long ago I quit asking. The end result was that because I knew next to nothing about him he was impossible to shop for. And he seemed to be insulted if I suggested he take some time off.

Did I really know enough about Jon to rule him out as the person who killed Glenda? Could he have? Before I went further with these ideas I reminded myself that I was the teensiest bit overloaded right now. Any thoughts about making up to Jon, or of him being a murderer, needed to be saved for another day.

Before leaving for the barn, I made one final call and left a message on Robert Griggs's machine asking for information about the opium equation. He was, after all, a nurse. And weren't nurses supposed to know about chemistry and such things?

Cat's Horse Tip #9

"When a horse blows a blast of air through her nose, she's clearing her nasal passages so she can breathe in new scent and assess her safety."

17

UNLIKE MOST OF THE OTHER PLACES on River Road my barn was located behind the house, thus offering the horses, rather than myself, a clear view of the Cumberland River. It was a beautiful view I hoped they appreciated.

The barn had originally been built more than fifty years ago as a semi-permanent residence for dried tobacco leaves—a big industry in this part of the country. A few decades later, and with little or no renovation, it served as shelter for beef cattle. By the time I bought the place the barn had been reduced to storing used tractor parts. The basic structure, however, was still sound, so I had repeatedly patched a few spots on the roof (not a fun job, especially if you are like me and get heart palpitations sitting on anything taller than the back of a horse), built some roomy stalls, and hung out my shingle. For now the barn was adequate, but obviously a day lurked in the not too distant future when I would have to make a decision whether to keep repairing and adding on, or tear down and build new. But, thank goodness, that day was not today.

Robert Griggs returned my call just as I was finishing up with Petey. It had been a good session, good to get back in his saddle again. Peter's Pride was a wonderful all-around horse, very versatile. But versatile didn't always win national and world championships. He was a tall, leggy, angular horse and would do well on a regional level in both hunt seat and the more stylish saddle seat classes. But it had to be either/or if he was entered in open classes at the nationals in July. Because each class was so specialized, this horse couldn't do both at the level needed to win a national title. He was built to handle the saddle seat classes but was more interested in the hunt seat discipline. Then again, if Darcy chose to compete in youth classes, we were back to needing versatility. We'd have to make some decisions soon, but that meant sitting down and assessing the prospective competition for the coming year, talking with Mason, and getting a firm decision from Darcy as to whether she was going to compete or not. In a nutshell, things I didn't have time for right now.

I took Robert's call in the office.

"I have what you asked for," he said without preamble. "But before I tell you what it is I want your solemn promise that you aren't going to make any of this stuff."

I agreed, my curiosity growing by leaps and bounds.

"It's laudanum," he said primly.

"Laudanum? What's that?"

"It's a pain killer, outdated now, but one that was used for centuries. It was also a preventative, administered orally, against malaria and diarrhea. And, it was a popular painkiller for dental problems for many years. From what I could find, each doctor tended to have his own laudanum recipe, generally a variation on two ounces of opium and one ounce of saffron dissolved in a pint of wine. Some people threw in a pinch of cinnamon or cloves. The stuff must have tasted like stale cow pee. Can't you just imagine? Are you having pain, Cat? Because if you are, you should see a doctor."

"Pain? No. Not me. It's for someone else I know. Knew. I think."

"Well," he said, unconvinced, "mixing up laudanum on your own is a risky business. Like all opiate-based drugs it's highly addictive so you need to go to a clinic at the very least. And soon, Cat. Don't mess with this stuff."

"I won't, Robert. But tell me, where can I find out more?"

After a long hesitation he suggested the Internet or the main library in Nashville. "But I want you to know that if I thought you were actually going to make up a batch, I'd have to do something about it," he finished.

"Like what, Robert?" I didn't appreciate his attitude.

There was a long silence on his end. "It would be for your own good," he said.

Was that a threat?

In lieu of a pleasant goodbye I heard a resounding click. Great, I thought, just great. Now on top of everything else, one of my students thinks I'm a drug addict.

I found it hard to believe Glenda was a druggie, but I kept coming back to it. I dismissed as incomprehensible that Glenda was dealing. So if she wasn't a druggie and she wasn't dealing, why bother writing down the formula? Surely she hadn't been manufacturing laudanum right there at Fairbanks.

Maybe, I continued, it wasn't Glenda. Maybe there was some other connection with Fairbanks.

The phone interrupted my thoughts.

"I'm at the library but I couldn't wait to tell you what I found," said Carole, foregoing the hellos. "This is so cool. Col. Sam was born in 1842 and was nineteen when the Civil War started. He was a big man, heavy too, and limped badly throughout his life from a hip injury received in a fall from a horse when he was young. Because he couldn't physically take part in the war, he geared up for the war effort. His father was into shipping, agriculture, trade, that kind of stuff, and owned twenty slaves in 1860, which apparently was a lot for someone living in Cheatham County, so he must have been wealthy. It says Col. Sam and his father, Hiram Goforth Henley, built Fairbanks in 1859. Hiram passed in 1862, but Col. Sam prospered during the war anyway."

Carole added that the colonel married late in life and fathered a son, Sam, Jr., in 1899 and a daughter, Alice, in 1903, when he was sixty-one. He lived to the ripe old age of ninety-five, when a housekeeper there at Fairbanks found him dead one morning sitting in a chair in front of his fireplace."

That made two whose lives had ended in front of that fireplace. I shuddered.

"What happened to his wife and kids?" I asked.

"Hmmm. Doesn't say, other than his wife's name was . . . oh get this, Alice Giles. Why does that last name not surprise me? She died in 1909. Doesn't say what from, or what happened to the kids."

I remembered the painting in Opal's room and wondered if the text said anything about the amount of hair on the colonel's head. Carole laughed and said, no, it didn't. There was a photo, but he was wearing a top hat.

Carole also said that she wasn't sure, but she thought "Charles T. at C.S." might be Charles Toner, a senior banker at

AmSouth Bank in Ashland City. AmSouth had gobbled up a bank that had gobbled up the old Cheatham State Bank a few years back, but despite large new signs and corporate logos, many still called the bank by the name their grandparents had called it. Cheatham State. C.S.

"Oh, and get this," she continued. "I talked to Hill. Glenda had plans to buy a mare from a client of his, but the transaction never took place. Hill was the one who thought Charles T. might be Toner because Glenda told him she had to transfer some funds. Poor Hill."

Being the nice, polite neighbor that I am, I asked Carole how Hill was handling Bubba's disappearance.

"He didn't mention it," she said after a pause. "But Cat, I know that's because he's hurting so badly. A man like that just doesn't open up easily."

I resisted the urge to harumpf into the phone. Instead I said, "Thanks, Carole. Great job. I don't know where this will lead, if anywhere, but I'll keep it in mind."

I hung up the phone slowly and leaned back in the creaky wooden office chair. Hank, a stick firmly in his mouth, plopped down at my feet and I massaged the base of his ears as I thought. Was I on the wrong track? Although the information from Carole was interesting, I wasn't sure it had anything to do with Glenda's death or with Bubba's disappearance.

I felt sick at the thought of Bubba, and that in itself, was odd. I thought I should be feeling more for the brutal ending of Glenda's life, but it was Bubba who was ever in my thoughts. I felt that his continual disruptions in the neighborhood happened not because Bubba was a bad kid, but because he was neglected and bored. I agreed with Carole that Bubba had never been offered any kind of guidance. He wasn't a bad looking kid either. He was overweight, but he had a strong chin, a straight nose, and clear blue eyes the girls would be sure to adore, once he grew up and got his teeth fixed. So what if his dark, wavy hair was in need of a cut, and his usual odor *du jour* indicated that a long, hot, soapy shower was in order. He was a kid who needed help. Badly.

Taking a line from Opal, I realized I couldn't help the dead. But I could help the living. And with any luck, Bubba was still alive.

Cat's Horse Tip #10

"Lead ropes don't lead horses."

18

THAT EVENING ON THE WAY TO dinner I gave my best impish wave to the press, who were camped out along the road between my driveway and Glenda's. After I passed them. I played unsuccessfully with the truck radio, trying to get a "traffic and weather together" report on WSM-AM radio, Nashville's "Air Castle of the South." Because of the high cliffs on the south side of the road, evidence that the mighty Cumberland River had once been much mightier than it was today, it was hard to get the station even in the best of weather. Of course, listeners in Arkansas and Ohio could probably hear every second of the fifty-thousand-watt broadcast quite clearly. Go figure.

I continued to wind up River Road and near the end of it turned left just before Sawyer Brown Road, which, if I had taken it, would have led me into Bellevue, a west-side bedroom community for Nashville. A lot of people thought Sawyer Brown Road was named for the country music band Sawyer Brown, but the opposite was true. The band took their name from the road. I don't know a lot about the history of country music, but living in the Nashville area you can't help but pick up a few things.

I made another left on Highway 70 and drove toward Walmart, but stopped before reaching the mega store. The neon sign placed high in Verna Mae's window repeatedly flashed its retro shades of turquoise and orange. Inside, the sounds of plates clattering, raucous laughter, and a TV Land showing of *Laverne and Shirley* made the little building vibrate all the way to its ancient foundation.

Verna Mae's had last been redecorated in the fifties, or at the very latest, maybe the early sixties. The well-worn booths were covered in patched turquoise vinyl and the walls were hung with pictures and pennants of local high school athletic teams from decades long gone.

I inspected the walls of the waiting area, playing a game with myself that I did every time I came in. The latest photo I could find was dated 1963, but the frame was different from the others, leading me to believe the shot had been added sometime after the restaurant's decor had been in place for a while. Nothing new. I didn't know if I'd be thrilled or disappointed if I ever found a later photo and hoped I'd never find out. I liked Verna Mae's because everything was spotlessly clean, the food unsurpassed, and the prices so reasonable the food could be considered cheap. My idea of heaven.

A large young woman in limp brown hair and clothes she'd outgrown thirty pounds ago sat behind the register eating a Snickers bar. When I first began coming to Verna Mae's, the very large young woman had been a very large teenager, or maybe this was her sister. Either way, I had the idea that she/they were Verna Mae's granddaughter(s). Verna Mae rarely came out from the kitchen, but when she did, she was inevitably clad in a brown plaid muumuu and a starched white apron that would have fit, had her height matched her weight. My grandma always said to trust a cook who looked as if she enjoyed her own efforts, and Verna Mae more than fit that bill.

"I need a table for two," I said to the probable granddaughter after I'd had a chance to survey the crowd.

The young woman's jaw methodically went round and round as she considered my request. Her mental processes clicked into gear a short second before she finished chewing and she slowly raised a heavy arm to point to a small table that was being cleared at the back of the room.

Verna Mae's evening patrons were a generation younger than the breakfast crowd. Those who farmed a few acres this side of Fairview, or the retired folk who lived in Pegram or Kingston Springs and wanted to spend an hour or two at the neighboring Walmart, were the early morning clientele. The evening diners were their sons and daughters—harried working parents with half-grown kids and middle aged couples who'd just sent their youngest off to college and didn't know what to do with themselves now they didn't have to ferry their children from one sport to the next. I saw these people every week. They were as regular as clockwork. And so was I, as Darcy and I met here for dinner every Wednesday night.

I wiggled carefully through the tightly packed tables and was within spitting distance of my own when a hand reached out and tugged at my sleeve.

"Right here." I knew the voice as Darcy's, but I hardly recognized the body that went with it. One reason was the fact that her hair was piled elaborately on top of her head and she had traded her usual grunge jeans and sloppy shirt for an elegant navy designer suit. The other was that she was sitting with a young man whose own attire made Darcy's usual sloppy jeans look like high couture.

The kid was thin and lanky, with pasty, spotty skin that reminded me of Elmer's Glue. He wore faded black jeans with lots of chains attached to the pockets and a multi-stained T-shirt that seemed to be missing its sleeves. I was so engrossed in his hair, worn in a long, spiked, neon Mohawk, that I almost missed the tattoo of a skull on his right shoulder. That would have been a shame.

Darcy nodded her head in his direction, "Cat, this is Frog. I met him at the barn one day a few months ago—he's . . . a friend of Bubba's."

I stood with my mouth agape. It was enough that this horrible creature was sitting at the same table with Darcy, but for him to have been in my barn . . . I felt violated.

Frog turned and eyed me up and down, pulling a cigarette from his pocket and twiddling it with his fingers. His eyes were a bright blue and he would have been handsome except for the numerous safety pins that pierced various parts of his face. The surly expression and sneering curl attached to his lip gave me an idea about his attitude.

"Yeah. The horse lady. Been to your place. Cool."

"Uh, yeah. Cool," I replied, unsure whether I should kill Darcy right now, or wait until after dinner when there wouldn't be as many people around. After, I thought. No use spoiling my fellow diners' appetites.

Frog grinned sideways out of his mouth. "Yeah, me and Bubba, we hang together sometimes. I live just up the road."

Instinctively, I knew just which place it was, a dilapidated mobile home partially hidden behind the old VFW on the way to Ashland City. I remembered hearing about his granny just after I moved to the area. Her name was Cherry Berry, and she apparently thought it would be cute to name all her kids after certain kinds of berries, so you had to look at this kid and figure in the mentality of his forebearers.

Thanks to Granny Cherry, we were now blessed with her sons Goose and Cran, and the twins, Black and Blue, who both happened to be blonde. Sister Ras left for parts unknown years before I arrived, so I'd missed the pleasure of getting to know her. Hopefully somewhere along the way Miss Ras had the presence of mind to change her name. If I had my genealogy straight, Frog's father was one of the twins. Guess it didn't matter much which one.

Frog kept leering at Darcy, so I casually moved behind her, as much to attract his attention as to get away from him. To take a word from Glenda, he smelled a "wee" bit stale.

"So. Frog. Aren't you a little old to be playing with kids?" I asked in my sweetest voice. "After all, you're what, seventeen, eighteen? Bubba's only ten."

Frog shrugged. "Sixteen next month. Age don't matter. Bubba an' me, we're soul mates, if you know what I mean."

"No, I don't."

"No skin off my ass," he shrugged. He surveyed the room and, after finding nothing of interest, elaborated. "Neither of us got ma's. Our pa's are drunks. We ain't got no wheels an' we're within walkin' distance. That enough?"

I sighed and nodded. What a world.

"Get this, Cat," Darcy said excitedly. "Frog says he saw Bubba Monday morning, late."

"Noon," Frog corrected. "It was noon. I'd got me an appointment with the law, if you get my drift. One o'clock over to

Nashtown. My ol' man, he had to take me. Warn't too pleased about it none, I can tell you. Just a little problem with some wheels I borrowed an' everyone goes an' makes a big deal about it. I don't get it. Me an' my ol' man, we left the house at twelve o'clock sharp. By the time you get a parking place and get to that courtroom, it takes 'bout an hour. Been through it lots of times before, so I know. Anyway, I seen Bubba when we went by. He was crawlin' through the fence that divides his pa's place from that fancy house. Where that lady got herself kilt. I reached over and honked the horn, but it don't work so I pulled the plastic off where the window used to be and hollered at him, but he didn't hear me none."

Frog pulled a lighter out of a pocket. Why wasn't I surprised to see the lighter had a chain attached to it? He flicked the instrument several times, as if to test the strength of the flame. When no flame appeared he scowled briefly and shoved it back into his pocket.

"Frog, did you know that Bubba is missing and that the police are looking for him?" I asked.

"'Course. Even we po' folk got the t-vee. Couldn't miss it."

"So why haven't you told the police? This is crucial information. It might help find Bubba."

Frog's response was to ignore me and lean in closer to Darcy. "You're pretty cute," he whispered. Flecks of spit displaced by two silver studs in the center of his tongue dropped onto the table in front of her. "Mebbe later, you an' me can go somewhere, an' you know . . . talk or somethin'."

Frog leaned back, his gaze traveling up one side of her and down the other. Then slowly, crudely, he winked. I suddenly remembered someone once told me that it takes forty-two muscles in your face to frown, but it only takes four muscles to extend your arm and smack someone upside the head. The thought was tempting.

Darcy's response to Frog's wink was a single bored sniff. Smiling, as if he thought he could get her to change her mind, Frog returned to the question at hand.

"Dunno 'bout talkin' to no cops," he said. "Jus' not my way, I guess."

"But the police are looking for Bubba to charge him with a murder he didn't commit," I said, raising my voice.

Diners on either side of our table looked up, their forks frozen halfway to their mouths.

I lowered my voice and put my face next to Frog's. "If I don't find Bubba before the police do, your friend's ass will be in jail for the rest of his life. Come on, Frog, the kid's only ten years old. Ten years old. He's still a little kid."

Frog slowly unfolded himself from his chair. Upright, he wasn't nearly as tall as he looked sitting down.

"Lady, get the hell off my back."

Briskly, he stepped past me and bumped directly into the path of a furious Darcy.

"That's right," she spat, "just leave. Like that will fix everything. Go ahead. I'm sure it won't be the first time you left a friend hanging. You're a real tough guy, Frog. Real tough." Darcy snorted. "So listen up. Tomorrow, if you haven't told the police what you know, I'll personally come by and string you up by your balls."

It occurred to me that Mason Whitcomb had not been as passive in Darcy's upbringing as I had thought. Whether or not she was up to Frog, however, remained to be seen.

Diners throughout the restaurant were still staring, waiting to see what would happen. I had that fluttery, jittery feeling in my stomach, the same as when I was searching Bubba's house, and I tried not to let myself understand that I was terrified.

The obese woman at the register reached for the phone, whether to call the cops or to answer a call, I didn't know. Frog stood staring at Darcy, apparently trying to decide if she was serious. I decided yes, she was, and I was proud of her for it.

Suddenly, Frog laughed. He leaned on the table and pointed at Darcy with a long, grimy fingernail. Around the room, others laughed too, and finished bringing their forks to their mouths.

The woman at the register put the phone down and reached for another candy bar. Next to me, Darcy managed a weak smile.

"You," Frog laughed, "are one dumb shit."

She gulped in a deep breath of air. "Yeah, I know. But Bubba's my friend, too. And I want him found. Alive and well."

I stepped in. "Frog, we're just trying to save you some trouble." This was a blatant lie, but I didn't think he was smart enough to figure it out. He was at least a half quart low on brains. "The police will find out that you and Bubba were friends. And they'll come calling on you. Don't you think it would go a little better for you if you went to them? Particularly in light of your recent, um . . . incident with the wheels?"

He laughed again, and pushed past me toward the girl at the register. She reached again for the phone, but she soon relaxed her grip and chuckled at something Frog said.

I didn't have to ask Darcy about dinner. Our eyes connected and I knew that we both wanted out of there. She turned, weaving her way through the tables, and I was right behind her. When we got outside I looked back, but Frog was chatting amiably with the register girl. A few more steps brought us to my truck. I smiled a shaky smile at Darcy and, with great relief, reached out to unlock the passenger door.

A long white hand reached from behind me and grabbed my wrist in a vice-like grip. Frog spun me around to face him.

"Don't you go telling no cops about me an' Bubba. I don't know nothin' 'bout that ol' lady's murder an' I ain't gettin' involved any more than I already am."

"What do you mean, anymore than you already are?"

"Jus' by bein' a friend of Bubba's I'm kinda involved, like. See?"

No. What I saw was that Frog wasn't telling all. But I wasn't going to let him know that. Evidently he figured he had shut me up and he turned his attention to Darcy, leering in the mistaken belief that a missing front tooth was quite sexy. I reached around him to open the door and Darcy slid in gratefully.

"Right now, we're cool," said Frog as I opened the door on my side. "But I hear you been talkin' to the cops 'bout me, then I got a problem. An' if I got a problem, then you got a problem. Stupid baby shit anyway, gettin' hisself in trouble. I ain't gonna let him bring me in on it, too."

19

AFTER THE SCENE WITH FROG, DARCY didn't feel up to driving, so I told her I'd have Jon pick her up in the morning and bring her to her car, which we left at Verna Mae's. I knew full well that offering Jon's services without asking him would give him one more reason to hate me. Sigh. We grabbed burgers at a nearby Wendy's and took I-40 back to Nashville. No matter what the problem, life always looks better after eating a cheeseburger.

Despite the underlying threat of violence during the encounter, I believed Frog's story. I believed he saw Bubba on Monday at noon exactly where he said he saw him, going through the fence toward Fairbanks. That put Bubba very close to Glenda at what could have been near to the time she was killed.

Maybe Carole was right. Maybe Bubba had seen something that scared him. Even worse, an ill-intended person may have seen Bubba. That person may even have taken Bubba and was now hiding him. I dreaded thinking of the alternative, which was infinitely more awful. But it all came back to why.

Glenda had been killed for a reason. When I figured out the reason, I would find the killer. And with luck, the killer would know what happened to Bubba and would lead me to where Bubba was. Maybe.

I took the 440 bypass around to Hillsboro Road and into Green Hills. I turned right just south of the shopping area and after a mile or so of left and right turns pulled into a long, paved drive that led to a faux antebellum home somewhat along the lines of Fairbanks.

I knew from past trips to Darcy's that no weed would ever dare poke its head up from the deeply mulched bushes along the drive. Wide stone paths connected the house to a few smaller outbuildings. I could see what I knew to be the gazebo and a tool shed from the glowing light of precisely spaced electric decorator lamps along the walkway.

Mason was once again out of town and Darcy asked if I wanted to come in. Realizing she must be shaken from the nasty encounter with Frog, I agreed. As we neared the house, a huge Doberman got up from a mat on the porch and snarled.

When Darcy said, "hush," Keno recognized her voice and his vicious snarl immediately changed to yelps of joy as he ferociously wagged his stumpy rear end. We both gave the ancient guard dog lavish pats as we opened the door. These days his hearing was much better than his sight.

Inside, the elegant home was spotless, no thanks to Darcy. Mason always hired good "help." We smelled apples and cinnamon and Darcy made a beeline for the kitchen. There was a large pan of apple crisp cooling on the counter beside the oven, doubtless the courtesy of Mason's latest cook. Yum! Even though I'd just downed a cheeseburger, I was still hungry. It was stress. I was sure of it. Maybe that's why cops are never too far from a big, fat doughnut. All the carbs must keep the stress at bay.

Darcy started assembling forks, plates, and napkins while I heated cocoa in the microwave. We plopped down in a pair of rocking chairs in front of an antique, but working, wood stove, our plates balanced on our knees, our drink mugs resting comfortably on the stone floor. There was not a word said between us until both plates and cups were empty and the cups newly refilled.

"All in all, an interesting evening," I began, lightly rubbing the heel of my scraped hand, which had begun to itch. "Not quite the evening I had in mind, but interesting all the same." When there was no response from Darcy I added, "Mind if I ask about your get-up?"

Darcy had not explained her sudden interest in high fashion. Very possibly that was because she'd had other thoughts on her mind, like how to get rid of a slimy, violent jerk.

"Oh, this," Darcy giggled and smoothed her skirt. "Daddy thinks I should dress more ladylike and had like a bunch of this stuff sent over from that frou-frou shop Glenda goes, ah . . . went . . . to in Belle Meade. Daddy and I got into a big fight before he left because I've had the stuff like since before Christmas and he found out the price tags were still on every piece. I just wanted to be able to tell him, you know, when he called, that I actually wore some of it. If," she added quietly, "he calls."

"Listen, Darce. Why don't you come home with me? Spend the night and wake up early with a ride on Petey?"

"No, but thanks. Really. I've got a major history test tomorrow. Besides I've got a ten o'clock date tonight with my Greek god. Like that must be what, four in the morning over there? And, oh," she squealed, her melancholy forgotten, "like I totally forgot to tell you what I found for you on the Internet. It's too cool."

Darcy had indeed come up with a few things, like Carole, that were too cool.

For starters, she found roughly the same information on the opium equation that Robert had. It still added up to laudanum. Then she found an old newspaper article from an historical archive that linked Col. Sam with large shipments of "agricultural items" from China during the 1860s. There was also a second article that linked the old man to bootlegging during the Civil War.

"I don't know about the China stuff," I said, "but the bootlegging is interesting. I wonder if that's what he was smuggling during the war. I don't know anything about what the laws were back then. Alcohol manufacturing and sale in the 1860s. I imagine they were a lot different from what the laws are today. Do you think you can find out anything about that?"

Darcy said she was sure that she could, and with her words, I realized I was exhausted. All I wanted to do was go home. With Hank performing security duty, maybe I could make my own kitchen seem as safe and cozy as this one.

I walked to the front door reluctantly.

"You're not afraid Frog or anyone will bother you tonight, are you?"

"Oh, Cat, no. Like I was really rattled when I got to Verna Mae's tonight because that Deputy Giles pulled me out of class at school today. That creepy Robert Griggs told him I yelled at Glenda and he wanted to ask me about it."

"What did you tell him?"

"Exactly what I said to Glenda. That I called her a bitch and that I hoped she'd die a thousand deaths." In spite of Darcy's bravado, big fat tears welled in her eyes and began to roll down her cheeks. "I didn't kill her, Cat. Really, I didn't. I was so mad at her for being mean to you that right then I wanted to, but it's not a thing I'd ever, like, really do."

Of course I knew that. But did Deputy Giles?

"Then, like, there was that scene at Verna Mae's," she continued, snuffing and wiping her eyes. "But Daddy has made sure this place is secured tighter than Fort Knox. There's Keno. And Ruby, you know, the cook, has rooms over the garage. I'm cool with everything. I didn't like invite him, you know. Frog. I got there early and he was just there. Like he recognized me, or was impressed with the clothes." She giggled. It was a good sign. "Maybe Daddy isn't so old and dumb after all. These clothes . . . they just might be useful sometimes. I'll have to look at the others more closely."

Darcy gave me a hug and reassured me again that she would be fine. But I still worried about her on the way home. She was too young to face so much responsibility alone. I hoped she was up to it.

River Road was shrouded with patchy fog. I carefully threaded my way through an "S" shaped curve roughly two miles from the county line and accelerated slightly as I hit the straight run that would lead me home. It was the tail end of a spooky stretch of road. A few miles back, and just to the right, was an Indian burial ground that was estimated to be about nine thousand years old.

When Walmart was trying to build their new store here, many Native Americans held protests on the site, as part of the burial ground was going to have to be relocated. They tied cloths of the four colors, red, yellow, black, and white, to trees along the roadside to represent the four directions of their Native beliefs, and held regular twenty-four hour vigils. Many Native people believe the spirit stays near the body and that it would be wrong to relocate the burial ground. And who's to say they are not right?

The powers that be in Nashville eventually decreed that the remains were so old they preceded the modern tribes, such as Creek and Cherokee; and because no direct descendant could be found, there would be no problem in relocating the burial ground and putting a Walmart in its place. I boycotted the store for a while. But I am weak and Walmart is convenient. Nevertheless, that stretch of road, on certain nights, to me seems very ominous.

I saw the lights of the oncoming car and the bulky object in the road at the same time. On this stretch of highway there is no shoulder. To my right was a deep, swampy ditch; to my left was one lane with a car approaching fast, and further left beyond that was a wall of rock. Straight ahead was . . . well . . . something.

I slammed on my brakes before I had time to think about it. The back end of the truck veered violently to the right and I corrected with a sharp right swing to the steering wheel. But not before the truck collided with whatever was in the road and ground to a screeching, shuddering halt.

20

I GOT OUT OF THE TRUCK cursing. I peered under the truck and cursed again. Wedged tightly up underneath the engine and extending back almost to the rear axle was a large, thick tree branch. At least it wasn't Bubba. Until the actual words popped into my head, I didn't realize that was what I'd been thinking. Vile tasting bile backed up in my throat, my stomach dropped down to my knees and my legs started shaking, obviously from the extra weight of my stomach.

I sat down on the damp road in front of the truck. Not a very safe place, I admit, but my legs refused to take me anyplace else.

I damned Goose Berry to hell and back. This was his doing. He lived near here on a house sitting on stilts on top of a flood plain. I don't know how he got a permit to build where he did. Some said he didn't bother with the permit. He just built. With his family, you just didn't know. Just look at his beloved nephew,

Frog. Come to think of it, I'd about had my fill of the Berry family tonight. As far as I was concerned, if you put them all together they were about as smart as a bag of hammers.

Geographically, this was still Davidson County, and when it came to Goose, county officials should have known better. Ever since Goose built the house, he had a vendetta going with the county over the speed limit on the road in front of it. This was a flat, straight stretch posted at fifty miles per hour. But he thought it should be thirty-five. And when the county repeatedly ignored his complaints, he took matters into his own hands by placing tree branches, just the size of the one lodged under my truck, up and down the road.

It was illegal, of course. And dangerous, too. The county had started with warnings, then fines and finally jail time. But Goose didn't care. He was bound and determined that the speed limit be reduced. He claimed it was a noise problem, but his house was at least two hundred fifty feet off the road, so it couldn't be that much of a problem. If he'd wanted complete silence, he should have chosen one of the lots over near the Cheatham Game Preserve. Quite a few of those land parcels were totally isolated and I'm sure there would be no problem of a speed limit on the old, bumpy, logging roads that led to many of the lots.

I looked at my watch. Almost nine o'clock. It was pitch dark. Any garage would be closed by now and a tow truck would cost a fortune. But maybe Jon could come to my rescue. Maybe. I pulled my cell phone out of my pocket with trepidation. Sure enough, there were zero bars. Over the past few years I had tried every possible cell phone provider and none gave coverage in this spot. Together, the cliff and the swamp conspired to provide a communications black hole.

I considered the dark road. I didn't particularly feel like walking two miles home in the murky mist. But given the lack of any other viable option, I gathered my courage together, put one foot in front of the other, and started out. I decided that I really did need to break down and join AAA. Have I mentioned that I tend to be miserly at times? And old-fashioned? My grandma raised me not to want what I didn't need, but my problem was that I often couldn't tell the difference—or so Jon kept telling me. Well, now he would be happy. It looked as if I was finally going to spend some money whether I wanted to or not.

I wished Hank were here. It's not that I am afraid of the dark. Okay, truthfully, dark places scare the bejesus out of me. And as long as I'm being honest, I still have a nightlight in my bedroom. I can trace my fear of the dark back to the time I spent alone in Chicago as a nine-year-old in a run-down apartment. At night, rats and mice would creep in and more than once I woke to the feel of a furry body scurrying over me. But that was a lifetime ago. No rodent would be out on a cold, rainy night like tonight. Or so I kept telling myself.

As I walked, nothing stirred. The fog smelled like sand and rotten wood. Stray breezes sent showers of rain from the cliffs on my left. I stayed off the soft, narrow gravel shoulder and walked just inside the white line on the road's edge. Eventually I stopped thinking about rats and congratulated myself for not sending the truck into the ditch. Now that would have been a mess. Dents and swamp muck all over. Of course there was the very real chance that someone would plow into the truck, even though I'd left the emergency flashers on.

I'd gone about half a mile and pulled two more of Goose's big branches off the road when I heard a car approaching from behind. Its headlights cast wide, shiny patches on the wet pavement, and its engine geared down as the driver saw me. Nervously, I stepped to the side of the road to let the car pass. But instead, the car slowed and as it slid alongside me, it came to a stop.

My heart thudded into double time as the passenger door swung open and a voice from inside said, "You'd better get in."

The voice, I realized, belonged to Deputy Giles. And now that my wits were gathering themselves together, I saw the car had the official Cheatham County seal stamped on its side.

"I saw the truck back there and called a report into Metro. Looks like Goose Berry is going to spend a few nights courtesy of Davidson County. You want me to call in a tow for your truck? Metro's already got a car there. They'll tow it to an impound lot if you don't call in your own tow."

I nodded, and he picked up some papers from the passenger seat. As I got in with a mixture of curiosity and fear, Deputy Giles made the call. It was, I admit, the first time I'd taken a ride in a cop cruiser and I had half a mind the deputy was going to take me back into Nashville and lock me up with Goose. Maybe there was the teensiest inkling of guilt in the back of my mind. Maybe I realized deep down in my subconscious that my sudden interest in snooping wasn't going to be met with open arms by the deputy.

As the deputy rearranged his stack of paperwork, I noticed that the dash of the car and the space between the two front seats had a lot of serious-looking equipment attached to it. Each piece was equipped with its own set of blinking lights, hissing noises, and the occasional semi-understandable squawk from the dispatcher in Ashland City. It was quite intimidating.

The deputy noticed my inspection. "Don't let the lights fool ya. All I got in here is a radio link to the dispatcher, a phone, radar, a computer, and a regular AM/FM radio. The Metro cars have all the cool stuff." His envy was obvious but I forgot higher technology when, to my relief, he nosed the car in the direction of the stable.

"I didn't know you ran a twenty-four hour traveler's aid service. Out of county too. I'm impressed." I tried to keep it light now that my heart had resumed beating normally.

He shrugged and said, "Don't be, Miz Enright. I'm just driving around thinking. The sheriff's been giving me a lot of grief."

"I guess he wants to wrap this up. Make a quick arrest, huh." I tried not to sound uneasy, but all of a sudden I remembered Glenda's notebook was burning a hole in my coat pocket. I didn't want to know what Sheriff Big Jim would think of that.

The deputy nodded. "Yeah. The sheriff isn't the most popular guy in town right now. With anyone on or off the force." He paused. "How 'bout you? You look like you've had better days. You can tell me, now. Anyone been bothering you?"

"Me? Why would anyone bother me?" I immediately thought of Frog and wondered if the deputy had talked with him since our very recent conversation at Verna Mae's.

"Oh, I don't know," he drawled. "Just thought maybe someone like Adam Dupree might be somewhat bothersome."

I looked at him in surprise. "Adam? No, not at all. Why would you think that?"

"I heard you were tighter than two peas in a pod," he said. "Neither of you mentioned it in your statements, so I wondered if it was a big secret—or if there was a reason you wouldn't want it to be mentioned."

I hadn't had much time to think of the possibility of Adam and me as an "us." The chemistry was there, but we hadn't spent enough time together to determine if there was enough to continue with it. There was too much else going on in both our lives. But, the thought of others gossiping about Adam and me as an actual couple, combined with the evening's events, was altogether too much. My Irish temper, which I now realized had been simmering for some time, boiled over.

"First of all," I replied, "I've never been on a date with Adam Dupree. In fact, I've spent a total of about three hours in his company. I don't know what constitutes a couple in your mind, but I certainly need to spend considerably more than three hours with a man before I decide whether or not I like him."

"Now, Miz Enright, uh, Miz Cat, don't get all in a huff. It's just that my Aunt Marybelle works over to the nursing home and says she saw you and Mr. Dupree hugging and holding hands. And then my cousin Sissy waits tables over to the Riverside Restaurant. I just been wondering. Seems to me if you're hugging and holding hands and breaking bread together then maybe you're an item."

"Holy bells, the grapevine is just humming around here isn't it? All right. You want to know how much of a couple Adam and I are? Here's the deal. Monday I gave a riding lesson that included Glenda, and she disrupted the entire class with her theatrics. As I am sure you know by now, Glenda Dupree could be a royal bitch. After the class, I went to Adam's office on Music Row in hopes that he could help me deal with Her Royal Heinie. He said the best way was just to go to Fairbanks and talk to her. As you know, I went over there because that's when I realized

Bubba was missing. Then the next day I found her. She was dead, but by God, I found her. You have that much in my statement.

"This morning I went to the nursing home to pay my condolences to Opal, Glenda's mother. Adam was there. I didn't know he was going to be there and he didn't know I was going to be there. It was a difficult time. I don't know if your Aunt Marybelle has mentioned it, but Opal's mind is not what it used to be. She upset both Adam and me. We held hands as we walked out to the parking lot and gave each other a friendly hug. Then we went out for a late breakfast and we talked. That is the total extent of Adam's and my relationship."

"I see."

"What do you mean, you see? What's that supposed to mean?"

"Just that I see the extent of your relationship now and it makes sense. He don't seem your type anyhow. Flighty." He glanced over at me and smiled. "To tell the truth, before I heard about you and Dupree I thought you might be interested in meeting my brother Brent.

I had to laugh, wondering what kind of impression I had made on Deputy Giles in the few days I'd known him that would make him want to introduce me to his brother.

"Brent's real quiet. But independent. A little stubborn, but caring. He's a veterinarian up in Clarksville. Small animals, though. He don't treat horses."

The deputy turned into my driveway, and wiggled around Jon's barrier. The lights of my house were a very welcome sight. Lord, I was tired.

"I mean," he continued, "if you're not interested in Dupree, maybe you'd like to meet my brother."

"You don't like Adam, do you?" It wasn't a question. The deputy's eyebrows went up. "Wouldn't say that. Not at all. I just can't get a feel for the guy, him being Hollywood and all. I ain't ashamed to say that my family is country as a bowl of grits, so I got no common ground with Mr. Dupree. Nothing wrong with that. There's lots of people I don't share ground with. But I tell you what, you want to meet Brent, I'll arrange it. You just let me know."

I shook my head. "Thanks, Deputy. I do appreciate it. But I've got too many things swirling around in my head right now to make room for anyone else. Maybe later."

He pulled the cruiser up to my front porch and put it into neutral. "Too bad. I think both of you'd hit it right off. I, ah, don't suppose any of those things swirling around in your head have anything to do with the kid's disappearance, or the lady's murder?" He didn't wait for me to answer before he continued. "I just was wondering if you maybe had happened on anything."

I hesitated. I knew the question wasn't an idle one.

"If you have come across something it sure would help me to hear about it. I told you Burns is making life difficult. He thinks you maybe had a hand in it, and I think everyone in that riding class of yours had something against the lady. The sheriff, he wants this case sewn up yesterday and he thinks staying on my ass is the way to get it done."

He looked at me, and told me that the search warrant had been to recover clothes I had been wearing—clothes from the night I reported Bubba missing and the day I found Glenda. I'd already figured that out. My wardrobe was not so extensive that a few missing items would go unnoticed.

"They found blood on your boot. Blood that his doctor's records say is of the same type as Bubba Henley."

My heart once again began thudding in my chest. This time the rapid thumps in my chest were accompanied by hands that were clammy with cold. "I tripped over the cap," I said in hot defense. "When I was outside Glenda's house. I scraped my hand! The cap got stuck on my boot and I had to peel it off. Remember? I gave the cap to you. That's how I found out Bubba was missing. I—"

"I know that. Calm down," said the deputy as he placed a large hand on my arm. "I'm just telling you how the sheriff sees it. That cap, by the way, didn't only test positive for the kid's blood type. It tested positive for the lady's as well."

Deputy Giles and I sat there in silence for a minute or more while I took several deep breaths and processed all that information, then I got out as he he shifted the car into reverse.

"Well," he said as I was closing the door, "if you run across anything, it'd sure help me out."

The car began to roll.

"Deputy, wait."

The car stopped.

"You were willing to share your information with me and I know you didn't have to do that. Maybe I have run across something. Some things. I don't know. Do you want to come in? I at least owe you a cup of cocoa for the lift home."

The smile on the deputy's face was almost enough to salvage my day.

21

BEFORE I COULD SPILL MY GUTS to Deputy Giles I had to check on the horses. I had been absent so much recently and had earlier told Jon that I'd take care of the evening walk-through tonight, even though it was his night to do that.

With the deputy in tow I opened the barn door to the soft rustling and munching that I associate with horses settling in for the night. If I had my druthers, I'd keep all the horses turned out. A horse, after all, is a horse, and does best in its natural environment. When the weather was warmer, and the ground not so slippery, the horses in my barn did spend time outside. In the summer, they often were turned out at night, when it was cooler and when the sun wouldn't fade their lustrous hair coats. But this past week had been so wet that it was too dangerous to turn the horses out. They were show horses after all. One playful slip in the mud could keep a horse out of competition for a year or more.

Tonight the ten horses in the barn all stuck their heads into the aisle when we entered. All except a striking three-year-old palomino filly named Tater. Tater was a western pleasure hopeful and had come in after the world show in November. Jon and I had put about eighty days of training on her—enough to know neither her gaits nor her temperament were suitable for the show ring. Her trot was too choppy and her mentality was more like that of a yearling. She needed more time than most horses to grow up and become a responsible adult. I'd tried to tell her owner that before I accepted her, had tried to turn her away. Her owner was a steady client of many years, however, so I finally said I'd give her a try.

I explained all this to Deputy Giles who looked uncomfortable as he stood in the center of the aisle. I checked on Tater, who was sound asleep, stretched out diagonally in her stall, snoring. All good there. Then I went into each of the other stalls to be sure the automatic waterers were working and that none of the horses had managed to cut, bang, or scrape themselves since Jon fed them a few hours ago. You'd be surprised at the damage a horse can do to him- or herself, even when there is nothing to get hurt on.

"Um, is this horse okay?" The deputy was standing in front of Sally Blue's stall and I walked up the aisle to join him. Sally was staring directly at the deputy. Then she dropped her head to the ground and pawed. She pawed for about ten seconds, and then repeated the process of staring, then pawing. It was a much stronger, firmer paw than horses usually use to move bedding around before they lie down, but I explained that was what she most likely was doing.

I pulled a stethoscope from my equine first aid kit and listened to Sally's stomach. The absence of typical stomach sounds, especially when combined with dull eyes and sweating, could mean colic. Horses are not able to throw up so when they get a tummy ache, it can be a serious thing. But Sally's eyes were bright, her coat was dry, and her stomach was gurgling as strongly as a babbling brook. She was fine. Physically anyway. I did give Sally a curious glance over my shoulder as we exited the barn, though.

Hank met us at the door to the house with the stick he had been carrying around for several days. I had quite a difficult time explaining to Hank that if he wanted to come in, the stick had to stay out. In the end he stayed out with the stick, but soon set up such a howling and moaning that I gave up and let both of them in.

"I don't think I've ever heard such a big howl on such a little dog," said the deputy.

"That's why I named him Hank, after the country singer, Hank Williams. They both have that country moan in their howls. Maybe I should see about getting Hank an agent."

The deputy shook his head, not even bothering to reply. But there was a quirk at the end of one side of his mouth that led me to believe he was trying to hide a smile.

I gathered cups, saucers, and spoons—a procedure I'd been doing so often lately I was beginning to feel like Miss Susie Homemaker. Now there was a frightening thought. We settled at the kitchen table with my third dose of hot chocolate for the evening. I wanted to add a large splash of coffee-flavored brandy to mine, but thought I'd better not tempt the deputy with such a delicacy while he was on duty.

I didn't know where to begin, so for lack of anything else I pulled Glenda's notebook from my pocket and placed it on the table between us. Then I told him everything, from more details of the scene with the riding class and Sally Blue finding the notebook in my pocket, to the strange meeting with Opal Dupree, Carole's find at the library, the encounter with Frog, and Darcy's investigations on the Internet.

As my grandma used to say, "letting the cat out of the bag is a whole lot easier than putting it back in." I tried not to squirm as the deputy scowled at me, but I couldn't quite pull it off. Guess he'd be having second thoughts about introducing me to his brother.

"You mean to tell me that a horse, that horse right out there in the barn that was staring at me just now, is responsible for finding this notebook?" he finally exclaimed.

I nodded.

"Now how in hell am I supposed to tell Sheriff Burns that I need to question a horse? Tell me that, huh. Tell me just how I'm supposed to go about doing that?"

There really wasn't an answer to his question, so I just shook my head and bit my lip—but whether it was to keep from laughing or crying, I couldn't honestly tell you.

"Well," he said after a long period of silence, "I can tell you right now I'd like to take your silly ass and throw it in the lock-up for your own protection, if nothing else. Why on earth didn't you tell me all this earlier? Especially the part about the notebook?"

Deputy Giles looked unhappier by the minute. "I've also been wondering when you were going to clue me in on your version of the details of the big barn fight. Do you have any idea, any idea at all, what Burns will say when I tell him you were trying to stop the deceased from slandering you, and now you've got her private notebook?"

He gave me another very dark look, which I did my level best to ignore.

"And then there's the kid. Bubba Henley," he continued. "You know who saw him last and where. You know all this. Why you? That's what Burns will say. Why do you know stuff no one else seems to know?"

"Give me a break!" My Irish temper was rising again and I made no attempt to stop it. "In all fairness, I learned about Bubba's noon stroll through the fence just this evening and believe me, I wasn't in a position to drop everything and say, 'I gotta go call the cops about this.' Secondly, yes, a horse did find the notebook in my pocket yesterday morning, but I just this morning remembered I had it, so it's not like I sat on information forever. And thirdly, don't tell Sheriff Big Jim squat about me right now. Just tell him you heard rumors from reliable sources."

And he had very reliable sources. Deputy Giles had talked to Robert Griggs today and pulled Darcy out of class. Jon mentioned that he had talked with the deputy, too, and I'd bet my spare tire that he talked to Carole as well. With the possible exception of Robert, those sources were as reliable as any I could think of.

"Nothing says you have to tell Burns I told you anything," I fumed. "The fact that you now have the notebook should be enough. Lastly, Deputy, I didn't have to tell you any of this and if I'd had one iota of common sense I wouldn't have. I don't need you to yell at me. This day has been rough enough anyway."

As quickly as it had risen, my anger subsided, washed away in a sea of mixed emotion. "Besides," I added, "even if I happen to be a suspect in Burns's mind—and I realize that I am—this case is going to look at quite a few people before it's all said and done. Isn't it?"

Another thing my grandma used to say was: "never miss a good chance to shut up." This was my chance.

I spent a full minute fighting the fidgets before the deputy began to nod his head slowly.

"So," I continued cautiously, "with all the new information I just gave you, Burns will have enough to turn his attention to other people and maybe even solve this case correctly."

He nodded. "Maybe. We talked with your students today."

"And?"

"Can't rule anyone out, but that Griggs, he's kinda cold. There's something there. Don't know if it has to do with the lady, but there's something."

"What about Carole?"

"Observant. Good memory. Pleasant. Dunno."

He didn't bring up Darcy and I didn't have the courage to ask. Surely she didn't have anything to do with this.

Deputy Giles swirled his chocolate. "Miz Cat, I appreciate the info. Truly, I do. But you gotta realize that it is your duty as a citizen of this fine county to turn this stuff over to us. You got to keep me more informed. See, the time Frog saw Bubba confirms what we already suspected, and it helps pinpoint the time of the murder. And," he added, rubbing a big hand over his face, "in all fairness, I do have to tell Burns about all this."

It was my turn to frown.

"And I will tell him. Just as soon as he gets back from that police convention up to St. Louis."

I stared and felt a wave of shaky relief wash over me.

"Burns left town about noon, just after he finished chewing *my* ass for not hauling *your* ass in. Won't be back until Saturday."

"And then what? What happens on Saturday?"

"I'll tell him I've had you under surveillance. He'll like that because he likes us to use those big, long words—thinks no one else in the county can understand 'em, like we're talking code or something. Beyond that, well, hopefully something will come to light before then."

I then asked the deputy something I'd been thinking too much about in the past twenty-four hours. "Tell me the truth, Deputy. Do I need a lawyer?"

His eyes were solid on mine for a few seconds before he said, "It wouldn't hurt to have one in mind. But, in the meantime. . . ."

The deputy pulled out a sheaf of papers. My statement. I looked it over, noticed and ignored the omission about the scene at the barn, signed it, and pushed it back across the table.

"That out of the way," he said, "I also need to tell you that the medical examiner is finished with the body. Funeral is tomorrow at noon."

"Tomorrow!"

"Family wanted it over and done with. Mrs. Dupree, Mrs. Opal that is, muddled as she is, still has a lot of pull out here."

He headed for the door, notebook in hand.

"Uh, Deputy? Martin? You . . . you don't think I killed her, do you?"

He turned, and his beefy hand once again rubbed his face. "No, Miz Cat. I don't. No rhyme or reason for it, but a man's gotta trust what his gut tells him. I've told you before and I'll tell you now, I don't believe you had anything to do with it." He sighed. "But that don't mean I can convince Burns of it. He's looking for a conviction and that election's coming up quicker every day. Wish me loads of luck. That's all I can say, 'cuz you're going to need every bit of it."

I wished him luck in persuading the sheriff. But as I watched his taillights disappear up River Road, I didn't feel much luck surrounding either Deputy Giles or me.

"Grrrraarrffff," said Hank, the stick still in his mouth. "Grrraarrffff."

"Yes, Hank," I said absently, giving him a pat on the head. "That's exactly my thought, too."

Cat's Horse Tip #11

"The sequence of footfalls for the horse at the walk is left hind, left front, right hind, right front."

22

WESTERN HILLS CEMETERY IS ENCLOSED ON three sides by a four-foot stone wall that was most likely a 1930s WPA project. The wall had seen better days, but they were long, long ago. The fourth side of the property featured a slightly lower wall with a wide gap on the left. The gap was bisected by a gravel drive that wound through several side roads and eventually circled around and led back out to Highway 100.

It was an old cemetery. Many of the crumbling markers decorated graves that had been there for over a century. Old Nashville names such as Harding, McGavock, Robertson and Demonbreun were prominent on the larger stones. And even though the grass was meticulously mowed, the paths carefully swept, the entire graveyard had a desolate air. It had a feel of incurable shabbiness. Only in the far right corner did the feeling lift, giving way to newer marble headstones that you didn't have to squint at to read the inscriptions.

It was in this area that Glenda's grave had been dug. And now she was about to be lowered into it, in a black lacquered coffin that was covered with a blanket of large, white roses. For obvious reasons, the coffin had been closed during this morning's brief period of viewing, the heavy veil of prickly rose discouraging even the nosiest of neighbors from the tiniest urge to peek. I wondered about the choice of cemetery, but Adam said many generations of Duprees were buried here. I think if I had the Dupree money, I'd send a little over to spiff up their graves.

Despite the short notice, the Hollywood contingent had turned out. Morgan Fairchild, a long-time friend of Glenda's was there. She looked fabulously beautiful and blonde. Bill Royce, a writer and casting director I'd met at one of Glenda's parties stood next to her as did Neville Johnson, Glenda's entertainment attorney. Someone told me that Warren Beatty sent the huge spray of lilies that stood next to the grave.

River Road residents had also turned out en masse for the event. Even though Glenda hadn't quite fit in, and even though by virtue of her caustic personality she wasn't well liked, she had been born in the Nashville area, and, like the prodigal son, had returned. When she was alive, neighbors alternately bragged about the fact that she was a star and moaned that she was the rudest person ever. But now that she had moved to the hereafter and wasn't quite so likely to say something to piss anyone off, all the neighbors were willing to let bygones be bygones and sink any differences along with Glenda to the bottom of the grave.

I had not wanted to come. Let's get that straight right away. I don't like funerals and prefer to do my mourning in private. In fact, I felt I had already done my grieving, what there was of it, Tuesday afternoon at the riverbank in the comforting fork of my favorite tree. But I knew my absence would be conspicuous, and ever after, had I not shown up, it would be added as a codicil to my name. I can just hear them now, "Oh, yes dear, this is Cat Enright, the one who didn't show up for Glenda Dupree's funeral."

I tried to imagine Glenda peacefully at rest inside the plush coffin, but couldn't quite pull it off. It was easier to imagine her screeching in protest, banging on the gates of heaven, yelling for someone to return her to her living earthly body. I could just see St. Peter grabbing Glenda by the waist and dragging her, kicking and screaming, to her life review with the Creator. The thought almost made me giggle.

Instead, I clenched my fists and hugged myself tightly. Glenda was dead. Even though I had found her body, it was hard to imagine. A weak midday sun reflected off the spray of roses on the coffin. On the other side of the grave, Deputy Giles stood, looking solemn in his tan-and-brown county uniform. He hadn't worn a coat, even though the temperature was hovering at forty, but you'd never know by looking at him that he might be cold.

Adam stepped forward and dropped a few clumps of dirt symbolically over the coffin. The priest said a few words. Two minutes later I remembered none of them. Then people were leaving.

Dickson journalist Chuck Dauphin walked next to Morgan Fairchild, as did Buffy Thorndyke from the *Ashland City Times*. I'd called Buffy earlier that morning to ask about the time of Glenda's phone call to her on Monday. Buffy said it had come right before she went to lunch at noon. Buffy wasn't carrying a notebook, but I was sure I'd read about the funeral in next week's paper.

Carole Carson was there with her husband, Keith. He must have flown in early this morning. I knew he'd been out on the road yesterday. I wondered if it was sinful to have lustful thoughts about your neighbor's husband while at a funeral, and decided I didn't care. There was no way around it. He was hot.

There were a few older women dressed in varying shades of gray that I assumed were contemporaries of Opal Dupree. Hill Henley was there too, looking white as a sheet, no doubt realizing that the next funeral he attended could be that of his son. I smiled at Jon and at Darcy. Darcy was inappropriately dressed in an old pair of chinos and a navy down-filled jacket, but she either didn't see me, or wasn't up to conversation.

Jon ignored me, which was a disturbing sign for our ongoing working relationship. Okay. I have not been communicating well lately. I should have told Jon about the funeral in person, rather than leaving a message for him. I could tell by his studious indifference that I would have to be the one to take the first step. But not here. Now was not the time.

Adam and Opal, of course, had ringside seats. I had worried that Opal would be so overwhelmed with the funeral proceedings that she'd have one of her spells, but she sat still as stone throughout the entire service. Most likely she was heavily sedated.

I, too, began to walk toward the parking lot, which was divided from the rest of the cemetery by an even lower stone wall. It was so low, in fact, that you could step over it in places where the top stones had fallen away.

The media vultures, whose cameras had been relegated to the parking area, jumped into action as the mourners began to make their way to their cars. Interest from national press remained high, as I knew it would. I watched as one cameraman approached Keith Carson and I felt a twinge of sorrow for Carole. The life of a celebrity did have its downfalls.

Deputy Giles caught up with me, having agreed last night to take me to and from the service. While a civilian shouldn't be in a county car without reason, the deputy said if he got any flack about it he could call my presence "close surveillance." It was either that or have Jon take me, and Jon was mad enough at me right now to bash my head in himself.

My truck had been towed to a garage near Verna Mae's and wouldn't be ready for another few hours. Goose's branch had done a number on my oil pan.

Deputy Giles exhaled loudly as we got into the patrol car. "You know, Miz Cat, I should have taken my dad up on that job at the co-op. Life would be a lot simpler. Find the right bag of feed, load it up, make change and you're done."

"Can I take that to mean a new development has taken place?"

The deputy made a wry face as he pulled the patrol car onto Highway 100 and headed west, toward Fairview.

"What happened is that after I left your place last night, I arrested a student of yours. Griggs. He was over to that catfish restaurant there on Highway 12. Drunk and disorderly, and hotter than a lit match. Didn't realize he had such a temper. Seems he got upset when the other diners wouldn't believe his story."

"I see. His story. And what story would that be, Deputy?"

"Seems Griggs was insisting the lady wasn't beaten to death. Said he knew it for a fact. Had it from a good source that she died from asphyxiation and not from head wounds."

Why would Robert say that, I wondered. Could he have killed Glenda? Maybe. But I just could not fathom it. There had to be another explanation.

"Poor Robert," I said, shaking my head. "I don't know him well but he's always so remote. I'm not surprised he snapped. He keeps everything locked up inside."

"Yeah," said the deputy. "There's only one thing. . . . "

I looked at him. "You can't mean that Glenda. . . ."

He nodded. "Bingo. Miz Dupree choked to death on her own blood. Time of death was late Monday afternoon, give or take a couple hours either way. Her head wounds were messy and were inflicted some time earlier than the death, but she didn't die from them. She might have, eventually, but she suffocated on all that blood first."

"Oh my God. How awful." I couldn't imagine the horror of Glenda's death. As much as I had disliked her, I wouldn't wish that kind of abuse on anybody.

Then I realized that late Monday afternoon was when I pounded on her door. If I hadn't slipped on Bubba's cap and gone off to look for him, would I have gone around to Glenda's back door? And could it have been open then as it was the next morning? If it had happened that way, then maybe I would have found Glenda alive. Maybe she could even have been saved! My mind was swimming with the possibilities. I mentioned my thoughts to the deputy, but he shook his head.

"Don't go playing 'what if.' That won't get you nowhere. From what I can tell from the medical report, even though she might technically have been alive late that afternoon, her brain was toast. She wouldn't have made it even if you'd found her at two o'clock.

"Thing is, Miz Cat," he continued, bringing us both back to more productive thought, "we haven't let the report from the medical examiner's office out to anyone. So how did Griggs know? You think he's been talking to your psychic horse?"

"That's a joke, right Deputy? Ha ha. You know, I know Robert's kind of strange, but I don't see him involved in this." He cocked his head. "Maybe. Maybe not. By the way, whoever bashed the lady was right-handed. And you . . . are a lefty." He glanced over and I noticed there was another slight lift at one corner of his mouth. Another smile. My heart gave a leap of relief.

"In addition to that," he added, "it rules Bubba out as well. Bubba is right-handed, but the medical examiner determined he probably wasn't big enough or tall enough to get this job done. No, we're looking at a right-handed adult here. And about Griggs. Well, I think he's a talkative drunk who knows more than he's told us. We're going to hold him as long as we can."

"But how did Robert know?"

"That, Miz Cat, I don't know. It's precisely the reason we're holding him. So he can tell us." He glanced at me again. "Just between you and me and the fence post, I'm having a heck of a time trying to figure it all out. You got time to take a little drive? My brother says it clears the head."

Considering the dismal scene we had just left, I thought a drive definitely was in order. We passed through Fairview, turned north on Highway 96, east on I-40, and took the Kingston Springs exit. But instead of turning right at the "T"—toward Highway 70 and Sam's Creek Road, which would bring us back to River Road—we turned left and drove past the block long area that passes for "downtown" Kingston Springs. Then we took another left and headed into a wooded area. After a while, the reason for the drive became clear. The deputy wanted someone to bounce his ideas to. Someone who would not dismiss his ideas without thoroughly considering them. Someone, well, kind of like me.

I was flattered. In several ways I was beginning to appreciate the slow-moving, quick-thinking deputy. The deputy was too young for me, but if his brother was anything like him, I just might give it a go. Maybe.

"All right," he said, holding up his hand. "We know the lady left your barn about ten forty-five Monday morning. We think she went directly home. No one admits to seeing her after she left the barn. So let's say she did go home. She's inside. The front door is locked, or so you say."

I nodded in agreement.

"That means the killer was either in the house waiting for her when she got back, or she let him in and locked the door after. We think he left via the rear door, the door you found open. My insides tell me she knew the guy."

I'd thought that all along. Glenda was not the type to let strangers into her house. She never scheduled an appliance to be serviced or the chimney to be cleaned unless Cinda Lu was there to deal with it. In fact, Glenda was not likely to even let friends into her house unless they had an appointment.

I told him about Glenda's call to Buffy just before noon.

"And Bubba was seen," I added, "by Frog at noon right outside the house."

"That reminds me," he said. "I checked up on that Frog character and it turns out he was the one broke into Fairbanks. Said he was looking for Bubba, but I think he wanted to see all the gory details for himself. I'm not charging him with nothing, at least not yet. He may have more to tell. On the other hand, he may be like the rest of his family and turn out to be as useful as the goose pee I used to find on my granny's pump handle."

Deputy Giles pulled the car onto a wide spot in the road, stopped and killed the engine. To our left a picnic table perched precariously on a wide ledge of scaly rock. Beyond the rock was a breathtaking view of stony cliffs and tall pine trees. I saw that a dozen or so industrial sawhorses cordoned off the rock slab. The sawhorses were all chained together and several were screwed into the ground.

"Lover's Leap," said the deputy. "Ever been here?"

I shook my head as we got out, passed between the wooden barriers and sat down at the picnic table.

"Usual story. Young lovers come here for privacy, a romantic view. The guy somehow falls over the ledge. It's one hundred and seventy-four feet to the bottom. A bunch of rock ledges along the way. He didn't make it, of course, so the girl wrote a note and pinned it on that tree over there." He indicated a sturdy oak with a nod of his head. "She threw herself off. They were both only sixteen. Happened in the twenties."

I asked about the sawhorse barriers and the deputy quirked his mouth in a smile.

"Got so's high school kids would drive up here and dare each other to see who'd drive closest to the ledge. One kid came so close the end of the ledge broke off. Took him and the car with it. That was in the fifties. Big, heavy car. Then there've been a few over the years who come up to party. The guys get themselves full of beer and go to the ledge to pee. Over the years, three or four of 'em lost their balance and took a quick trip to the bottom."

He looked out at the peaceful view. "The lady might even have been glad to see the guy who killed her, assuming she knew him . . . or her," he said, switching mental gears with ease. I struggled to keep up.

"Assuming it's a he, why did he want to kill her?" I asked.

"If we can figure out the why, maybe the who will follow."

Martin looked at me. He seemed to be taking my thoughts quite seriously.

"Think, now," I said. "Who would want to kill Glenda Duprce? It probably was someone that she made incredibly angry. Of course, that includes everyone in the riding class and at least half the county. Or maybe it was someone she had dirt on, a piece of information that would destroy a life if it got out. Maybe it was information that she stumbled across, something she didn't set out to find, but she did, and she told whomever it was that she knew. So they killed her."

He nodded. "Could be, but you left out a big piece. Bubba Henley. What happened to Bubba? The murder weapon—the twitch—was his. It was covered with his clean, unsmudged prints. There were no other prints on it. You do realize that it's all tied together, that Bubba somehow is mixed up in this?"

A lightning bolt flashed through my head. "No other prints?"

"None."

"No blood?"

"A few drops on the far end, but it was enough for us to know the blood belonged to the lady."

"But," I said slowly, my mind racing. "I grabbed the twitch away from Bubba that morning. I remember it feeling cold. I'd left my gloves in the truck. Shouldn't my prints have been on there too, along with quite a bit of blood? Bubba's cap was covered with blood and the fireplace mantle was liberally streaked with it."

He frowned. "You're right. You can thank the good Lord that there wasn't a trace of your prints, though. Left-handed or not, Burns would never let that slide. You'd be eating off the county by now."

"But Deputy, listen. If there was no blood to speak of, and Bubba's fingerprints are on the twitch, and no one else's are on it, why there's only one way that could happen."

The deputy stared at me. "If the prints were placed on the twitch after it was used to bash in the lady's head."

"Right," I said. "The twitch was wiped clean and then given to Bubba to handle. Whoever wiped the twitch must have missed the few drops of blood on the end. Either that or some blood was intentionally left there."

He nodded, but still looked troubled. "As far as it goes, it's reasonable," he said. "But it ain't enough. There are too many blanks to fill in."

"What about the Society Lady killer, the one who killed those women in Springfield and Dickson?"

"No go. That guy was picked up on a drunk and disorderly in Arrington Sunday night. They had some good evidence and he confessed. He claimed the women were aliens from the planet Jupiter and he was protecting the world by killing them. I know you're too busy to watch TV, but it's been on the news."

"Hmmm. So it all goes back to who Bubba saw that Glenda had pissed off."

The deputy frowned. "Say that again?"

"Deputy, didn't you advise me to keep my nose out of events that don't concern me?"

His mouth quirked again. "I did. Several times. But not until *this* case is over and done with. So say it again."

That was another quality I found myself liking about Martin Giles. He wasn't insecure. He didn't care where ideas came from, or who did the work. He just cared that the job got done. He was a hard worker, but not above realizing that others could work hard, too.

"Okay," I said. "Someone killed Glenda. Then, bad luck. Bubba shows up. Maybe he was there when the murderer arrived and the killer didn't know it. Maybe Bubba was heading over to my house for lunch, heard a noise and went in to check it out. Or, maybe Bubba saw someone leaving Glenda's house. In any case, the killer saw him. Now that would be inconvenient for the killer, don't you think, to have Bubba see him? Or her. So the only solution, as far as the killer can see, is to get rid of Bubba and rig the evidence to show that Bubba murdered Glenda."

The deputy sighed and stood up. I followed him to the car. The only words the deputy spoke all the way back to town were, "Not a bad thought at all. At least, not bad for a rookie."

ᴏ ᴐ ᴐ
ᴐ ᴐ ᴐ

We passed Verna Mae's and he dropped me at the service station.

"Thanks for the lift," I said, and got out.

Deputy Giles nodded and pulled away, a puzzled look on his face. I had been turning several ideas over in my mind during the ride back to town. Apparently the deputy had, too.

I hadn't been comfortable with the idea that Bubba had done something awful to Glenda. I thought it much more probable that Glenda's murderer had done something awful to Bubba. He'd gone from suspect to victim, and between the two, I realized that I liked the second possibility a whole lot less.

If you are found guilty of murder, at least you have a chance to redeem yourself, to turn your life around. Even if the rest of your life is spent in a jail cell, you have the chance. But if you

are found dead, you have no chance. Bubba was still very much
a kid. And I was starting to be very much afraid that Bubba was
a kid who was very, very dead. That thought made me mad.
Every child needs a chance. My grandma had given mine to me.
Bubba deserved the same. In addition, if Bubba was dead, I was
sure Sheriff Big Jim would try to hang another murder charge
on me.

I walked into the service station to find that my truck's vital
organs lay in pieces on the floor. There had been other damage,
in addition to the oil pan, and parts wouldn't arrive until the next
day. Goose Berry was costing me a lot of money. Maybe I
should call that lawyer after all. But not now. Torn between calling Jon and a nice hot lunch at Verna Mae's, the thought of
deep-fried chicken, corn bread, and sweet potato pie won hands
down.

23

I REACHED DARCY ON HER CELL phone and she agreed to rescue me. Jon had gotten the message on his voice mail that I had left last night about the funeral and Darcy needing a lift. He picked her up before her history test, and then brought her back to Verna Mae's and her car. I guess that half explained her inappropriate attire at the funeral. She'd come directly from school. I hadn't finished buckling the seat belt when Darcy told me we were making a detour via the cemetery.

"You'll never believe what I found," she exclaimed. "Like, you know, after the funeral. I hung around and, oh man, this is way cool."

She declined to tell me more and I resigned myself to the fact that I would never get back to the barn and Jon would hate me forever.

We parked in the shabby graveyard parking lot, walked toward the back corner, opposite from where Glenda had been laid to rest, and stopped beside a large pillar. Darcy pointed to an elaborate carving of a name on the old stone. Henley.

Curious, I examined it more closely. Carved below the family name were all sorts of Henleys, including Col. Sam, his young wife Alice, and their children, Alice and Sam, Jr. I noted with interest that the younger Alice had the same name as her mother, Alice Giles Henley. I wondered if she married another Henley, or if she'd never married at all. There weren't any names of offspring credited to her, but that didn't necessarily mean anything. Sam, Jr. on the other hand, had been almost as prolific as the Giles clan, which, via his mother, he was part of.

I noticed the first Hill Henley was also a Hilton. He was the son of Sam, Jr., and his other sons also followed the "H" theme with Heath, Hampton, Hagan and Houston. The last no doubt was named for the Texas version of our Col. Sam. I wondered what had happened to them all, and if there ever was a Sam, III.

Darcy said she knew how to find out. We walked toward the front of the graveyard, but stopped short of the parking lot. Here, hidden among a few scrubby pines and lilacs, was a small, whitewashed stone building. The painted wooden sign over the door said Western Hills Cemetery Office and Historical Society.

The woman inside was cheerful and quick.

"Here you are," she said, pulling a large book from the center of a huge stack on the far wall. "Colonel Samuel Henley. Born February 8, 1842. Died March 15, 1937."

I looked at the entry she was pointing to. Not that I didn't believe her. I just have to see things for myself.

"Col. Sam," she mused. "We don't get too many requests for that name anymore. Oh, are you by any chance the lady who called about him a few days ago? The reporter from the historical magazine."

I was about to admit that no, I wasn't the lady in question, when a swift kick to my right shin, courtesy of Darcy, convinced me otherwise. I put an honest expression on my face and nodded in earnest.

Assured of my legitimacy, she continued. "It's just the biggest coincidence that you should stop in here today. I just found out that poor movie star, Glenda Dupree, interred here just this morning, was a great-granddaughter of Col. Sam."

The luck of the Irish was with me in such force that I had to catch my breath and wait for the world to right itself. After a brief moment, during which I hoped the woman would believe my deep sorrow at poor Glenda's demise, I gave what I trusted would pass for an encouraging smile.

"I must say that the family wasn't too forthcoming with information regarding Miss Dupree's genealogical background, but we do have to keep our records," she said. "Let's see now. The way I understand it, Miss Glenda Dupree's mother, Mrs. Opal Dupree, is the only daughter of Alice Henley, that's Alice the younger. There was some hush-hush scandal involved with Alice the younger, but I don't know if anyone remembers what it was anymore."

I acknowledged that I hadn't been in the county long enough to hear about such a dishonor.

"Guess it's died off with the old folk," said the woman, glancing at her watch.

She was losing interest and I wasn't done with her yet.

"Oh," I said, slapping my forehead, "Miss—"

"Watson. Penny Watson."

"Of course. Penny. I did hear a rumor. Not about Alice . . . um . . . the younger, but about her father, Col. Sam."

She nodded for me to continue.

"Someone mentioned he was a smuggler during the Civil War. Have you heard anything about that?"

I smiled brilliantly while Penny Watson pretended to rack her brains. A known smuggler was obviously a besmirchment to her fair cemetery and she was reluctant to hand out the sordid details. But she eventually decided I already knew about it and she'd better fess up.

"Now that you mention it, yes. He was rumored to have brought in illegal goods during the War of Northern Aggression—solely for the benefit of the Confederacy, of course. But what the nature of those goods were, or how he got them in, I don't know."

My Irish instincts told me she was telling all she knew so I asked one final question. As far as Miss Watson could tell, there never was a third Sam Henley. Darcy and I bid our farewells and headed for the car.

On the way home, I imitated Deputy Giles and Darcy took my role.

"So Glenda had family connections to Fairbanks," I exclaimed. "I wonder if she knew that when she bought the place. Surely she did. She must have."

Darcy nodded her agreement.

"Then the two big questions are: Do Opal and Adam know? And what does this new information have to do, if anything, with Bubba's disappearance and Glenda's murder?"

I was willing to wager the farm that the connection had a lot to do with everything. But what? Connections were what I had wanted in the first place and connections were what I got. I guess that old adage, "be careful what you wish for because you just might get it," is true. The trouble was, the connections didn't line up. Not that I could see. Not even that Deputy Giles or Sheriff Big Jim could see. The connections didn't produce any answers, just more questions. And now I had more questions than fleas on a dog and nothing to squash them with.

When we got back to the stables, Darcy and I both headed for the barn. Jon was evidently taking a late lunch. Either that or he heard me coming and made himself scarce. I could hear him stomping around his apartment overhead and had to admit I was glad for his absence.

Hank, however, was very glad to see us. Stick firmly in his mouth, he alternated greeting each of us, his tail wagging his body so hard that his stick hit us on the legs with each wag. We both lavished affection on him until a bird mistakenly thought it could hop up and down the aisle looking for grain droppings. Hank dropped his stick to dash off to the all-important task of bird chasing.

Darcy threw her hunt seat gear on Petey while I put my western saddle on Sally Blue. From Sally's eager expression, I sensed she hadn't been out of her stall yet today. Of course Agnes would say Sally was sending me her thoughts telepathically. Who knew, maybe Agnes was right. If nothing else, schooling Sally would take my mind off Bubba and Glenda. Darcy was engrossed in her own thoughts, so I was spared conversation.

In the horse world, all horses turn a year older on the first day of January. Sally's actual birthday wasn't until the end of March, but for show purposes she was already three. There were a lot of trainers who started horses under saddle right at two, mainly for the purpose of competing in the financially lucrative two-year-old western pleasure futurities. These were classes that were judged at a walk, trot, and canter, and were entered months in advance of the competition. Every month or so the horse's owner or trainer paid an additional fee to keep the horse eligible for the class. By the time the class was held, there was a big pot of cash waiting for the winners.

I, however, felt that most horses' leg and bone structures were not yet developed enough to withstand training early in a horse's two-year-old year and started mine in November, when they were considered "long," or older, two-year-olds.

To date, Sally'd had just ninety days under saddle and was thriving on her slow schooling pace. Of course, the term "slow" is subjective. Dressage horses undergo years of training before they are ready to compete. Unfortunately, in the world of stock breeds and western pleasure, the system requires a much speedier return on an owner's investment.

At ninety days, Sally walked with a long, loose stride. She could jog trot slowly on a loose rein with her head nicely balanced and her legs underneath her, and she could lope both directions from a walk on the correct lead. Sally was bending nicely on the turns and we were just starting to work on her extended trot. In a few more weeks Sally would be ready for her debut under saddle at a small schooling show and Agnes could barely wait for that day.

I ground-tied Sally in the center of the arena and set up four cavaletti poles, each about three feet apart, and about eight feet in from the rail. Cavaletti poles look like eight-sided fence poles and are anywhere from eight to twelve feet long. They are placed either flat on the ground, or on low risers, and spaced evenly in a row so the horse can stride over them.

The object today was to get Sally to trot over them without ticking any with her hooves or breaking her stride. Once she could do it consistently at a slow trot, we'd gradually increase the distance between the poles and the pace.

It didn't take long for me to realize that this would not be an ordinary training session. Today, every circuit we made of the arena, Sally came to a dead stop at the gate that led back into the barn, wheeled her butt toward the center of the arena, looked through the open aisle, whinnied in the direction of Fairbanks, then stomped impatiently.

It was only after much prodding and encouragement on my part that Sally would deign to continue, but as soon as we came by the gate, even though I strongly encouraged her to keep moving, she'd repeat the behavior. This was no ordinary case of being barn sour. Something was going on with her.

One of the keys to working with horses is to understand the motivation behind the behavior. Another was the idea that the horse was never wrong; the human partner just had to figure out why the horse was acting in a particular manner. Today, I was discouraged that I didn't have a clue.

"Maybe Agnes isn't all wrong when she says Sally is psychic," observed Darcy, riding by at a posting trot. "Just think, what if Agnes is right?"

As I looked at Darcy, I noted that her hands and lower leg position were as good as any I'd ever seen, and reminded myself that very soon we'd have to make some decisions regarding the show season for the pair. Darcy and Petey had the potential to win some big classes—but only if Darcy wanted it badly enough to put in some hard work.

"Well, I'm about ready to agree she is," I said. "Sally certainly acts as if she knows something is going on over at Fairbanks, don't you?" I added to the horse who had by now turned her head around to observe me on her back, an exasperated expression on her face.

I gave her a pat and dismounted, knowing we wouldn't get anything good done that day. Another good trait of a trainer was knowing when to quit. Heading into the aisle, I was surprised to find it growing dark.

I brushed Sally down and tucked her away in her stall. But instead of checking her surroundings once, then dozing off as she usually did after a training session, Sally put her nose to the ground and began pawing. And, rather than pawing with one hoof, as she did when Deputy Giles was here, she used both hooves, like Hank would do if he were burying a bone. Then she stopped and looked at me for a minute before digging again. Lucky for me there were durable rubber floor mats in the stalls, so she wasn't doing much damage.

Darcy appeared next to me. "What is she doing?"

"I have no idea. I've never seen a horse do that before."

"I'm telling you, she's giving you a message."

"What? That she doesn't like the way the shavings are spread in her stall?"

Sally raised her head after another bout of digging and stared at me. Darcy offered to run upstairs and ask Jon to keep an eye on Sally, just in case she was beginning to colic. I debated asking Jon myself, but decided there were no olive branches handy.

After another few minutes puzzling over Sally's strange behavior, I headed for the house. Once inside, all the worries and problems of the world once again descended upon my shoulders. Some bit of information I picked up during the day didn't fit. Something was not quite right. But I didn't know what.

The next morning I had a blistering headache. But I also had part of an answer.

Cat's Horse Tip #12

"Desensitizing is never about scaring horses. Instead, it is about making horses comfortable in all the unusual situations the human world puts them in."

24

As soon as my alarm rang I tried to call Deputy Giles, but the line was busy. Just after I hung up, the phone rang. Looking back, it would have been infinitely better if I had waited to answer that call until I had talked with the deputy. But then, foresight has never been one of my virtues.

I quickly did the morning feeding. The nozzle had come off Sally's automatic waterer so I put a bucket of fresh water in her stall and added a scoop of powdered cherry flavored electrolytes, just in case she was coming down with a bug. Electrolyite were like Gatorade for people, and cherry was a favorite flavor of many horses. Agnes would be devastated if anything happened to the mare, and so, actually, would I.

I wrote another long, sincere and apologetic note for Jon and checked Sally one more time. Instead of drinking her water, she had buried her nose in the bucket, almost up to her eyeballs, and was blowing bubbles. Then she lifted her head to look at me and repeated the process. Maybe she didn't like the smell or taste of the electrolytes, I thought, although she never seemed to notice anything different when I had added them to her water in the past. If Sally *was*, as others had suggested, giving me a message, I had no clue as to what it could be.

Concern for Sally was added to my already heavy list of worries, but it wasn't enough to override my growing concern for Bubba. I remembered my early morning phone call, ducked out of the barn, and jumped in Jon's vintage Toyota Camry. Well, he did always leave the keys hanging in the office, and as my truck was still in the shop. . . .

A few thin rays of sun shone on the wet grass along the sides of the road, and when I reached my destination, the low brick building seemed to shimmer in a hazy glow, almost like a mystical vision from the past. But a friendly wisp of smoke curled from the chimney. And beyond the chimney lay a flower garden, which in spite of our cold weather, was beginning to send fragile shoots skyward.

I wondered who cared for the flowers. I remembered that last summer there were tubs of begonias, impatiens, and marigolds that sent brilliant cascades of color tumbling throughout the paved yard. Climbing roses and peonies planted decades ago thrived under someone's watchful hand. The memory was similar to a painted garden I had recently seen. The sun gave up its quest and disappeared under a thunderous cloud as I entered the main door and walked down the long hallway.

"We need to talk," Opal had said on the phone. It sounded more like a summons than a request, but I had planned to speak with her today anyway. Now was as good a time as any. When I reached Opal's room there was a nurse with her, assisting her into her wheelchair.

"I'm sure I don't know, Miss Sanders," Opal said as she struggled to sit. "It ought to have made me feel better. You gave me two of the blue pills, and one red capsule. It should have been one blue and two red."

She waited while the unfortunate Miss Sanders checked the chart and confirmed that she had indeed given Opal the correct medication. Opal nodded, frowned, said a few more sharp words, then dismissed the young woman.

It seemed strange to be with Opal again, and I glanced involuntarily at the portrait of Col. Sam. I expected it to look different, but it didn't. For some reason I thought the painting should reek of death, his death, Glenda's death, but it didn't. It looked the same as it had before. I guessed I was just nervous.

I sincerely hoped Opal wasn't going to have one of her bad spells. It had been difficult enough with Adam there, and I didn't know if I could handle such a scene on my own. I peeked out into the hallway and was reassured to see Miss Sanders at a desk that was within shouting distance.

I sat tentatively on the gold plastic chair. Opal's eyes were bright, and as I looked closer, I saw that the brightness came from rage. Color dappled her cheeks and her lips were clamped tight with anger.

"Miss Opal, are you all right? Is there something I can help you with?"

"Yes," she said shortly. "I understand you are poking your nose into my Glenda's murder."

It took a moment before I realized that's what she was angry about.

"You need to stop. Right now. Today," she demanded, waving an arthritic hand wildly about her face. If possible, she looked more shriveled and gnome-like than she had a few days before. It must be hard to lose a child, no matter what the age the child is when they pass.

"I heard from that Watson woman over at the cemetery," she said. "I thought I was done with her. Nosy bitch. It's an historical cemetery, you know. She had to know which of their illustrious skeletons my Glenda was related to so we could bury her there. Of all the nerve. And our plots have been bought and paid for for more than fifty years. But I told her. And I told her to keep quiet about it, too. But then she had a visitor. It was you, from the description."

Opal looked at me accusingly.

A big fat poo on Penny Watson. What business was it of hers if I asked a few questions? I opened my mouth to speak, but Opal jumped in ahead of me.

"All those years," she spat. "All those years of respectability and peace of mind." Her eyes darted like an angry bull.

"I thought," she said, "that it was forgotten. I thought we had stopped it, that we had finally laid it all to rest. But I was wrong. Wrong! And now you are going to stir it all up again. And to what purpose? It will only cause pain. Too much pain."

"You laid what to rest, Miss Opal? I don't understand. All Penny told me was that you were the daughter of Alice Giles Henley."

For all I knew, half the county was related to the woman. I couldn't see the crime in that. Penny also mentioned there was a scandal in connection with the woman, but I got the feeling that now was not quite the right time to bring that up.

"Hush your mouth. Don't you think you've caused us enough trouble?"

"Miss Opal, I am sorry if I've upset you. Please tell me what you're talking about, because I don't understand."

Opal made a snort of disgust. Then she began shaking, trembling violently. A vein throbbed in her temple and all I could think of was that she was going to have a stroke. Not to be selfish, but I couldn't handle another dead person quite so soon. That was one thing I was sure of. But then, neither could her grandson. When I'd seen Adam at the funeral yesterday he was so pale and drawn that he looked like a candidate for a rest home himself.

"You need to let sleeping dogs lie," Opal managed to say, her face the color of beets. "If you must dredge up old scandals, wait until I'm dead. Give me that, at least. At this rate, you won't have to wait long."

"And if I don't?"

"If you don't, whatever truth you find, I promise you on my grave that I'll say you're wrong. I'll tell the world that you made it up. I'll fight you to my dying day—in court and out. But more importantly, I'll ruin you. I may be an old lady, but I know people. Just whose horses do you think you'll be training after I'm done with you?"

Well, now I knew where Glenda got her repertoire of threats. She'd been taught them by her mother.

I looked away from Opal's angry, demanding stare. Beyond the small window I saw a tiny redwood tool shed. The door to the shed was open and inside I could see a series of rakes, shovels and other gardening tools neatly lined up against the wall. In the center of the shed there was a large piece of equipment, possibly a tractor or riding lawn mower, neatly covered by a bright blue tarp. An older gentleman, indistinguishable between resident or staff, was puttering inside, moving small pots from one shelf to another. My mysterious gardener. I turned back to Opal.

"If I stop, will you tell me why it's so important that I don't continue? Not just for me, but for Bubba Henley. He's still missing. If I understand what's going on, I might be able to find him."

Her face distorted into an ugly mask. "You are being ridiculous. That boy'll show up on his own. Mark my words. Forget about him. Now, I don't want to talk to you any more so you go on. But you think about what I've said. I meant every word."

I believed her. I got up and moved toward the door. "But Miss Opal, please. If you can just tell me why?"

"Because I said so," she spat as I stepped toward the hall. "Isn't that enough? I'm old, too old to live down another scandal. All I'm asking is that you leave me alone."

I escaped down the hallway, passing Miss Sanders's desk on the way. She gave me a baleful stare and I knew exactly who was going to be the next victim of the wrath of Opal Dupree. Miss Sanders knew, too.

ↄ ↄ
ↄ ↄ

The phone was ringing when I got home. I was too upset to talk, so I let the machine pick it up.

"Oh, Cat darling, I just heard," squealed my effervescent client, Agnes. "How ghastly for you. Your neighbor bludgeoned to a bloody death mere inches from your happy home. I've been meditating the last few days, dear. And I spoke with two of my dearly departed husbands and this time they both got along amazingly well. Amazingly. Hopefully Ira will join us next time but he always was a little shy, poor dear. Anyway, I didn't rejoin the real world until this morning. It's hideous. Absolutely hideous."

I wasn't sure if Agnes was talking about Glenda's murder, meditation, her departed husband's shyness, or the real world. I pictured Agnes, hands flying as she talked, the sparkle in her eye, her outlandish wardrobe, and I smiled.

"And," she continued, "you're trying to help the police solve the case. That is so like you, to get involved like that. I read it in the paper, so I know it must be true. It's just below the picture of the calf triplets on page three. Aren't they just the cutest things you've ever seen? Holsteins it says they are. Just adorable. By the way, did you know you're never supposed to kick a cow chip on a hot day? My neighbor's nephew told me that. Said things get real messy if you do.

"Anyway I'm calling to let you know I'm sending you a trench coat. Black. You don't have one, do you, dear? I don't think so. But I know you can't do your best to help the police unless you are properly dressed. It'll arrive later today, I think. Now, please, please, please let me know if I can help. Oh . . . but I don't know what I could do."

There was silence for a moment while Agnes, bless her heart, was trying to think. I debated picking up the phone, but decided not. She'd keep me there for hours.

"I know," she finally shouted. "I can lead a pep rally in front of the police station. Encourage the troops. Show my support. Gracious me, I'll have to get pom-poms, won't I? And I'm not sure where one might find those. Oh, *The Yellow Pages*. That's it. I'll get it all organized here and call you back. Toodles."

I almost laughed. Pom-poms. A pep rally. Won't Sheriff Big Jim love that? The imagery that thought conjured up was worth at least one national championship. If I had the slightest inkling that Agnes could get organized enough to pull it off, I'd call her back and dissuade her. But if I knew Agnes, she'd never make it past the pom-poms. Thank God.

I returned Jon's car keys to the office and sat in the one good chair, the one Glenda had commandeered in the last hours of her life. Opal Dupree was a very determined lady. In one way she was as country as mud, but in another, she was the shrewdest woman I'd ever met.

Whatever the scandal was, or had been, I wouldn't find it out from her. And if she had any say in the matter, no one would find it out from me because I would never learn what it was. I had no doubt that Opal could—and would—carry out each and every one of her threats. Opal not only had a great many contacts in the Nashville area, she had them across the country. Probably she had them across the globe. I was sure there were more than a few big shots in banking, government, media, and business who owed Miss Opal one last favor.

I wandered out into the aisle, and wondered what life would be like if I were mistrusted and disliked. What would I do if I didn't have the stable, if I couldn't be around the horses I loved like family? It wouldn't be pleasant. Probably I couldn't afford to live here anymore.

My little worn-out house and my battered barn entered my thoughts. Much of my feeling for the place came from all the work I had put into it. Seven years. Not a lifetime by any means. But time enough.

I rubbed an inquisitive Gigi on her shiny, chestnut forehead. I liked my life just the way it was. But I knew I couldn't live with myself if I let Opal run me out of town. I also couldn't live with myself if I didn't do everything I could to find Bubba. And that was one thing, I knew, Opal Dupree did not want me to do.

My mind made up, I raced back into the office and called Deputy Giles. This time I got him.

Cat's Horse Tip #13

"A bad attitude is the first sign a horse is sore or hurting."

25

"Deputy? Cat. Guess what! I am absolutely, positively, completely sure that Glenda Dupree was the great-granddaughter of Col. Sam Henley."

"So?" His tone was skeptical.

"So," I said, "I think her mother, Opal, is the illegitimate child of Sam's daughter, Alice Giles Henley."

I heard the sounds of conversation on the deputy's end of the connection. "Hang on," he said to me. There was more muffled conversation before Deputy Giles came back on the line. "I'm sorry, Miz Cat. I know you're trying to help. But what actual proof do you have? And even if you did, being illegitimate ain't cause for arrest. It ain't a crime. I can't pull someone in just because their parents weren't hitched. And I honestly don't see that it has anything to do with either the murder or the disappearance of the Henley boy."

"Okay," I said, deflated. "Sorry I bothered you."

"No, Miz Cat, it's not a bother. You never know, and Lord knows I got on your case when you didn't say something. So please feel free to call. Anytime. Hey, gotta go, but I'll call you later." He hung up the phone.

Disappointed, I sat at my desk and thought. That had to be it. The scandal involving Alice. Opal had gone out of her way to make sure it wasn't dredged back up. What could be worse for a woman of Opal's generation than for her parents not to be, as the deputy put it, hitched? She must have been ostracized a great deal as a child to harbor such strong feelings about it today.

My mind shifted gears and I jumped to the day I found Glenda. I remembered it was raining. I was mad and went to her house to confront her. There was no answer at the front door, so I went around to the back. The house was so still, so quiet. But I went in the back anyway. I thought no one was home. So why did I go in? Anger? Curiosity? I decided the question was unimportant and shoved it aside. The fact was, I had gone in. I found Glenda. I was sick and then I called the police. I sat outside on the steps. I heard a car and Adam was there. Then Deputy Giles showed up. The sheriff and the press arrived. I talked with all of them and then watched with Adam as they got ready to load the body.

My mind jumped again. Robert Griggs knew, somehow, that Glenda had choked to death. How did he know that? Hill Henley lost a sale of a prized Tennessee Walking Horse due to Glenda's death. Or was the death due to the loss of the sale? It was all too confusing.

I called Adam to let him know I wanted to come over to look at the crime scene. There was no answer at his office, on his cell, or at the number next door, but I left messages at all numbers anyway. I grabbed my jacket to ward off the rain that had started and once again hightailed it over to Fairbanks.

Well before I arrived, I could see remnants of the crime scene tape fluttering in the slight, wet breeze. Either Adam, the police, or the elements had taken their toll on the bright yellow strips.

The front door was locked and there was no response to my repeated bell-ringing. I couldn't tell from the windowless garage if Adam's Jag was housed inside, so I splashed through a muddy patch in the yard around to the back and once again the back door eased itself open after a few loud knocks. Adam really needed to get that fixed.

Inside, it was deathly still. The clock above the stove had stopped, the curtains were drawn and the whole feeling was tomblike—dark, damp and chilly.

"Adam? Adam, it's Cat. Are you home?"

I tiptoed across the hard bricks to the plush dark red carpet that covered the dining room floor. My heart was thumping to beat the band and my breath was coming in short, sharp gasps. I'd either have to stop sneaking through other people's houses or get a prescription for Valium. I glanced at the stairway as I entered the hall and was relieved to see that someone, probably Cinda Lu, had cleaned up my mess. I stopped cold at the cordoned off entrance to the living room.

Glenda had always been a stickler for perfection. And to the casual eye, the living room was as she had always kept it. But I noticed a small brass vase had been knocked on the floor underneath an antique end table, and the table itself was out of alignment with the sofa it stood next to. The carefully arranged copies of *Architectural Digest* on the coffee table were scattered here and there, and the portable phone, which was always kept on the table next to the sofa, was still in its cradle, but lay sideways against the base of the wall.

I went back to the dining room, a room that had fed generation upon generation of Henleys. Despite the chill in the house, I was sweating in my warm, down-filled jacket, so I took the jacket off and hung it on a chair. Then I wandered around the room for a few minutes, taking in details I had missed on previous visits.

Finally, I sat at the huge table and tried to think back, to recover from the murky depths of my meager mind exactly what the living room had looked like when I found Glenda. I couldn't remember anything except the bloodied mantle and that grotesque hand reaching up from the fireplace. Ugh.

The slight disarray in the living room was most likely the work of the paramedics and the police. I think I would have noticed right away if the room had been trashed the day I found Glenda. If it hadn't been, then that meant there wasn't a struggle and that Glenda had probably known her killer.

I had just made a mental note to ask Cinda Lu if she'd straightened the room when the hairs on the back of my neck prickled and I sensed I was not alone. I whirled my head around to check the kitchen door—the door directly behind me. Nothing, yet I couldn't get over my unease. I slowly turned my head back around and was immediately knocked off my chair with a blow to the left side of my head.

"Just give it to me and I'll forget you were here."

I blinked. Standing over me were two blurry, hooded, and draped figures that slowly merged into one. "What?"

"The notebook," said the figure. "Glenda Dupree's notebook. You have it." The voice was gravelly, distorted, rough, unrecognizable.

Since the night I realized Bubba was missing, I'd battled a nervous, shaky, fluttery feeling. But now a horrid, icy calm filled my being. It was a feeling of paralyzing fear. Of the two feelings, I definitely preferred the former.

My ears were ringing and my head was throbbing so much I couldn't think. The figure took a step toward me. It was the kind of slow, careful step you take when you mean to catch an unwilling colt, but you don't necessarily want the colt to know what it is that you have in mind.

"I . . . I don't have it." I said through the fog, pulling my feet toward me and away from the approaching hood. I silently thanked the guardian angel that made me invite the deputy into the house Wednesday night. He'd left with the notebook tucked deep into an evidence bag, otherwise it probably would have been left out on my kitchen table, easy for anyone to find.

The cloaked figure took another step toward me and I somehow struggled into a squatting position. There was blood dripping on the floor near me but I was too frightened and concussed to realize it was mine.

"Give me the notebook. She knew about the basement medicine."

I tried desperately to think. I couldn't remember anything Glenda's notebook had said about a basement, and the only thing that could be construed as a medicinal notation was l=opium+saffron+wine. The opium equation. "L," as I later found, had stood for laudanum, a concoction that had been used for centuries as a pain killer, and was still being used during the Civil War. As in back in Col. Sam's day.

They said in his later years the colonel was crazier than a mad cat. I wondered if his madness was consistent with addiction to laudanum and bet that it was. That solved the big mystery surrounding Col. Sam and the smuggling. Probably, opium was not a big crop in the Mid-South during the Civil War. But I bet it was grown in boatloads in China. And Darcy had connected him to China through information she found on the Internet. When the war ended, I wondered, did the smuggling stop, or had it continued? And if it had continued, what, if anything, did it have to do with my crouching on the floor with an insane cloaked person hovering over me? And why could I think so clearly about this when I couldn't figure out how to stand up?

Basement medicine, I thought. What was it Carole said about safety and her kids? I blinked my eyes to try to speed up my thoughts. Didn't work. Codeine. Basement. Kids. Keep it locked up. I blinked again. Surely this can't all be about some cough syrup? And surely that's not hunky Keith Carson, or worse yet, Carole, under that hood?

Before I had a chance to look closely for identifying characteristics, the figure said, "The notebook is mine. Mine." Then large, strong, gloved hands flexed, and the cloak, hood and all, charged at me.

I was physically strong and quite fit from daily workouts in the saddle, but I had been weakened from the blow to the head. I tried to stand, to run, but was overcome with dizziness. Instead, I started to crawl toward the front door, but the figure kicked me against the stairway. It pulled an object out of thin air and suddenly I realized what that object was. For the first time I felt that I was going to be killed, right then and there.

Outside, a banging came from the thick, antique front door at the same time the figure viciously swung the long metal hoof rasp at me. It looked like the same hoof rasp I had picked up out of the back yard that morning and had laid on my kitchen table. Shaped like a long, quarter-inch thick metal ruler with a

wooden handle on both ends, Hank had found it in the barn
and thought he'd appropriate it for his own use. However, the
flat part of the metal hoof rasp had hundreds of small sharp
points, like the gigantic nail file that it was, and Hank's tender
mouth doubtless had found it a bit too much.

I was dimly aware of the front door flying open at the same
time the rasp whizzed by, a centimeter from my left ear. Deputy
Giles filled the doorway, saw us, and the world stopped.

"You know, Miz Cat," he said as I somehow scrambled upright, "after you hung up I just got an awful feeling. Like maybe
I should have listened between the lines. Like maybe you'd head
over here and this is the one time I'd get here too late. I'm telling
you, I—"

Then the world jump-started with an explosion. The figure
swung simultaneously at the Deputy and at me. Ducking too
late, Deputy Giles grabbed his ear and melted into the floor. I
distinctly heard the solid thunk of his head hitting one-hundred-
fifty-year-old wood.

Then the monster smacked me twice from behind, knocking
me through the police tape and into the living room.

ᴐ ᴐ ᴐ ᴐ

I lay on the floor with no particular interest in getting up. I had,
in fact, no particular interest in anything at all. Everything
around me was pulsing and throbbing in a way that was sicken-
ingly psychedelic. I thought it very unfair that my dying moments
should be so blank. My life should be flashing before my eyes;
my loved ones should be gathered around me. I felt nothing.

There was only the smell of blood and a warm stickiness along the upper left side of my body.

I was sure there was something I ought to do. Something important. My body paid no attention to my brain. My brain seemed to feel I had gotten us into this mess and I damned sure had better get us out. I kept trying to focus, to stop the world from throbbing, but it kept on, getting bigger and louder until I was consumed with it.

Then, after an eon, the throbbing slowed and eventually stopped. In fact, everything was stopping. I couldn't hear. My vision was getting spotty, like I was looking through a heavy, dark veil. And it was getting hard to breathe. I considered this development with great interest. Maybe it was all a dream. Maybe I was already dead. Maybe I didn't care. Then I got the giggles, but that was too painful for belief, so I tried to find something else to focus on.

Glenda's portable phone was under a table, just inches from my fingertips. I stretched for it and giggled again at the hilarious distance between it and my hand. I stretched my right shoulder and brushed the phone with my fingers. The floor screamed with my pain. I paused as the scream eventually died.

I brushed the phone a little closer and could now see the keypad out of the corner of my eye. It made no sense, but there was a pretty red sticker by one of the buttons so that's the button I touched. The pretty one. While I was trying to figure out what to do next, I heard a voice from inside the phone. Now wasn't that interesting? I giggled, but I don't believe the voice in the phone could hear me over the screaming of the floor.

26

I WOKE UP IN A HIGH, narrow bed. Gray walls and a window with matching gray blinds completed the faux-designer decor. Even noting the industrial gray tile floors, it took me a while to realize I was in a hospital.

"Well, you're finally awake," said the handsome man in the chair by the window. He was garbed in green medical scrubs and provided the only color in the room. "You were lucky, you know."

I could have argued the point, but didn't want to waste the energy. My left shoulder seemed to be immobilized under mounds of bandages, and it hurt like the dickens every time I drew a breath.

He noticed my confusion. "Your upper arm is broken, along with a few ribs, and you got a bash on the head for good measure. If that creep had hit you much harder, you wouldn't be here now."

I refrained from snapping that being here wasn't tops on my list of places to be, only because the alternative was unthinkable. Instead, I asked, "The deputy?"

The man in the chair leaned back and closed his eyes. He looked just as good with his eyes closed as he did with them open.

"Martin is checking alibis for everyone in the county and for half of Nashville," he said. "He will find whoever did this and he will get a conviction if it's the last thing he does. He said to tell you that. For some reason, he thought it would make you feel better."

It did. A lot. Water started running from my eyes. "So he's not dead?"

The man opened his eyes and grinned. For the first time I had an inkling of whom he might be. He was taller and leaner and darker, and his chin wasn't quite as prominent, but otherwise the resemblance was striking. "Oh, no way," he said. "My baby brother is tough. A little bash on the head's not going to slow him down. At least not for very long. By the way, I'm Brent. Brent Giles."

I sniffed a few times and he handed me a Kleenex. I took it with the hand I could still use.

"I heard that before you passed out you had sense enough to dial 911," said the deputy's brother. I vaguely recalled a red button and a voice. "Martin came around just before the ambulance pulled up. I had the day off so I came down to fix a window on Mama's house. Martin called me to come over and sit with you while he went off to find that hooded scumbag. I wish he'd gotten a doc to look him over—he's got a nasty lump on the side of his head—but he was stubborn as all get out about it. Just grabbed an ice pack from the ER and left."

I heaved a sigh of relief that I wasn't the target Deputy Giles was looking for.

Brent said his brother had not gotten any better look at the hooded person than I had. We both, apparently, were in agreement that whoever it was, was probably male, stocky of build, and right-handed. Because of the strength and agility, the person was most likely less than fifty years old, and very possibly much younger. The description fit a thousand people in Cheatham County alone.

Where we differed was in the opinion of the attacker's height. Since I had spent most of my time on the floor looking up, I guessed he was about seven-foot-three. Allowing for my somewhat concussed state, I agreed to somewhere in the neighborhood of six-feet to six-foot-two. The deputy, on the other hand, thought more in the neighborhood of five-foot-ten. Neither of us was in a position to be a good judge.

I told Brent about my conversation with my attacker, and my belief that he was speaking through some kind of voice synthesizer. I almost forgot to add the part about the basement medicine and Keith Carson's safety measures for his kids. Brent said he'd fill his brother in, as soon as Martin came in from questioning everyone he could think of to question.

"So what did you do," I asked finally, "bring out the horse sutures and sew me up?"

He grinned widely. "Oh, no. I'm a small animal vet. I would have used canine clamps. Actually, by the time I got here an ortho specialist by the name of Williams had already been in to see you. He said it's a clean break there in your upper arm. Apparently the doc owns one of the horses in your barn. And, he said to tell you he had a lawyer friend of his lined up for you should the need arise."

I wasn't sure if the lawyer was to defend me or to sue the person who smacked me. Either way, Doc Williams had a vested interest in keeping me sound and out of jail if he wanted Hillbilly Bob to go the nationals this summer.

"You have a lot of surface cuts and bruises. Nothing serious there. Most of the blood was from the rough edges of the rasp," Brent continued. "Martin showed the thing to me. Nasty piece of metal. You'll be right as rain in a month or two."

"A month or two! Nope. I'm right enough to go home right now." I eased myself into a sitting position and the room suddenly turned upside down.

"Uh, I think maybe you should wait." Brent jumped up in alarm. "You've suffered a concussion, a pretty severe shock, and you're barely out of anesthesia. You need to stay in bed here for a few days."

"Can't. I've got a lunch appointment with a client tomorrow," I said. "She's coming down from Louisville."

"I don't mean to burst your bubble, but I don't think you're going to be up to having lunch with anyone tomorrow."

I considered the statement and realized that it quite possibly was true. "Well then, if I can't eat, I'll watch her eat. I really do have to meet with her. We're going over the new ad campaign for the show season. Deadlines are coming up and we need to make some decisions."

"She can come here and you can make decisions."

"Oh no, not Agnes. You don't know Agnes. She's . . . well, she's Agnes. If she showed up here she'd have the nurses so confused they'd probably kill someone by mistake. No. Really, Agnes doesn't need to come here."

Okay, so I exaggerated. I was taught that the difference between exaggeration and a lie was that a lie was done for selfish reasons and exaggeration was done for the good of all. It really was in everyone's best interests to keep Agnes away from the hospital—and come to think of it, me. Trust me on this.

"Well, maybe you can go home tomorrow," said Brent.

I hoped he didn't think I was always this difficult. On the other hand, what did I care what he thought? Well, he was kind of cute.

"Promise me," he said, "that you'll get someone to stay with you at your house and I'll see if they'll consider letting you go tomorrow."

I hadn't asked exactly where I was. But the few times I'd been to the Cheatham Medical Center in Ashland City to visit a patient led me to believe I was now one of their guests. Even though I desperately wanted to get out of there, I knew deep down that I was better off staying put. But there was a vague idea that kept nagging at the back of my mind. Something important. Something I couldn't quite catch. If I could just get into my own bed in my own house, I knew I could figure out what it was.

"You know," I joked, easing myself back into the flat lump they called a pillow, "this is one hell of a first date."

Brent laughed. It was a good laugh—one that held a lot of promise. "We'll make up for it later. I make great lasagna. Maybe you'll be up for it sometime next week."

Well gee, anyone who makes great lasagna was okay in my book. We made a date.

"Martin has told me a lot about you," he said.

I didn't know if that was good or bad. Or if saying bad things about me would be good, or if saying good things would be bad. It must be the medication.

"When you're up to it, I'd like to see your place. We have

one other vet at the clinic where I work who treats large animals. Sometimes I get called in to assist. I've got a few questions on working with horses that you could help me with."

I supposed aloud that I probably could.

"Good," was all he said.

"Do you really think I can leave tomorrow?"

He looked at me appraisingly. "Well, it's not my decision. I'm sure there's a doctor around here somewhere who can answer that for you. But if you're bound and determined to leave and if you aren't running a fever, if you're taking fluids well, and if you can walk out of here on your own two legs, I think they'll probably let you go."

This last requirement made me think. At the moment, a trip to the bathroom seemed equivalent to going on an African safari. And speaking of the bathroom, it was time to go.

By the next morning I could stagger woozily down to the end of the hallway and back, and I only fell into the wall once. The thought I couldn't put my finger on kept coming into the outer reaches of my brain, only to whisk itself away like a leprechaun who didn't want to be caught.

Doc Williams reluctantly released me only after I promised to go directly home to eat, sleep and do nothing. I agreed to it all just to get out of there, then I finally made the call I had been dreading for days.

Jon picked me up in the middle of an early afternoon rain, and had enough sense to remain gracious about recent events. I know he was furious with me for leaving him to take care of the barn and also for getting so involved in events over at Fairbanks. I also knew that his fury originated in concern and that, when it came right down to it, he was just glad that I was all right. Of course, he'd never admit all that, but I knew it anyway.

I counted my steps as Jon carefully led me from the car to my bedroom. Twenty-eight. All so very painful. I lay on my bed with a feeling of intense relief. I'd recently splurged and redecorated the room in shades of pale yellow and deep plum, and I loved it. I had every intention of calling Deputy Giles the minute I got settled in bed to find out what was going on, but before I knew it, I was sound asleep.

Cat's Horse Tip #14

"Horses put their ears back not to show aggression, but to protect the ears in what they perceive as a potentially dangerous situation."

27

WHEN I WOKE UP I CALLED the deputy, but he wasn't in. Then I took one of the nice pain pills the hospital had sent home with me and settled back in a pile of pillows.

I tried not to mind very much that the barn was strictly off limits for a few days, not only because Sally Blue had been acting so strangely, but because my absence would serve to drive another wedge between Jon and me. I knew Jon and I would have to talk soon but I so hated confrontations—especially when I was the one who was wrong.

In the horse business, the horses always come first. Or should. It was a rule I had not followed this week. However, I reasoned, if one of the horses were missing, or God forbid, murdered, I would be just as focused on that situation as I was with the events that surrounded Glenda and Bubba.

Hmmmm. Maybe that was an argument I could use when talking to Jon. Technically, I was employer to his employee so I could do as I liked. But with such a small operation, Jon and I were both integral parts of this team, and it didn't take a rocket scientist to figure out that one half of the team was a little miffed at the other.

In addition to carrying both his and my share of the barn duties the past few days, yesterday Jon had taken care of Agnes for me, telling her I'd been unavoidably detained in the course of my investigation, and would call her the first of the week. I'm sure there was a lot more to the conversation than that. With Agnes there always is, but Jon spared me the details and for that I was thankful.

Her package, I saw, had arrived safely and a glossy, black, lined trench coat now hung from my closet door. I couldn't wait for my arm to heal so I could wear it.

Although the short trip home from the hospital had been brutal, I figured I was lucky to have been released at all. And I knew they never would have let me go if they realized there wouldn't be someone fussing over me all day. But I had it all figured out. After Jon helped me settle in at home, he made sure the security system was turned on and that my phone was within reach. Although Jon wasn't staying in the house, he was on the property and easily accessible.

I figured if the medical staff at the hospital knew the situation, they wouldn't be happy. But, oh well. I was safe, and lots of people were available if I needed them. I hate to be fussed over.

Before he went back to the barn, Jon made sure I had water and a stack of magazines and books. On top of the pile was my friend Lisa Wysocky's book, *My Horse, My Partner: Teamwork on the Ground*. I wanted to look through the book again to see if I could find any ideas that might help Gigi. But not today. Today, printed words did a conga dance in front of my eyes, which were once again becoming hard to keep open.

While I tried not to doze, word got around that I was out of the hospital. Cran Berry, widely thought to be the only "normal" Berry in the bunch, brought the mail up to the house instead of leaving it in the box, as he usually did. With it, he brought a to-die-for double chocolate layer cake that his wife had baked.

Carole sent over some organic liquid vitamins via her oldest, who asked me if getting bashed hurt very much. I said that it did and we talked for a while about how she should avoid it, if at all possible. She agreed that she would try. I found it increasingly hard to believe that either Carole or her hunky husband was behind all this, although I guessed at this point just about any right-handed adult who didn't have an alibi was still a suspect.

As she was leaving, another, more unexpected, visitor came in the door. Robert Griggs. He turned into two people as he moved across the room, which I thought was a bit odd, but then as the pain in my arm simultaneously subsided, I realized the wonder drugs were kicking in. Robert looked uncomfortably around the room and, not finding any place to sit, perched uneasily at the foot of the bed. He said he came to mend fences, that he was sorry about the tone of our discussion the other day and he hoped I realized he had just been concerned. He realized I was not a druggie.

I glanced at the small cache of pill bottles the hospital had sent home with me and giggled as they paired up and began to tango across the table. Damn those pills. In the midst of the awkward pause that came next, I asked Robert about his drunken brawl.

He blushed. "I, uh . . . I'm not much of a drinker, but then I've never known anyone who was murdered before," he said. "I'd had a few, thought I'd better eat. You understand I was pretty upset."

I nodded. And waited.

"All right, I told the police, so you might as well know. I have a close friend who assisted on the autopsy, on Glenda's . . . Cheatham County doesn't do autopsies so they sent the body to a private firm in Nashville. I was there when they were starting the . . . at first I didn't realize it was her. Glenda. And when it finally dawned on me who it was, I was so shocked I didn't say anything. I should have. I should have left. But it was so compelling, once they started to, uh, examine her. Later, it was . . . awful. I got drunk."

"So that's how you knew before anyone else that Glenda had suffocated, that she didn't die from the beating." The drugs might have impaired my vision, but I could still think.

"I . . . I didn't kill her," he said.

I so hoped he was telling the truth. There was another awkward pause. "Okay, Robert. Now it's my turn to level." I told him the reason I asked about the opium equation, the laudanum—that it was a notation I found in Glenda's notebook. "I didn't know what it was," I said. "Only I had a feeling it was important."

"And was it?" he asked, eyeing my mound of bandages.

"I think so," I said. "I think it was very important."

Later in the day, after yet another nap and yet another pill, I heard the phone ring. I debated letting the machine get it. I was still pretty drowsy, but, thinking it might be the deputy, I answered.

"Cat, this is Opal Dupree."

I shifted a pillow to better balance my elbow and the phone. Which Opal was calling now, I wondered, the shrewd businesswoman or the rambling elderly octogenarian?

It turned out it was the businesswoman, but instead of lambasting me, as this version of Opal had before, she commiserated with me about my injuries. I tried to figure out where she was going with all this concern, but couldn't quite manage it. Instead, I told her I had given up on finding Bubba. Dead or alive, for better or worse, that boy was now on his own.

"Oh, no!" she cried, alarmed. Opal was wholly coherent and I prayed her condition would last at least until the conversation ended. I wasn't up for another round of her ramblings. "You've been through a good deal on account of that Bubba boy, haven't you?" she asked.

Surprised at her perception, I agreed that I had.

"And you care about him, too, I suppose. You must, to have gone through so much."

I nodded even though she couldn't see me. "I hate that I haven't been able to find him," I said. "He's just a boy and I am convinced he is a victim in all this. He hasn't had much of a life, but he deserves a fair chance at it, just as everyone does. It must look foolish to you, the way I've gotten so involved."

As I said the words, I finally realized why I was so concerned about Bubba. He was only a year older than I was when my dad had abandoned me for a whiskey bottle and just two years older than I was when my mother abandoned me in favor of death.

And, while I knew the latter was not my mother's choice, I felt abandoned all the same.

Apparently my dad did, too. He was so devastated by her death that he eased the pain of her passing with alcohol, and ended up living on the street too drunk to realize he had a home, or a daughter who needed him. I clearly remembered the confusion of being alone at nine years old and my poor attempts at making survival choices. If Bubba was alive, he most likely also had survival decisions to make. I didn't wish that situation on any child, Bubba included.

Opal was silent while we each clarified our thoughts, but I was afraid her silence meant her mental capacity was draining away. "No," she said finally and with clarity, "your involvement doesn't look foolish and I think you'll find that you have done some good. I think, in fact, that you will find him."

"But how? Miss Opal, I know you can't see me, but I was beaten by someone so badly when I was over at Fairbanks that I have several broken bones. My upper body is covered in bandages, and I'm forbidden to get out of bed for the foreseeable future. Besides, I don't know anything more now than I did yesterday. That knowledge wasn't enough to find Bubba, but it was enough to practically get me killed. Not to mention poor Deputy Giles.

"Probably," I concluded, "Bubba is dead. Or maybe he just got tired of being ignored by that sack of garbage that calls himself 'dad'—and I use that term loosely by the way—and took off on his own, like some people are saying."

"The boy," she said strongly, "is not dead. I am certain of it. But he may soon be if he's not found."

I tried to sit up and instead gasped in pain. "How do you know that?" I asked.

"Now don't worry, Cat," she said, ignoring my words. "Everything will be fine. You'll see to it. Just remember that in spite of everything that's happened between us, I believe in you. Just think very carefully about the information you've learned in the past few days and you'll find that Henley boy."

Then with out a ho-hum or a good-bye, she hung up.

Before I could call Deputy Giles with a suggestion that he question Opal Dupree a little further, Darcy arrived with huge, mouthwatering helpings of baked chicken, green beans, macaroni and cheese, and fried apples from Verna Mae's. We shared it along with most of Mrs. Berry's cake. If my appetite was any indication of my health, I'd be jumping hurdles by morning. I couldn't believe how hungry I was, then I remembered it had been a couple of days since I'd last seen a good meal.

Darcy's a sweet girl and I love her dearly. But her constant chatter was tiring, so I sent her with a leftover piece of cake out to Jon and the barn. I knew she'd end up spending an hour or so with Petey and I hoped by that time that I'd be fast asleep.

After checking the security system and the locks, I wrapped up in my down quilt. I sat propped up in bed and gazed out the window, sleepily watching the fog roll up to the house.

Although I should have been, I wasn't worried that a hooded monster would jump out of nowhere to finish me off. In fact, I had no worries or fears at all, probably because I was still somewhat sedated. I wished I knew what was in the pills I was taking. I'd forgotten to ask Doc what they were. Maybe Jon knew. I tried to read the label, but the letters all looked like Greek to me. Probably, I thought, it wasn't anything I'd heard of before anyway. The pills took care of the strong muscle cramps in my broken arm, but I didn't like the lethargic feeling they gave me, or the distorted sense of vision, and I knew I wouldn't be taking any more.

As the evening wore on, my mind turned introspective, something it doesn't often do. I thought if I had to live someplace, it was just as well that I lived in a place where I had lots of friends. If I didn't realize it before, today I'd found that almost everyone I knew was full of unconditional kindness—the type that surfaces when one of your own is down.

I've always thought of myself as an independent, self-supporting person, but my neighbors' responses taught me otherwise. It was surprising to discover that although seven years was a short enough amount of time to qualify as a newcomer here, I had also been accepted as an honorary native. My friends and neighbors cared about me, and that was comforting knowledge.

I never thought I'd subconsciously seek a place to live that was similar to my hometown of Bucksnort. But apparently I had. Both Bucksnort and my River Road neighborhood were filled with people who would band together to help others. But Bucksnort is so small; it is the kind of place that many young people run from as soon as they are able. Me included. It was reassuring to realize that even though I had voluntarily severed my ties with the little town, I had created similar roots right here on River Road.

My butt was falling asleep so I shifted positions amid great protests from my arm. The pain was so great that despite my earlier vow to take no more medicine, I reached for the bottle on the nightstand.

And then I stopped. The medicine. That was it. That's what had been elusively pulling at me all the time I was in the hospital. That's what I had forgotten. The basement medicine. And Opal said that Glenda knew about it.

My mind was still slow and I wondered vaguely if the deputy had found his prey yet. Considering what had happened the last time I'd had an impulse, I supposed I ought to just stay put and wait for the officials. But suddenly I knew without a doubt where Bubba was. Opal's veiled message had gotten through. Time was of the essence, and I hoped with everything that I had that it wasn't too late.

Cat's Horse Tip #15

"The horse population in the United States peaked before World War I at about 26 million. Currently, there are just over 9 million horses in the U.S."

28

YOU CAN HIDE A LOT OF stuff in a basement. Cursing myself for my stupidity, I left the pills on the nightstand and picked up the telephone. I once again dialed the police station only to be told, once again, that Deputy Giles was out. Seems like cops are always around when you don't need them, but when you do. . . .

Instead, I called Opal Dupree. I glanced at my watch. It was after ten. The old bat was probably asleep by now, but if the nurse wouldn't wake her, I'd go over there and shake her awake. Unfortunately, I wouldn't get the pleasure, as Opal answered on the second ring.

"Miss Opal." I said, after she had again inquired solicitously after my health. Maybe she finally felt some guilt here. She should, I thought. For I believed that while Opal didn't know *before* the fact of the crimes, she figured out what was going on *after* the fact and didn't tell a soul. I believe in loyalty, but this was carrying it too far. Especially when Bubba's life was at stake.

"Miss Opal, who besides you knew that Col. Sam was your grandfather?"

"What's that got to do with anything?"

"Nothing, but it may have everything to do with the life and safety of Bubba Henley. Miss Opal, you've got to believe me, no one cares if your parents weren't legally married or about anything else that went on in the past. But I need to know who knew."

There was a dreadful silence while she contemplated her reply.

"The family," she said finally. "Just the family."

I listened with growing horror as Opal described to me the peculiarities of her family tree. When she finished, I not only had my suspicions of Bubba's whereabouts confirmed, I had the old lady's tearful prayer that I be lucky enough to find the boy alive.

"By the way," she said, as I was about to hang up. "I'm not as strong as I once was and in a different way neither are you. I am choosing not to deal with any more of this trouble and because of your injuries, you can't. That boy needs to be found, but let someone else go to him. You stay put, wherever you are, but I don't suppose I have to tell you that."

I agreed that she didn't have to tell me, but you know me, in one ear and out the other. It was only after we hung up that I realized I had lost my quite substantial awe of the Dupree family matriarch. The awe had turned into pity.

I slowly eased myself out of bed, wincing and holding my upper arm firmly with my right hand. By use of some innovative ankle movements, I was able to slide my feet into an old pair of slip-on paddock boots. I pulled Agnes's new, black slicker from its perch and managed to slide my right arm into the sleeve, and, by twisting and ducking my upper body, draped the rest of it around my left shoulder. It took me another five minutes to button the top button, but I got it done.

If it says anything about me, I knew I wasn't supposed to be doing what I was going to do. I knew it wasn't safe. But I also knew that I had to do it. Bubba's life depended on it. If he still had one.

It did occur to me that I should call someone to go with me. I had seen the lights of Darcy's car go down the drive a few minutes ago, and Carole was probably reading bedtime stories to the kids. So that left . . . let me see . . . Jon. I was horribly sure of what I would find in that basement and knew that I would need help moving the body. If Bubba was down there, alive, surely someone would have heard him. In all the times people had been in and out of there the past few days, no one had heard a single peep. Which meant Bubba was no longer alive.

I sighed and gave Jon a call, just telling him I needed him to help me with something. He probably was in horror thinking I needed him to help me to the bathroom. The thought almost made me smile, but before I could, there was a knock on my door. So sure it was Jon, I switched off the alarm and, without checking to see who was on the other side, swung open the door.

Damn those pills.

"I've spent the entire day trying to get to you."

Adam's hair was splattered with mud, his jeans torn and soaked in mire. His voice was full of rage and I refrained from looking at his eyes, for fear of what I would find. "In case you're wondering," he said, showing me the frighteningly large switch-blade he was carrying, "I don't have a gun, but I think you'll come with me anyway. If you say one word, I'll use the knife on the dog."

It was only then that I noticed that Adam had a subdued Hank on the end of a piece of baling twine. Hank looked wor-riedly from Adam to me, trying to understand this strange situ-ation. His floppy ears, sad expression, and hopeful half-wag of his tail brought tears to my eyes. I looked Adam dead in the eye and realized that if he thought I was going to make a sound he would slice Hank's jugular in a second.

Adam's eyes were dead, but the rest of him was gasping from excitement, or maybe rage, and his face twisted into a ma-niacal grimace as he looked at the bandages peeking from un-derneath Agnes' stylish coat. It was a vivid reminder that I was in no shape to fight him. Indeed, I could barely stand. If he gasped any harder, I'd probably fall over from the force of his breath.

We made our way slowly out the door. My only hope was to stall for time in hopes that Jon would see us. What in the world was taking him so long? And why had Agnes sent me a *black* trench coat? Wasn't white much more practical in a situation such as this? If I was wearing white, Jon might be able to see me in the dark.

We were now walking away from my house and barn, and toward Fairbanks. I was trying to make as much noise as I could walking, but bare, cold ground is pretty silent, even when it's damp. The more I tried to stomp around, the more it jarred my fragile, broken bones. I prayed for a diversion, something, any-thing, that would make Hank bark and attract Jon's attention.

Jon must be walking from the barn to the house by now, mustn't he? Surely he was. But no one, including Jon, arrived to interrupt my walk with Adam.

I will say that Adam treated me as carefully as a treasured piece of art. So carefully in fact, that it was spooky. It had been drizzling when we left the house, but now the rain was coming down much harder—like a cow peeing on a flat rock, as my grandma would have said. After a few more steps and a few deep gulps of cold, foggy air, the last of my sedative wore off. Along with the clear thinking came deep, thudding waves of pain, but as long as my mind was clear, I felt I could handle anything. Well, almost.

In the distance I heard a horse whinny and the sound of hooves banging on wood. It sounded like Sally Blue. Maybe that meant Jon had exited the barn and was headed this way. If he had done so without giving Sally a pat, she would whinny and stomp. Or did Sally know what was happening here? Adam didn't seem to hear the noise.

Away from the house it was much darker, and I knew any chance of Jon seeing us was gone. With Plan A down the tubes, I was doing double duty battening down my fear of the dark while also scrambling to come up with a viable Plan B.

Billows of fog rolled heavily over Col. Sam's mansion, where a single light shone in the hall. Beyond the house, I could hear the waves of the Cumberland River as they slapped against the steep, rocky bank. The fog thinned here and there, revealing windswept trees and angry, leafless branches.

"Listen," I said, "I'm not so sure this is a good idea, Adam. I just got out of the hospital and I'm not feeling all that well. Maybe I should go home."

Hank whined his assent, but Adam didn't bother to reply.

The air was full of the smell and taste and dampness of the river. The only sound besides the waves and the high, gusty whine of the wind was the irregular splattering of the rain as it hit the ground.

I stiffened as we turned away from Fairbanks's massive stone steps and headed behind the house toward the river. Adam still guided me gently, but his grip around my waist was much tighter. We stopped at the top of the wooded riverbank and a wave of wooziness swept through me. Adam sensed my faintness and pulled me to him. It was almost as if we were back in the parking lot of the nursing home, embracing each other for the ordeal to come. Only then, Adam was not going to kill me.

"Is there a reason why you and I are standing here freezing to death and getting soaked?" I asked as I jerked away. I couldn't believe myself. Here I am waiting to get killed and I'm pissing the guy off.

"I wanted you to see the river," he said quietly, so quietly that I had to strain to hear his words. "During much of the Civil War the river here was filled with boats. Rafts, barges, you name it, they all passed by here. When the river was high, big boats—ships almost—could come in and dock right here at Fairbanks.

"There was a warehouse just to our right, near where the Henley trailer is. It's long gone, but it was there. They'd pull the goods up the bank and store it until Col. Sam could sell it at a profit. Neither side ever bothered Col. Sam's shipments. They knew he carried needed supplies for each Army.

"Once in a while, though, they'd unload and leave the goods locked in a big shed on the dock. Then when the ship had left, and when the river had receded, Col. Sam's slaves would bring the goods in a different way, to another storage place."

He must be talking about the smuggling, I thought.

"Cat, I'm going to take you to that other storage place. I just wanted you to see this first."

"And what if I don't want to go?" I asked, my voice rising. "What if I just refuse?"

"You won't," he said turning me roughly and jerking Hank and me toward Fairbanks. I didn't think my arm could hurt much more than it already did, but I was wrong.

It was even darker now. Black clouds rolled across the dark gray of the sky and it was difficult to see even a few feet ahead. Adam pulled a small flashlight out of his pocket; the light glowed eerily through the water soaked night as we moved in an odd pattern of disjointedness toward Fairbanks' back door. I wondered if the lock was still broken and, bizarrely, I wanted once more to giggle. Maybe the last of the medication hadn't worn off after all.

Adam escorted me to the door and flung it open. For the first time since we left my house, I could see Adam's features. His face was hard, expressionless, his aqua eyes now the color of ice. In that instant, reality set in and I knew he was going to kill me. Soon. My brain sent panic signals to my body and the now-familiar shakiness began.

"Adam, listen, I—"

Suddenly he was kissing me, forcing his tongue down my throat. His hands were everywhere at once, pulling at me, pleading, needing. I resisted the impulse to gag and tried to get in a good deep breath. I managed to, sort of. Then suddenly he stopped.

"I love you, Cat," he said in a ragged voice. "I knew it the first time I laid eyes on you."

He reached up to gently wipe a tear from my face and that was the first I knew I was crying.

"Just remember," he said, "whatever happens, I'm doing it out of love."

Then he gave me a hard shove and sent me sprawling butt first onto Glenda's very hard, very brick, kitchen floor.

Cat's Horse Tip #16

"Horses on pasture spend about 60 percent of their time grazing, while stalled horses spend only 15 percent of their time eating—one reason behavior issues develop more often with stalled horses than pastured horses."

29

THE PAIN WAS INDESCRIBABLE. I LAY on the floor without moving. Indeed, movement of any kind was no longer within the realm of possibility. I don't know how long I lay there unable to breathe; I only hoped it wasn't long enough to qualify for brain damage. After a while I was able to take tiny puffs of air. Only when I was breathing close to normally did I open my eyes.

Adam was sitting on the kitchen sink, staring at me. No, through me. His eyes were lifeless. As he made no move toward me I closed my eyes and concentrated on becoming mobile. Eventually I was able to move each limb, with the obvious exception of my left arm, and carefully rolled myself into a sitting position. My broken ribs felt as if they were on fire. I looked again at Adam and couldn't believe how frightened I was of him. Wordlessly he held out his hand to help me up. Hesitant, I accepted, for the fact of the matter was, if I didn't have help, I wasn't getting up.

The house was cold. Rain was dripping in the back door. Apparently Adam hadn't thought to close it. Or maybe he liked wet kitchens.

Through the door I could see Hank on the wet patio trying to decide what to do. With his tail curved into a question mark and confusion in his eyes, guard dog he definitely was not. My heart ached for him and I hoped he'd have the sense to run away before Adam noticed he was there. Maybe Hank would run to Jon. With the length of baling twine still tied to his collar, Jon would know something was wrong. Shouldn't Jon be calling the deputy by now?

"Now that you know I'm serious," said Adam slamming shut the kitchen door along with any fantasies I might have had about a Hank-engineered rescue, "you'd better come on." He then threw open the basement door and pulled me through it. "You know, if you hadn't started all the snooping, you wouldn't be here now."

The steps were dark and endless, and when we reached the bottom one, I stumbled. Adam jerked me back to my feet so abruptly that I bit back a scream. I wanted to tell him there was no need to be so rough, but I didn't want to upset him any more than he already was. I didn't know if I could withstand another session with a Fairbanks floor.

The basement reeked of mold and age and decay. If there were lights, Adam didn't use them, so the only illumination we had was the small flashlight he still carried. But, it was enough to see that there wasn't much down there. What I did see looked older than the mountains with twice as much dust. Definitely no Bubba.

I could make out a pile of ancient newspapers in one corner. A stack of wood full of dry rot was piled next to them. The only item that could qualify as furniture was a large, ornate dresser complete with an elaborate antique mirror against the center of the far wall.

"Go on," said Adam, as he propelled me toward the dresser, "open it."

I was sure he meant that Bubba's body was stuffed in one of the large drawers, so one by one, and with mounting horror, I awkwardly juggled the bigger drawers open. They were sticky with age and trying to open them one-handed was next to impossible. With an impatient grunt of disgust, Adam grabbed the handle of a smaller drawer nestled along the top row and gave it a twist. With a creak and a groan the entire dresser, mirror and all, slid away to the left, revealing a hidden room beyond. I knew without a doubt that I was finally looking at Miss Opal's gopher hole, the "water and darkness."

Adam shone the flashlight around the room, which measured in feet about fifteen by fifteen and was lined with a series of shelves full of glass bottles, vials, and sealed jars of powders. Some of the jars looked spotlessly clean and others looked positively ancient. Here then, was Adam's "medicine," the remains of Col. Sam's huge stash of drugs left over from the Civil War, supplemented by fresh supplies and a small, but modern, laboratory.

I stared at the many shelves of drugs, and the words Miss Opal said about Col. Sam "helping those boys" came vividly back to me. Old Sam must have been supplying addicted Civil War soldiers, and later, veterans, with drugs. Bet he made a ton of pretty pennies on his sales, too. A lot of pain was generated from that war.

If the stories were true, Col. Sam had died mad, possibly a casualty of addiction to opium. And like many who are addicted,

Col. Sam surely had one fear, that of running out of drugs. That fear now belonged to Adam.

"Impressive, isn't it?" Adam asked when he saw my eyes widen. "Col. Sam not only smuggled opium in from China, he grew it right here in the fields. As you probably know, poppies are the source of opium, which can then be turned into a variety of drugs, including heroin, and the old Henley/Dupree family standard, laudanum. Tennessee was one of the leading poppy producing states during the war, along with Virginia and South Carolina, and I think Georgia. Bet you didn't know that, did you?"

I shook my head, too overwhelmed to answer.

"Oh, I've done all my homework. In 1860 it was estimated that close to seventeen thousand acres were dedicated to poppy farming in China. That's a huge amount of land Cat. It created a severe lack of food production and also caused mass starvation in several provinces. By 1887, seven of ten adult Chinese males were opium smokers, and Chinese opium was considered the best, and most potent, in the world. Of course, it was still illegal over there, so people had to be careful. Not like here, where both armies wanted and needed the opium that poppies produced for laudanum. So old Sam mixed the two—the harvest he grew here, with the smuggled imports he got from China—making his opium, and his laudanum, the best in North America. That way both the Northern and Southern armies would want to buy from him. And they did."

"But—" I interrupted. He shushed me with a hard slap to my cheek.

"I'm not finished yet, Cat. Please listen."

I nodded mutely, my anger building as I realized he was reciting lines he had rehearsed for a sole audience of one. Me.

"In addition to dental problems, opium was used to cure dysentery. A very large number of Civil War soldiers became addicted—more than sixty thousand returned home as addicts. That's a pretty high number, wouldn't you say so, Cat?"

I just stared at him, fury blazing into my eyes. This time, I refused to acknowledge his little lesson with a nod. He continued anyway.

"Well. Opium addiction was so widespread back then it was called the 'army disease' or 'soldier's disease,'" he said. "After the war, laudanum was so common that it was marketed commercially. You could get a third of an ounce at the general store for about a penny. I got that figure from some notes Col. Sam left down here. He left a lot of notes.

"Of course, when Sam became old and feeble, it all stopped. But then someone found this room and it started all over again. You think that person was me, don't you?" he asked. "Well, you're very wrong in that thought, Cat. Did you ever wonder how Aunt Glenda got started in her film career? How my grandmother got the attention of the Hollywood moguls for her daughters? It's all right here," he said, spreading his arms and turning around to look at the room. "Gran supplied the biggest studio heads in Hollywood with laudanum for many years. Aunt Glenda and my mother never knew, of course.

"Yes, my grandmother is a very smart woman," continued Adam. "She never used, never introduced the drug to her daughters. She just traded movie roles for a little of the good stuff. But both Aunt Glenda and my mother were good actresses and soon the roles, the parts, came on their own.

"When I was visiting here a few years ago I found all this by accident as I was exploring the house. Of course, even though my grandmother was initially able to use what was left of Col.

Sam's original supplies, time has since eroded that possibility for me. Remember that field I showed you earlier, the one just past the Henley's where the warehouse used to be?" Adam did not wait for me to respond. "If you look carefully at that field beginning in the spring and continuing into the summer months, mixed in with the different varieties of native grasses and wild flowers, you will see the blooms of the poppies planted there years ago. They are doing quite well, actually.

"Months ago, I knew Aunt Glenda suspected I was on something, but she couldn't prove it. Then a few days ago she followed me down here. I didn't see her, didn't even know she was home. But she saw it all. That day, that fateful Monday when Aunt Glenda came skipping back from her riding class, she was in a great mood. She said she felt as if she could conquer the world. But all she really wanted was to conquer was me.

"Aunt Glenda said she was going to send me to rehab. I, well, I didn't want to go. You see, I need my 'medicine' and I knew they wouldn't let me have it there," Adam took a deep, ragged breath and rubbed a hand across his face, as if the thought were more than he could bear. "Cat, I hurt all the time. My back. I was in the car when my mom was killed. I was just a little kid, but I've had incredible back pain ever since. My medicine is the one thing, the only thing I've found, that helps.

"When Aunt Glenda picked up the phone to make the call to the rehab center, well, I just couldn't let her do that. We had an argument, a very loud, heated argument. Then all of a sudden that kid, that Bubba, was there. He tried to stop us. Aunt Glenda and I were screaming at each other and pushing each other. He got between us and I grabbed that damned twitch from him. I knocked Aunt Glenda on the head with it. Several times. I didn't mean to, but she had the phone in her hand. I didn't mean to kill her, I just wanted her to put the phone down. Then I turned around and there was that damned kid bawling in the entryway.

"I didn't know if Aunt Glenda was dead or alive, and I couldn't come back to see. I . . . well I just couldn't. So I put the kid's cap on the steps and when you showed up at the office later that same day, well, it was easy to get you excited about coming out right away to confront my aunt. I waited up all night, sure the police would call. But they didn't.

"Then, on Tuesday, I couldn't wait any longer. I had to find out. So I came out that morning and parked my car on the old field road—the one just past the county line. You can see both the front and the back of Fairbanks quite clearly from there if you park so your line of sight goes between Hill Henley's barn and house. I waited. And before too long I saw you go in, and then come out and sit on the steps. I knew by the way you kept your head between your legs that you had found Aunt Glenda and that she must be dead."

The man was truly mad.

"Then yesterday you came over. I heard you come in but I knew you were on your way because of the phone message you left. I was home, you see. In the pantry. Well, it's the laundry room now, but when the house was built, it was a pantry. It's quite a sizeable room and Aunt Glenda stored a lot of her old clothes there. You were getting too close and I couldn't let you do that. I didn't want to hurt you, Cat. I didn't. But you see," he said pleadingly, "I have to have my medicine."

I reminded myself that Adam was a skilled actor. There was some semblance of reality in what he was saying, but the actor was there all the same.

"Did you like my costume?" he asked brightly. "I found the hood and cape in the laundry room. Aunt Glenda wore the cape in one of her last movies, *Night Escapade*. Remember that wonderful scene by the cliff? It was glorious!

"But getting back to yesterday. It was chilly when you came. Remember? I had my heavy down parka on. I was ready to go to the office. So I threw on the cape and hood over my parka and used that gag voice synthesizer from the Halloween party last year. . . .

"You have to understand I was afraid Aunt Glenda had told Gran about it, about my medicine," he continued. "I couldn't have that happen. Aunt Glenda went to Gran all the time for advice. I was afraid of Gran, of what she would do, so I started switching her medication to make her more confused. She's so old anyway, no one would think it odd if an old lady started getting confused."

No one except the old lady herself, I thought. Adam underestimated Opal Dupree. It was a crucial mistake. I felt hollow inside as I realized the only question left to be answered was, "where was Bubba's body?"

It was a question that soon answered itself.

"Help!"

I couldn't believe my ears. It was a faint cry. I had to hear it again to believe it, and I did.

"Help me!"

Although it was distant, I knew it was Bubba and now I could hear him crying.

"Bubba!"

The crying stopped, to be replaced with an ominous silence.

"Bubba, it's me, Cat. Are you okay?"

There was a continued silence of such length that I was afraid Bubba had cried his last. Then I heard him again, and as he spoke, I began to turn around, frantically searching for the body that went with the voice.

"Cat, it's dark. I can't get out, I'm stuck."

"Bubba, stay calm. I'm here and I'm going to get you out." Adam or no Adam, I was going to find Bubba and he'd better not try to stop me. "Bubba, listen! I can hear you but I can't see you. Where are you?"

He began to cry again. "I don't know! It's dark. I can't move. There's water. Lots of water."

"Okay, Bubba. I'm coming."

His crying grew louder, as if the possibility of being rescued only made him more afraid that he might not be.

"Bubba, listen closely. I'm coming. You might not always hear me, but I'll call out to you every few minutes, understand?"

The sound of hysterical weeping was his only answer.

I had been looking about the dank, gloomy room as I was shouting, trying to find an opening, a door, a hallway, a place where Bubba might be. He was some distance off, that I could tell, but I didn't know where to begin to look.

Through it all, Adam watched me silently, thumping the switchblade lightly against his thigh. I whirled toward him. I was so angry that I could have killed him myself if Bubba's life hadn't been at stake.

"Where is he?"

Adam sat there stonily, back in his staring mode.

"Please, Adam. Tell me where he is!" I fought to keep myself from physically attacking him. Fat lot of good that would do. "Don't cause another death. He's a boy. A little boy. Think how you felt when your mother died, think of the boy you once were. Please, Adam. Please."

Adam could have been comatose for all the response I was getting. I grabbed the flashlight from him and played the dim light across the room. Only now I could see that it wasn't a room. Not a real room. A cave, I thought. We are in a cave.

On a whim, Jon and I had once gone with friends to a cave on the other side of the river. I don't know if it had an official name, but the locals called it Junk Yard Cave, because you entered it through a tiny hole in the ground in an abandoned junkyard.

I remembered crawling on my belly through the slimy muck, climbing mountains of subterranean rock and being amused by the sightless but harmless bats that inhabited the cave. I also remembered squeezing through almost invisible cracks in the rocks, cracks that led to a maze of passages and tunnels and additional huge rooms. So I adjusted my thoughts and almost immediately saw the slim opening at the end of an ancient set of shelves.

I poked my head and right shoulder into the crevasse and found a fairly tall tunnel, about four feet wide. What I could see of it sloped down and to the right. I knew if I followed it, I would find Bubba.

I turned back to Adam, to the room.

"Bubba's down there," I screamed. "You knew all along. How could you?"

"Because I'm not a killer," he said. "Despite what you might think, I'm not a murderer. I didn't kill Aunt Glenda. Not really. If she had rolled over she wouldn't have choked on all that blood and she would have lived—"

"She was unconscious. How do you expect her to roll over when she's unconscious?" I was furious and had forgotten with whom I was arguing.

"—had to get the kid out of the way. Down here it's up to him. I even threw his cap out for someone, for you, to find and I brought him food once or twice—"

"Once or twice! He's been here almost a week! Damn you, Adam, he could have died. Could still die!"

"And so might you."

That brought me up cold. Adam now stood next to me, next to the crack in the wall.

He sighed, "Cat, I am so very sorry, but I'm sure you can understand that this is something I've just got to do."

I took a slow step back, a slow step back into the creviced entrance to the tunnel. All of a sudden the tunnel seemed very small and confining, and I didn't like to think how dark it would be without a light. When we went to Junk Yard Cave, my friends insisted everyone have three sources of light, just in case.

We'd been inside the cave for over an hour, hiking to a subterranean waterfall where we'd rested and ate lunch. Then we all turned our flashlights off. I have never known such total blackness; not even the rat-infested apartment of my childhood home was that dark. The blackness was so thick you felt as if you could cut it with a knife. It was so thick I couldn't breathe until someone mercifully turned a flashlight back on. The thought of Bubba down here, alone in the dark for close to a week, made my blood boil.

There were other thoughts running through my mind. Thoughts that also made my blood boil. One of them was the idea of Bubba and me starving to death in the tunnel. Another was me going mad from the blackness once the flashlight went out. I wasn't sure I could handle that, or any of this for that matter. How does one come to terms with being killed?

For once, common sense took over and I knew I had to get help. I had to get out of here and call Deputy Giles. Now.

I turned and started to slip past Adam, but the crevasse was too small for the both of us. He put his hand with the knife out and I backed off. I knew what those hands and that knife could do and I didn't want any part of it. If he killed me, Bubba would die, too. There had to be another way.

"I need my medicine," Adam said with the pleading of a child, "and anyone who knows how badly I need it has to be dealt with. Oh, Cat, you must understand the joy I felt when I discovered this room. I found the latch on the dresser by accident.

"When I saw the room, I realized the air down here in the cave is perfect for preservation of this kind. Do you understand? The consistent, cool temperature was perfect for keeping a little of the opium ready for my grandmother to make laudanum all those years later. And then I discovered Col. Sam's notes and recipes, and the poppy field. Every time I visited Aunt Glenda I brought stores of saffron and wine and when the poppies could be harvested I mixed a batch for myself. Can't you understand?"

I understood that I wanted to shriek. I understood that I wanted to lie down and cry myself into a stupor, that I wanted to pound my fists into the wall and to bang my head against the cold, hard ground. But most of all I understood that I wanted to kill Adam Dupree. I wanted to wring his neck until his throat was crushed. I wanted to kick him in the balls, to pull a two-by-four from one of the shelves and bash him senseless. But the total unconditional rage and fury unleashed inside of me was what stopped me and I realized that I wasn't going to kill Adam. Adam was going to kill me.

"If you'd stayed out of it, Cat. If you'd just stayed away."

Boy, ain't that the truth. Hindsight, as they always say. But then Bubba would surely have died and I'd have gone to my own grave knowing I could have done more, and that was not acceptable.

"Okay. Let's think about this, Adam," I said, my voice surprisingly steady. "You don't have to do this, you know. There are other ways. We can work it out."

The blue in his eyes had returned and never been so deep, his smile never more sincere. It was the smile, the eyes, I realized, of an opium addict. It was the smile of a person whose own needs totally superseded the needs of everyone else around him, including their very lives. The powerful cravings had so engulfed his mind and body that all this seemed normal to him. This for him, was a reasonable situation.

"No, Cat, I'm sorry. We can't work it out," he said, and amazingly, I believed he was truly regretful about this fact. "I do have to do this. You know you'd never let me get away with it. But I am sorry. I am. And by the time anyone finds you and the little brat it will be too late. I'll be long gone with all my medicine and no one will ever catch up with me."

Did that mean he wasn't going to kill me right here and now? It was a slim ray of hope, but one I caught just the same.

"No, Cat, I've got to do this, and I've got to do it now. Go. Go find your little friend."

And with that he gave me another shove. I staggered backwards into a jut in the wall just as a heavy wooden door slid across the slim opening. Realizing that the door had cut me off completely from Adam and the outside world, I banged on the door and screamed Adam's name over and over again until I was hoarse.

I stopped only because during a break in my screaming, I heard Bubba crying, and knew I had to get to him before it was too late.

Cat's Horse Tip #17

"Horses distinguish tones and vowel sounds rather than words. Consequently, saying no, go, slow, toe, so, oh, hello, or low in a firm tone will probably produce a halt in your equine friend's forward motion."

30

"Bubba?"

I groaned as I eased myself forward, step by step, fully conscious for the first time of the additional damage sustained to my ribs and left arm. I also was conscious of the fact that it probably didn't matter any more. But for the time being, I was alive. I was ahead of the game.

I was also conscious of the fact that whatever you are most afraid of, chances are you will have to deal with that exact fear at some point in your life. There couldn't be any more fearful situation for me than to be in a blackened cave. Yet here I was. I'd rather walk barefoot through a roomful of snakes. Well, almost.

"Bubba?" I called again. I hadn't heard anything from him for quite a few minutes. I flashed the light backward. I didn't think I'd missed any turnoffs. Nope. Hadn't. I turned the light once more dead ahead.

Carefully, cautiously, I walked down the descending slope of the tunnel. Here, while still dry, it was considerably damper than at the beginning of the passage. It was hard not to notice I was getting cold. Cave temperatures hover around fifty-five degrees. Add to that the fact I was soaking wet from the rain, badly scraped from my encounter with the bricks on the kitchen floor and now covered in mud. I longed for a hot shower and almost lost control of my battered emotions when it hit me that I might not get one. Ever.

Ahead was a sharp turn to the left that opened on to a room similar to the one barred to me by the wooden door. I stopped at the wide entrance. The ceiling was lower here, barely six feet in most places. In the gloomy light, I could make out an old picnic table, much longer and taller than those seen today. There were several old washtubs, some scraps of musty material that had once been rags, and bits of broken glass. I guessed that this was where Col. Sam had mixed his special brand of laudanum. At the far end were two openings.

"Bubba?"

Silence.

"Bubba can you hear me?"

"Cat, I'm here!" Although still muffled, Bubba's voice sounded closer. Quite close, in fact.

"Where, Bubba?"

"I don't know!" He started crying again.

"Bubba, think. Tell me what's around you. What can you see?"

"Can't see nothing," he hollered between crying spells. "It's pitch black and there's water. All around there's water. It's up past my knees."

Shit.

"Okay, Bubba, hang tight. I'm coming."

First, I tried the passage on the right. It was a cramped, level path, but I turned back when it took a sharp upward swing and narrowed to an impenetrable slit. Besides, Bubba had said there was water. To me that meant I should be descending, not ascending.

Going back, I noticed that the flashlight was dimmer than when I started out, but so far it was holding its own. Back in the room, I entered the second passage. My shoulder felt as if it was going to fall off. Actually, as much as it hurt, I thought it would be an improvement if it did. I had to breathe in short, tight breaths to avoid the Exacto knives that were twisting around my ribs.

The second path also began fairly level. But before too long it began a sharp downward turn.

"Bubba?"

"Yeah! Cat?"

I was getting close. I slipped as the damp ground turned to water and landed butt first with a thump and a splash. The jar of the fall hurt my arm and ribs so badly that my abdominal muscles began pushing up the remains of Verna Mae's cooking. After, I realized I had instinctively kept my right arm raised— so the flashlight wouldn't get wet. I take back what I said earlier. I'd *crawl* through a room full of snakes before choosing to be down here without a light.

"Cat? I can see you. I can see your light!"

I stood up in six inches of muddy water and waved the light around. The passage grew wider here and continued ahead for another twenty feet or so, where it stopped abruptly, the walls meeting not a floor, but a large pool of water that covered most of the chamber, including where I now sat.

I saw movement to my left and pointed the light in that direction. My heart stopped. A round, slime-covered shape that I assumed was Bubba was tied by his hands to a long chain that led to a large metal ring set about seven feet up. Around his wrists were tight, padded cuffs, similar to those used on training farms to hobble the front legs of horses. The water was indeed up past his knees.

I splashed over to Bubba as quickly as I could and enveloped him with my good arm. We both cried with relief, the water swirling gently around us.

"Cat," he finally gulped, "I'm sorry I smell so bad."

I told him truthfully that I hadn't noticed.

"I couldn't help it none. I had to go and my hands were all bound up, so I . . . well, I peed all over myself. And number two, too."

The confession brought on another round of tears. I felt a renewed spurt of anger against Adam. For Bubba to be humiliated so was unthinkable. I wished Adam could be tied down here for a week. See how he felt after peeing all over himself. On second thought, where Adam was concerned, a week wasn't long enough.

Bubba eventually rallied with a big sigh and a final round of snuffles. "What happened to your arm?"

"I, ah, fell," I said. I didn't want to upset Bubba more by telling him the truth.

"I bet that sorry bastard Adam had something to do with it, din't he?" When he realized I wasn't going to answer that one, he asked, "You think you can get us out?"

"I don't know," I replied. "But I'm sure going to try. First, we've got to get you untied from here."

On closer inspection, I realized Bubba *was* bound by a set

of horse hobbles, two sets actually, as his ankles were also bound. I wondered, briefly, if the hobbles were missing from my barn or Hill's. Neither, I guessed. I only had one set, and no one could pull anything from Hill's barn with his dogs around. Both of these sets had been modified by removing the six inches or so of chain between the two padded nylon cuffs, and replacing that with one heavy link.

The result was that Bubba's hands and legs were so closely bound as to render them totally useless. The heavy link between his hands was attached to a long chain of equal weight that led to the ring in the upper wall. At least the chain was long enough to let Bubba move around a little, sit down, and keep his arms moving,

"I think the best way is to try to get the cuffs off. It doesn't look like that chain is going to cooperate," I said.

"They're awful tight," he replied.

I agreed. They were. There were small padlocks on each buckle, but nothing I did released the lock.

"Bubba, listen. Back up the hill there is a room with a table and a washtub. Do you remember it?"

He shook his head as huge tears dripped from his eyes. "All's I remember is waking up here."

"Well, there's some broken glass there. I'm going to go to that room, get the glass and come right back. Do you understand? I'm coming right back."

Bubba's body was shaking with cold and fear, but he nodded that he understood. I sloshed through the cold water and up the incline, picked up as many of the larger glass pieces as I could, and sloshed my way back.

Bubba was still shaking when I returned; I was afraid he was going into shock.

"Deep breaths, Bubba, deep breaths." It felt cold enough to hang meat in here. Bubba must be freezing, starving, exhausted and who knew what else. I prayed that after all he'd been through his body wouldn't let him down now. He had to make it. I gritted my teeth. He would make it.

I have no idea how long it took. It could have been ten minutes or it could have been an hour. My fingers were bloodied with cuts, but I was able to cut through the heavy fleece and nylon to free Bubba's hands. Together we splashed and hopped to dry ground where I immediately went to work on the hobbles around his legs. Thank goodness that didn't take nearly as long. Weakened by the continual exposure to water, the material cut more easily.

As soon as he was free of all restraints, I started Bubba swinging his arms. First, one by one, then together. Back and forth, up and down, around and around. I was hoping the movement would bring some warmth into his body and feeling into his fingers.

I didn't know much about human first aid, but I was a regular pro when it came to equine medical emergencies. When horses were stiff and cold, you wanted to keep them moving. The principles couldn't be all that different, I thought. Bubba was just a small horse in a human body.

When the numbness was history and he protested that he could swing no more, we both collapsed on the floor. Eventually, I knew, we'd have to figure a way out. But for now this was enough. I positioned Bubba so he was lying with his head lower than his feet, and hoped the blood would rush to his brain. I also pulled every stitch of his wet lower clothing from him, shoes, socks, jeans, underwear, and it said a lot for Bubba's physical state that he didn't protest.

Although Agnes's new trench coat that I had so painfully draped over my shoulders was now mostly wet, there were still a few dry spots that I used to wipe the worst of the damp off Bubba before I covered him with it. Then, with a warning to Bubba, I turned the flashlight off and the darkness descended.

I waited for the panic to arrive, for the hyperventilating to begin, for the sheer terror to come. But although I waited, nothing happened. I'd been through so much my body was too busy to be frightened. My body had its hands full just trying to stay alive.

After an eon, I said, "Hey Bubba, you awake?"

He groaned in answer.

I was, meanwhile, asking myself the same question and getting a very painful answer that I knew meant yes. In addition to everything else, my fingers now throbbed from all the glass cuts. Lord, I thought, when can I give up? Sooner or later, I need to just lie down and die. But not yet. Not just yet. First, I had to get Bubba out.

Somehow, my body continued to function. My heart pumped great amounts of blood to my head and injured arm. My fingers bled freely. My rib cage felt as if it had been kicked by a mule. I wanted nothing more than to stop, to stay right where I was and rest. Let the angels come and get me. But, I thought, getting out of here was simply a case of mind over matter. I could do this. Had to. Bubba was counting on me.

Finally, Bubba groaned, rolled over, sat up and said in a clear, sensible voice, "Okay, how the hell do we get out of here?"

It was a valid question and unfortunately it was one I wasn't sure there was an answer to. The way I came in was out. Chances were slim to none that someone would hear us banging around way down here. I hadn't seen any additional passages, other than the one dead end I'd tried. I'd been watching closely, so I was pretty sure I hadn't missed anything. That left the pool of water, which was straight ahead.

I thought hard. If I was right, the basement was directly under the den, which meant the room behind the dresser was under the back porch. I'd zig-zagged a few times to get where I was, but by my reckoning the zigs and zags had all evened out and the tunnel was headed directly behind the house. And if you went far enough, what was directly behind Fairbanks? The Cumberland River. Then it dawned on me. This must be the tunnel Col. Sam's slaves used to bring in the smuggled goods. This was why Adam had shown me the river from above. Deep down, he wanted me to find a way out. I wasn't sure how I felt about that, except I really hoped he wasn't waiting with a meat cleaver if I made it that far.

"Bubba, when you first got here, was the water this deep?"

"No way. There warn't any water here."

"None?"

"Dry as an old cob of corn."

"So when did you notice it was starting to get wet?"

"I'm not sure. That prick Adam come down a couple times and give me a sandwich and a jug of water. I was real hungry but the stuff he gave me musta had drugs or something in it 'cause after I ate it I got real sleepy. That chain was long enough so's I could move around some, and sit down. I 'member sitting against the wall and I musta' fell asleep. When I done woke up there was water and there was fish nibbling at me."

"Fish?"

"Well, I think it was fish. Couldn't see 'em none. But I felt things swimming 'round my legs. They din't bite me or nothing but I could tell they was there."

Fish. Now that was interesting.

"Bubba, do you think the fish are still there?"

He said he thought they probably were. I felt around for the flashlight and went to take a look. I couldn't see anything by the edge of the water, so I waded deeper into the underground pond—and deeper and deeper until I was waist deep and almost to the far wall. I shone the light as far as I could down into the water. And then I saw them. Blessed little things they were. I don't fish, so I don't know a whole lot about them. I didn't even know what kind of fish these were, except I knew they were the right kind. I knew they were the right kind because they had eyes.

"Okay, I've got a plan," I told Bubba after I'd splashed back over to him. I was so excited I could hardly breathe. Not that I could breathe all that well to begin with anyway, but now I was having some real trouble. "Those fish are from the Cumberland River. I know this because cave fish don't have eyes. They don't need them in the dark so they don't have them." I'd learned this interesting tidbit during my foray into Junk Yard Cave. "Can you believe it, Bubba, these fish have eyes!"

My theory was that as it had rained almost constantly over the past few days, the water level in the Cumberland had risen enough to flood the outside entrance of the tunnel, the entrance that opened to the river bank. The fact that there were dams on the river to control flooding made me believe that we were very close to the entrance. If the water level in the river rose too much, someone would turn a crank somewhere and drop the level back down.

"So we've got to be close to the outside," I finished.

"You mean we're supposed to swim outta here through that pond?" asked Bubba.

"Well, not exactly. I thought I'd leave you the flashlight, then I'd swim out and call Deputy Giles and we'd come back and get you."

"Nooooo," wailed Bubba. "No, don't leave me. Anything but that. Please, please." He broke into hysterical sobbing and latched on to me tighter than a horsefly on a colt.

"Do you have any better ideas?" I asked after he had settled down.

"If you go, I'm going with you."

I considered that. If I went alone, there was a sizable chance that I'd drown. Even if I were healthy the chances were very slim that I'd make it. If I drowned, then Bubba would surely die holed up in here, so why shouldn't he drown right along with me? Then, of course, there was the very remote possibility that we'd both find our way out.

"All right," I agreed. "I'm not going to lie to you and say it's not dangerous, so you have to make up your own mind. If you go, you can't panic half way there and decide to turn back. It's all or nothing. Do or die."

He looked at me for the first time adult to adult. "I'm in."

In a way, I wished I had kept my mouth shut and forbidden him to go. He was so young. Too young. But I could feel his determination as he straightened his shoulders and I realized he had just made a man's decision. From here on out, I'd treat him as a man.

We both waded to the center of the dark, cold pond, shining the fading light and feeling with our feet for an opening, however small. But after precious minutes of searching, we found nothing.

"Let's feel around the walls," said Bubba. He went left, and I right. At the far corner I felt a small gap with my foot. I probed deeper and felt no resistance.

"I found it!" I called. The opening was at the base of the floor where it met the wall. I could tell the opening was narrow, not more than three feet wide. But it sloped down gradually, and was just wide enough for Col. Sam's boxes of supplies . . . and for us.

"Let's do it this way," Bubba said. "Let me go first. Even though I'm kind of tubby I'm still smaller than you are. You grab my ankle with your good arm. Then you kick hard with your legs. They're strong from riding and I'll pull with my arms. They're strong from batting things around, and you only got the one arm. We'll go faster that way. But . . . I think . . . you need to . . . you know, get rid of some of them clothes you got on or you'll drag us both down."

And someone had said Bubba wasn't bright.

Bubba helped me get rid of boots, socks, and sweats. The top part was complicated because of all the bandages, so we left it alone.

Just in case, Bubba, wearing only his T-shirt, and I, clad only in panties, tank top, and bandages, joined hands and said a prayer. I don't recall now exactly what it was that we prayed for, but it had something to do with ensuring our safety and, barring that, us being instantly teleported to heaven. That last part was

Bubba's. We agreed to keep our eyes open and to turn back if we hadn't gotten out by the time we counted to fifty.

It was tough. But after wishing each other good luck, we stood near the hole, took three long, slow, deep breaths. And then we dived.

Cat's Horse Tip #18

"The horse's hoof corresponds to the middle finger of a human."

31

I COUNTED. ONE ONE THOUSAND, TWO one thousand. . . .

The water was shockingly cold, and foul tasting, and as darkly black as ink. I pushed off as hard as I could with my feet and we were on our way.

Fifteen one thousand, sixteen one thousand. . . .

Bubba was heading toward a lighter patch of water a short distance ahead. I desperately hoped that patch meant the outside world was near. We swam into the light and Bubba started up.

Twenty-nine one thousand, thirty one thousand. . . .

My lungs were beginning to burn, my legs to ache. We were losing speed. Ahead, Bubba floundered and kicked his ankle free of my hand. I looked up in sheer terror as Bubba became tangled in a large clump of fresh water seaweed. My heart constricted as the tendrils clung tighter and tighter to him.

Forty-three one thousand, forty-four one thousand. . . .

Please, God, please, please, please.

As my injured left arm was still wrapped close to my body, I started an upward sidestroke using my other arm. Bubba had stirred up all sorts of underwater sludge, and I couldn't see. Somehow I bypassed the seaweed and hooked Bubba under the armpit as I passed. We went about a foot and jerked to a stop. I wanted to scream, to hyperventilate. I so wanted, needed, air.

Bubba began thrashing more violently. The kid was terrified and so, I admit, was I. I grabbed his face and pulled it close to mine, shaking his face until he opened his eyes and looked at me. I mouthed the word "relax" to him several times. Relax. It was the last thing I could will my own body to do, but Bubba had to relax if he were to survive. Priceless seconds passed as Bubba slowly loosened his body.

Fifty-two one thousand, fifty-three one thousand. . . .

Frantically, I tore the offending weeds free of his body. Bubba helped me with the last, but as we once again began our ascent Bubba began to choke. Seconds. Fractions of seconds. I knew that's all we had.

I grabbed a fistful of his hair and forced my exhausted legs to kick for all they were worth. They did and before I knew it, our heads broke free of the water. I allowed myself two wonderful, exhilarating, gasping lungfuls of precious air before checking my surroundings. There was an idle thought in the back of my mind that Adam would be waiting for us on the bank of the river. I quickly scanned the gray shoreline. If he was there, he was well hidden.

We were not far from the riverbank. Maybe fifteen feet or so. But Bubba had stopped choking before we surfaced and now, as far as I could tell, was not breathing at all. I kicked for all I was worth and with a final powerful surge, landed us both half in and half out of the river along a slew of muddy rocks.

Bubba's face was colorless, his lips blue. He was unconscious, his eyes partially rolled back. Water streamed from his nose and mouth. Come on Bubba, I thought. We've come this far. Don't leave me now.

I kicked myself out of the water and slapped his face. Hard. His eyelids fluttered faintly. Thank you God. I had no breath for myself, much less him, so CPR was out. I couldn't recall if I knew how to do it anyway and the thought that it required two hands crossed my mind. I slapped the other side of his face. Harder. He took one ragged breath, then a century later, another.

"Wake up, Bubba. Come on, wake up!" I cried. His hands still floated in the icy water, his wrists mottled a swollen red and blue from his vain attempts to free himself from the hobbles. Oh, Bubba.

I slapped him again. His head rolled sideways, but his eyes opened. He took another ragged breath.

"Come on, Bubba, breathe, dammit, breathe."

I pulled him further out of the water and heaved him onto his side. Then with all the strength I could muster, I punched him in the stomach.

Immediately he heaved up a huge stream of mud-colored water. And he began to breathe. I lay beside him, exhausted, tears streaming down my face, watching the rise and fall of his chest. I had reached my limit. There was nothing more I could do without killing myself in the process. Bubba would live or die. It was up to him—and the man upstairs.

I don't know how long we lay there, although I think it must have been half an hour or more. When we first broke the surface, there was a gloomy light; it was barely dawn. But the day gradually got brighter, in spite of the heavy gray clouds that blanketed the sky. Morning. I'd been in the cave all night and it was morning.

Eventually Bubba began to groan and he heaved up another massive load of water.

I sat up and put my hand on his chest. "Bubba?"

He moaned yet again and threw up a third time; he must have swallowed half the river. Finally Bubba raised his head and looked fuzzily at me.

"That Adam is such an asshole," he said.

"Of course, I never should have opened the door last night," I said to the deputy. "I should have checked to see who it was. But I really thought—no I knew—it was Jon. Shows you how much I know."

Jon, Sally Blue, Agnes, and Deputy Giles had found us as we straggled up the muddy, rocky riverbank behind the Henley place. The deputy immediately called for assistance and also called Carole to accompany Bubba to Vanderbilt Children's Hospital in the ambulance. Hill Henley, of course, was nowhere to be found.

It turned out that Agnes had called Jon just after I did and it had taken him forever to get her off the phone. He could not convince her not to drive down to take care of me, and she was in her car and headed to the stables minutes after she hung up. She'd told Jon she knew I was in trouble because Ira, the shyest and most reticent of her deceased husbands, had told her so in a dream. Guess I owe Ira a thank you.

Jon was upset that he hadn't arrived in time to stop Adam, but in actuality, if he had, we never would have found the secret room—or Bubba. Funny the way life works out sometimes. When I think about it too much it scares me.

When Jon finally arrived at my house, only to find Hank and me missing, he called the deputy, the Carsons, and Darcy. Then, when Hank showed up an hour later dragging the twine leash, he called everyone else he could think of.

The police and my friends and neighbors had searched for me all night. I have to admit that it gives me a little thrill to think of that hunky Keith Carson out searching for little ol' me at two in the morning. I know. It's shameful how twisted I am when it comes to that man.

Sally Blue was the one who eventually gave the searchers a clue. She burst out of her stall when Jon left to do the morning feed and jumped two fences to run to the field above the river where Bubba and I lay. Agnes insisted Sally was onto something and even Jon's curiosity was aroused when Sally wouldn't budge from her spot. Nor would she quit pawing or looking toward the river. Jon had just wrapped a lead rope around Sally's neck when we came straggling up the bank.

"Fairbanks was the first place we checked," said the deputy. "We hunted from top to bottom and never found one sign of either of you."

We were now driving very fast up River Road toward Ashland City. One look at me, and the deputy had wrapped me in a blanket, started the sirens and headed toward the medical center. I didn't argue with him because I'll admit I have never felt worse. Adam had yet to be found.

"We're checking the airlines, the bus schedules, car rentals. My guess is he's driving back to California. Back to his own stomping grounds. We've put out a bulletin for the car. If he's driving it, someone will spot him."

I wasn't paying attention for I had remembered a horrible thing.

"Stop," I said. "We've got to turn around."

The deputy looked at me as if I were nuts. We were flying up the curvy hill that eventually drops motorists back to the river and into the county seat. There was no place to turn around, even if he wanted to.

"Please, Deputy, we've got to turn around."

He tightened his grip on the wheel in reply, but I reached over and pulled imploringly at his sleeve.

"Martin, please. Stop the car. Turn around. Now."

"What the hell for?"

"I just remembered that I talked to Opal before Adam. . . . Anyway, now I understand what she meant."

"I don't care what she meant," he said gruffly. "I'll talk to her later. Right now you need to see a doctor and the closest one is at the medical center."

"Deputy, Opal Dupree will commit suicide, if she hasn't already. I guarantee it. We just passed the nursing home. Please turn around."

During our last conversation, Opal had said she "chose not to handle any more of this trouble." Not "can't" but "chose" not to. Chose meant she had a choice. She also said she wasn't strong anymore.

At the time I took it to be a reflection on her arthritis. Now I knew she meant mentally. Opal meant she no longer had the mental fortitude to cover up the family demons. The only way out, for her, was suicide. That there'd be another scandal didn't concern her. She wouldn't be around to deal with it.

I told the deputy what was whizzing through my mind. He considered it briefly, then stopped the car at the driveway to the Riverview Restaurant.

As he headed the car in the opposite direction, he called ahead to the nursing home and alerted them to the potential problem. When he hung up, he gave me that half grin that I was coming to know so well, "Cat, you know I like you and all," he said, the grin still on his face. "I even introduced you to my brother. You're smart, and you've been a big help to me and I appreciate that." He accelerated quickly up the big hill. "But I gotta say I'm getting awful tired of you being right every single dad-burned time."

Martin insisted I stay in the car while he went in, using my disheveled state and sheer exhaustion as excuses. And very good excuses they were, too. I waited until he entered the building, then followed him inside. We found Opal in bed staring thoughtfully at the portrait of Col. Sam, a surprisingly large stockpile of pills on her bedside tray, while a nurse measured her vital signs.

"Mrs. Dupree has only been swallowing half her meds," the nurse said as she made a notation in Opal's chart. "We found that pile of pills rolled up in a sock in her drawer. Luckily, she hadn't yet begun to take them."

"I wanted to see Adam one more time," Opal said. "He's a good boy at heart, but he changed. The drugs changed him. When I realized all he'd done, I knew I couldn't go on. It's all too, too much."

And with that, a single tear rolled down her cheek.

While the medical professionals were seeing to Opal, I sat in the familiar gold plastic chair and quietly told the deputy that when we had talked the night before, Opal told me she felt she had spent her entire life covering up the doings of family members. Her grandfather, Col. Sam, had sexually abused his daughter—the same daughter who grew up to be Opal's mother, Alice the younger. It started when Alice was a young girl and continued until Alice had the courage to break away and go to Nashville.

By then the many years of laudanum use had turned the old man into a raving lunatic and Alice was close to thirty. Alice tried to start a new life in Nashville. She found a teaching job. She even fell in love. But the man was unsuitable—a gambler, a hustler. She was soon expecting a child, but before she could tell her lover, he was killed in a barroom brawl. The resulting child was Opal.

Opal grew up in the 1930s with the stigma of being an illegitimate child. Due to the dual problems of Opal's questionable parentage, and the family's perception of Alice's desertion of her father, Alice was shunned.

When Opal was ten, poor Alice died of pneumonia. Opal was farmed out to distant cousins, an elderly couple from the Giles clan who often helped out at the big Henley place: Fairbanks. There, in innocent childhood wanderings, Opal first discovered the legendary "gopher hole."

Opal married young, bore her two daughters, was tragically widowed, and scrambled to make a better life for her young family. Opal felt they were blessed when Hollywood showed an initial interest in her daughters and it was a relief to leave Tennessee and all the problems behind. But this savvy woman soon realized that the plush roles, the starring vehicles that paid real money, were as politically assigned as were staff at the White House.

Opal didn't have much clout at the time, but she did have access to the gopher hole and she made liberal use of its contents. Even though the gopher hole eventually gave Opal and her daughters what they thought they desired, what lay ahead was less than a blessing. Drunken orgies. Forbidden affairs. Death. When Adam was born to Amie, starting once again the cycle of illegitimacy, Opal deftly covered up the name of the father. The family curse would continue.

"I understand how Opal feels," I said. "She'd reached her breaking point. I was at my own breaking point in the cave last night, and again on the riverbank this morning. Opal had gotten to where she couldn't continue for one more second with all that had happened. All her life, by the very circumstances of her birth, Opal felt obligated to make things right. But she couldn't fix Glenda's death or Bubba's disappearance."

"Cat."

Opal beckoned to me from her bed. I gave a questioning look at the doctor and he nodded.

"I'm glad you found that boy, the Henley boy."

"I'm glad, too, Miss Opal."

"You understand that both my girls are gone and that Adam is my only grandchild, my only living descendant," she looked at me and I tried unsuccessfully to give her a smile. "I had to protect him, but then I talked to you. When I realized what you'd gone through for that boy—that Bubba—what you'd sacrificed, how hurt you'd been, I realized that boy, too, was someone's grandson. He couldn't be as worthless as he seemed, even though his father leaves a lot to be desired. So I had to help him in the only way that I could."

"But then I got so tired. I couldn't keep any of it secret any longer. I was just too worn out. So I decided to go home, to go to the Lord. Only I guess," she said with a glance at the doctor, "the Lord isn't quite ready for me yet.

"I know Adam was switching my pills. It took me a while before I figured it out, but I did. Adam almost killed me, but I've forgiven him. He's a troubled boy and I hope you can find it in your heart to forgive him, too."

I dug around in what was left of my heart. Nope, couldn't seem to find any forgiveness anywhere in there yet. Maybe someday. Or not.

Cat's Horse Tip #19

"Horses use their entire body to communicate with us. Our job is to understand the language."

32

"I DON'T UNDERSTAND," SAID BUBBA TEN days later.

I was finally out of the hospital, with strict instructions to stay in bed for another week. My upper arm had been reset, my ribs still burned when I took a deep breath, and the cuts on my fingers had been stitched.

Bubba was riding slowly around the arena on Sally Blue. I sat in a corner in a high canvas chaise watching them, thoroughly enjoying the thought that my doctor wouldn't approve if he knew what I was doing.

"You don't get what?" I asked. By the time Deputy Giles had wrapped everything up, Adam had been apprehended in Oklahoma City, and Hill had surfaced, drunk, of course. Bubba spent three wonderful days at Vanderbilt Children's Hospital and had only recently stopped talking about the great playroom they have. I spent a week at the Cheatham Medical Center, only because the deputy and Doc Williams realized that as soon as they released me, I'd be doing things I shouldn't. So they kept me a few days longer than necessary. At least that's my theory.

Bubba was spending a lot of time at the Carson home and seemed to have great respect for Keith. Or maybe it was Keith's many guitars. I was helping out with Bubba as much as I could, but I knew we'd be heading out for the summer show season soon, and I didn't think it would be good for Bubba to get too dependent.

In my lap lay the entry forms for half a dozen horse shows. Darcy had decided to go for it and I was glad. She was a tough competitor and we were shooting for at least one national championship for her in July.

Bubba reined Sally in from the rail and walked her over the raised boards Jon had nailed together to serve as a bridge obstacle in preparation for for trail classes.

"What I don't understand is why Adam got so crazy," he said. "I mean, you should have heard him, wandering 'round that big old cave, mumbling to hisself. Sometimes he'd think I was his dead Aunt Glenda and he'd start screaming at me. Then he'd bring me something to eat, say he was so sorry, and run outta there like a turpentined cat. It was weird, you know?"

I debated as to what I should say. Bubba had only just started talking about his ordeal. It was obvious the memories bothered him greatly. I decided to counter with a question.

"Bubba, if you understand that Adam wasn't in his right mind, what specifically is it that you don't understand? Ask me what you really want to know."

I prayed it was a question I could answer. There were some things I didn't want to explain to him and others that I couldn't, because I didn't understand them myself. I thought of Adam killing Glenda, holding Bubba hostage in that miserable cave, switching his grandmother's medication, bashing the deputy and me, then kidnapping me and leaving me to die with Bubba in the thick darkness, all so he could have his fix. Then I stopped thinking about it because it made me too angry. I wasn't ready to deal with it yet.

"So what do you want to know?" I asked again.

He rode over to me, and Sally rubbed her nose gently against my good arm. Bubba still had a beaten look about him and his eyes were brimming with worry.

"Well, Miss Carole said Adam probably had strange experiences when he was a kid."

I said I thought he probably had. It didn't sound as if Adam had had the most stable of childhoods out there in Hollywood. And instability can lead to drug use, I've been told. So can mental illness and hereditary factors. Then there are those people who don't need a reason. I believed Adam, though, when he said he started using to help manage his back pain.

"So Adam had problems to begin with and the drugs made it worse?" Bubba asked.

I said that the drugs had certainly helped things along. "But," I continued, "weird experiences or an unhappy childhood isn't enough to cause that sort of behavior on its own. A person has to be susceptible to start with, and have extraordinary conditions moving things along, such as the drugs. Some drugs, like the ones Adam was taking, are highly addictive. Once his body began to crave drugs he was helpless. Then there's the issue of free will. Adam had to choose to hurt people for his own gain. Adam made a very selfish choice: to hurt people so he could satisfy his need for drugs. It's not a choice that most people, even people who use drugs every day, would make."

I am not the one to explain all this, I thought with a sigh.

I'm not a child psychologist, which is what Bubba needed.

Bubba continued looking troubled.

"But Cat, I've had a weird childhood. You know, Ma running off and my dad being like he is. And there's lots of other stuff you don't know about neither."

Oh, I have no doubt, I thought.

"So—"

Bubba climbed off Sally and sat on a chair next to me.

"So I think I'm susceptible to being crazy," he blurted. "Like Adam was."

He looked up at me with huge tears in his eyes. "I cry a lot. When I think about stuff. Like that stuff in the cave, and—" He stopped to wipe away his tears. Sally turned her head and snorted gently into Bubba's neck. Bubba gave a wan smile and patted her cheek. "—and other stuff. I think 'bout lots of weird stuff. Sometimes I think my brain's not hooked up right. You understand?"

I did understand. So well that I thought I might burst out crying any minute. It hadn't taken much to get me going the past few days either.

"So I'm afraid I'm going to go crazy, too," he said. "Maybe not now, but someday. Sometimes when I start crying I think I'll never be able to stop. So what I want to know is, is there any medicine or anything they can give you to, you know, stop me from crying?"

"Yes, of course there is, Bubba. There's medicine for that. But I don't think you need any of it."

"How come?" he snuffled. He wasn't sure whether to believe me or not.

"Well," I said. "Remember when we were in the cave and we were trying to find a way out?"

"Yeah, I remember."

"Do you remember what you did?"

"Oh, yeah," he said with disgust, "I nearly kilt both of us. We got out into the river and the light hurt my eyes so bad I closed them and swum us right into a pile of weeds."

"No, Bubba! No. You had no control over your eyes. You'd been in a dark cave for a week. Your eyes had gotten used to the darkness so you did what you had to do. And besides, it was hard even for me to see. I didn't know the weeds were there. Anyone would have swum straight into them. What you did was this: you came up with the plan to get us out. And it was a great plan, because it worked. You swam out of there first. You led us out. Bubba, you got us out of there."

And it was true. With only the one arm, I never would have made out it by myself.

He still looked doubtful.

"So how come I'm still crying all the time?"

I had to think about that one for a minute.

"Well, okay," I said, "when we were finally out of the river and you were breathing again and we knew we were going to be okay, do you remember what you did?"

"Um, nothing, I just lay there."

"Exactly, you just lay there because you didn't need to do anything. Everything there was to do was done. You were out. You were safe. When you didn't need to do anything, you stopped. And it's the same idea here. You'll cry for a while because you need to. Then when you no longer need to cry, you'll stop."

I hope.

"So, the crying is like something I gotta do and when I don't gotta do it anymore, I'll just stop?"

"I think so. Bubba, don't worry about the crying, It's your body's way of healing. You need to do it. I think you'd be crazy if you didn't cry. So let yourself go. Cry all you want. And I'll tell you something else. If you need a place to cry, there isn't a better place in the world than Sally's stall. She's a good crying partner. I know that from experience."

Sally nudged Bubba again with her nose.

"See? You feel free anytime you want to come over and spend some time with Sally."

"Really?"

"Really."

Bubba looked relieved. He climbed back on Sally and rode to the end of the arena, talking to the wise, gentle horse all the way. I couldn't hear what he was saying, but it didn't matter. Sally could. And I couldn't think of a better way for Bubba to heal, or me for that matter, than from the quiet, comforting presence of a horse.

In fact, I felt Hillbilly Bob was in need of some company right then. So I climbed down from my chair and headed for his stall.

EPILOGUE

I AM HAPPY TO REPORT THAT, so far, Adam Dupree remains in jail and is awaiting trial. Now that Opal is off the mind-numbing drugs and is once again mentally strong, she has hired Adam the best criminal defense team in the country. She is still operating on the assumption that while she can't help the dead, she *can* try to save the living.

Deputy Giles received a commendation from Sheriff Big Jim Burns. It was a formal ceremony held last month on the courthouse lawn. If you think it was a big gesture on the sheriff's part, think again. The sheriff made sure all the media turned out and he twisted everything to look as if the deputy was just carrying out the sheriff's orders. Deputy Giles gave the medal to his mama and then spent a week fishing on the Kentucky side of Land Between the Lakes.

Speaking of the deputy, his brother Brent and I have gotten together for a meal or two. And Brent was right; he does make great lasagna. I enjoy his company very much, but we're taking things slow. I believe that good things come to those who wait. If we still like each other after the coming show season, then I think it's a relationship that just might stick. It would be nice to have a man like him in my life, but time will tell.

To my great disappointment, Carole Carson decided not to compete this year. About the same time the decision was made a brand new cabin cruiser showed up in their driveway and Keith announced that they planned to spend their free days this summer on the river.

My guess is that with Keith's heavy touring schedule they take the thing out three times max. I like Carole very much as a neighbor and friend but know, that despite her full life, something is missing.

Robert Griggs also decided not to compete, and resigned his position as a nurse in Vanderbilt's pathology department. Last I heard he was volunteering at a therapeutic riding center in Franklin.

Other than a real and ongoing concern for the stability of my body, Jon Gardner has withheld comment on the entire affair. We never did have that little talk. As the boss, I know it is up to me to initiate the conversation and give him my thanks and apologies, all the while begging forgiveness for leaving him in the lurch and endangering his livelihood. But you know how I am. I don't like big, messy, emotional scenes. Jon continues as my assistant, but I know until the day comes when we have that big discussion, we won't be the best team we can be.

Hill Henley went on a major bender when he realized Glenda had died without paying him for the horse. But the episode scared him enough to begin rehab at Cumberland Heights a good rehab center just up the road from us. He says he wants to be a better father to Bubba, but I don't think he knows how. Still, it's a good beginning and I know Bubba is worth everything Hill does to make himself a better parent. I'm keeping my fingers crossed.

Despite Hill's wish that Bubba stick close to home, between time at Carole's, and with us out at the barn, he isn't home much. Jon and I put Bubba to work cleaning tack or mucking stalls whenever we can. Most of the time, however, Bubba can be found sitting quietly crooning to Sally in her stall. I think it's time well spent for both of them, so for the most part, I leave them alone.

Since the "incident," as I tend to call it, Darcy has taken over the daily training of Peter's Pride and she's doing such a great job that it scares me. Their first show of the season is coming up in several weeks and I feel that this time around, Darcy's mind is eager and focused. I have no doubt they will beat the pants off all the competition.

Agnes finally got her pom-poms, albeit too late to stage a rally at the sheriff's office. But she was able to put them to good use at Sally Blue's first competition under saddle last Sunday. I'm not sure whether the pom-poms had any influence on the judge, but Sally won first place and Agnes is now in the process of developing an official Sally Blue web site, Facebook page, and fan club.

As for Sally, maybe she really is psychic. I thought about all the "clues" she gave us. Her obsession with pawing and digging into the ground could have symbolized the cave. The blowing of bubbles in her water might have indicated the wetness of the underground cavern. She often looked toward Fairbanks, and there was the riding session when she whirled toward the old mansion every time she came to the gate. And, Sally did find

Glenda's notebook. It probably was all coincidence, but I love her anyway.

Someone else I love, Hank, continues to chew sticks and howl at the moon. However, he just attended his first horse show and has found a new calling as official stable greeter. He is looking forward to a long and illustrious career.

As for me, well, against all advice, two weeks after my release from the Cheatham Medical Center I took an inaugural ride on Hillbilly Bob. Doc Williams, Bob's owner and orthopedic genius, has me undergoing daily whirlpool sessions along with an entire assortment of state-of-the-art physical therapy. The end result is that after six weeks, I'm almost back up to snuff. I try not to think about all that has happened. But it's hard not to look at Fairbanks without it all rushing back. We'll be heading out for the summer show season soon. I think the time away will be good for all of us. And as Opal would say, "time heals the deepest of wounds."

I think we'll be gone a very long time.

THE END

CAT'S SCRUMPTIOUS HOT CHOCOLATE

Ingredients
1 large mug milk*
1 single serving of your favorite hot chocolate mix
1/2 tsp. vanilla extract
1 large dollop whipped cream*
1 tbsp. chocolate sprinkles

Directions
Heat milk in a large mug so it is hot, but not boiling (Cat uses the microwave)
Add vanilla and hot chocolate mix
Stir
Add whipped cream
Top with chocolate sprinkles
Enjoy!

Depending on the circumstances, Cat may add a generous measure of coffee-flavored brandy—for medicinal purposes only, of course.

*Cat uses 2-percent milk and real whipped cream, but those whose metabolisms aren't as efficient as Cat's may substitute nonfat ingredients. For a creamier taste, try soymilk.

ACKNOWLEDGEMENTS

Many people nurtured Cat and me along the path of publication. While the list is too long to mention everyone, I thank each of you. You know who you are. Several book industry professionals went above and beyond. Claire Gerus, Mel Berger, and Eric Myers are all agents who took on earlier versions of the manuscript. Thank you for your kind and gentle suggestions, all of which improved Cat's story. Sharlene Martin at Martin Literary Management has championed me for many years and I treasure her invaluable friendship and expertise more than I can say. Special thanks to my publishers, the fabulous Neville and Cindy Johnson, who were eager to gamble on Cat and her adventures, and especially to Cindy for her eagle eye. Thanks also to Mary Isenman and my mother, Pat Wysocky, who helped with proofing.

Throughout my life there have been many horses with whom I have been privileged to cross paths, and I have learned something from each one. Special recognition goes to Dondi, Snoqualmie, Ben, Rebo, Ghost, Nelson, Nacho, and Valentino. Their wise and thoughtful perception of the world around them was the inspiration for Sally Blue. Over the years I have learned to trust equine instinct more than human and have learned much about myself through these, and other, very special horses. Thank you.

My apologies to the good people of Ashland City, Tennessee; Bellevue, Tennessee; and to the residents of Cheatham County, Tennessee. The law enforcement and journalistic teams there are much better in real life than in Cat's world. I also took some literary license with geographic locations and other details, including the positioning of the Cheatham/Davidson county line. However, the basic history of the area is accurate.

Many Tennesseans will recognize that information on Bucksnort, Tennessee (which is west of Nashville) and Mimosa, Tennessee (which is south) was merged into one town. Also, I have many friends who live in Belle Meade and know for a fact that not everyone who lives there is as snooty as Glenda or as superficial as Buffy. Goose Berry only lives in Cat's world, but there really is a "stick lady" in Tennessee who places branches on the road in front of her house to slow speeding cars.

Thank you also to Chuck Dauphin, Dr. Geoff Tucker, Bill Royce, Neville Johnson, and Morgan Fairchild, all of whom crossed boundaries from my world into Cat's. Next time any of you see Cat, please ask how the repairs on her barn roof are holding up. She does not always tell me these things.

To you, the reader, I have to say that Cat and I so appreciate you picking up *The Opium Equation*. I hope you enjoy Cat's story. If you do, please tell others about it and her. Many adventures lie ahead for Cat, but she has told me that public demand is the only reason she will agree to share them with you. So let us know what you think. In the meantime, please visit Cat and me online at: LisaWysocky.com or at CatEnrightStables.blogspot.com, or via email at lisainfo@comcast.net.

Lisa Wysocky
July 2011

FOOD FOR THOUGHT: BOOK CLUB QUESTIONS

1. How did the entire experience change Cat? Are the changes for the better or for the worse?

2. What could Cat do to smooth out her relationship with Jon Gardner?

3. Do you think Sally Blue really is psychic?

4. Is there a future for Cat's new relationship?

5. Do you think Cat should forgive the murderer? Why or why not?

6. Is Jon just a private person, or does he have something to hide? If he is hiding something, what do you think it is?

7. Do you think Sheriff "Big Jim" Burns will win the upcoming election?

8. What will happen to Fairbanks now that Glenda is dead? Will her survivors sell it? Keep it? Or. . . .?

9. Should Bubba go to a foster home, or is Hill Henley responsible enough to parent him?

10. How do you think Darcy will do in the upcoming show season?

11. Will the murderer's attorneys get the charges dismissed? Should they be dismissed?

12. How do you think Cat really feels about Agnes?

13. Would you have looked as hard for Bubba as Cat did? Why or why not?

14. What purpose does Hank serve in Cat's life?

15. Do you think Cat would make a good parent? Who does she "mother" now?

16. Can you relate at all to the person who murdered Glenda?

17. Which of the horses is your favorite? Give specific reasons why you like him or her.

18. What do you think Robert Griggs's background is?

19. How does Cat's childhood affect her today?

20. Do you think Carole will ever get back to her riding?

21. If you met Cat in person, would she be someone you would like as a friend? If so, why?

ABOUT THE AUTHOR

Lisa Wysocky is an award-winning author, editor, clinician, riding instructor, and a horsewoman who helps humans grow through horses. She is also a PATH·International instructor who trains horses for therapeutic riding and other equine assisted activities and therapies. In addition, Lisa is the executive director of the nonprofit organization Colby's Army, Inc. (ColbysArmy.org) formed in memory of her son. Colby's Army helps people, animals (including needy horses, and people with mental illness and addiction who can heal through horses), and the environment. Lisa splits her time between Tennessee and Minnesota, and you can find her online on Facebook at Power of a Whisper or at: LisaWysocky.com or CatEnrightStables.blogspot.com.

Author photo by Colby Keegan. The horse in the photo is Nacho, a Haflinger gelding who is a therapy horse at Saddle Up! in Franklin, Tennessee.

IF YOU ENJOYED *THE OPIUM EQUATION*, YOU MAY ALSO ENJOY THESE, AND OTHER, AWARD-WINNING BOOKS FROM COOL TITLES.
Learn more at CoolTitles.com

ForeWord **Book of the Year Finalist!** Kidnappers have snatched Judge Luna Cruz's daughter. They will kill the girl unless Luna releases a Hollywood movie star who is making a film in New Mexico. Public Defender "Conflict Contract" Attorney Dan Shepard journeys around the state on a desperate race against time to save Luna's daughter, all while avoiding judge who want to throw him in jail on contempt.

Mom's Choice Winner! IBPA Benjamin Franklin Book of the Year Award Winner! *ForeWord* **Book of the Year Finalist!** Human reason tells her she's crazy; the voice she hears tells otherwise. Emerald McGintay experiences dreams and visions and is diagnosed with schizophrenia. When she stumbles upon a trail of hidden secrets, her father decides to send her away to a special clinic. She flees her luxurious home in Philadephia to a safe haven in the Colorado Rockies where she meets a rancher who suggests he recognizes the voice she hears. Battered by a relentless storm of strange encounters, Emerald struggles to discover her reality.

Special Offers for Friends of Cat Enright